MASTER
OF THE
ROYAL
SECRET

PRAISE FOR
THE INVISIBLE COLLEGE

"Jeff Wheeler weaves a deep and unique world filled with magic, danger, and hope. Readers will fall in love with the characters and root for their triumphs. (And I may have a crush on Robinson now.)"

—Wall Street Journal bestselling author Charlie N. Holmberg

"What a ride! Jeff Wheeler really brings out the big guns—literally, there are cannons—with this amazing introduction into the world of The Invisible College. From the prologue, I was absolutely hooked! With a world of inventive magic, a doomsday war on the horizon, and a romance you can't help but want to cheer for, this story showcases some of Jeff Wheeler's best work. Old and new fans of his masterful storytelling are going to gobble this right up and come back begging for more."

—Allison Anderson, author of the Cartographer's War series

"Jeff has written an engaging story full of ancient magic, secret handshakes, devious antagonists, and a charming hero just discovering his power."

—Luanne G. Smith, author of The Vine Witch

ALSO BY JEFF WHEELER

Your First Million Words

Tales from Kingfountain, Muirwood, and Beyond: The Worlds of Jeff Wheeler

The Angel Sworn Series

Queen Mother

Tyrant Queen

The Invisible College Series

The Invisible College

The Violence of Sound

The Alchemy of Fate

Master of the Royal Secret

The Dresden Codex

Doomsday Match

Jaguar Prophecies

Final Strike

The Dawning of Muirwood Series

The Druid

The Hunted

The Betrayed

The First Argentines Series

Knight's Ransom

Warrior's Ransom

Lady's Ransom

Fate's Ransom

The Grave Kingdom Series

The Killing Fog

The Buried World

The Immortal Words

The Harbinger Series

Storm Glass

Mirror Gate

Iron Garland

Prism Cloud

Broken Veil

The Kingfountain Series

The Queen's Poisoner

The Thief's Daughter

The King's Traitor

The Hollow Crown

The Silent Shield

The Forsaken Throne

The Poisoner of Kingfountain Series

The Poisoner's Enemy

The Widow's Fate

The Maid's War

The Duke's Treason

The Poisoner's Revenge

The Covenant of Muirwood Trilogy

The Banished of Muirwood

The Ciphers of Muirwood

The Void of Muirwood

Whispers from Mirrowen Trilogy

Fireblood

Dryad-Born

Poisonwell

The Legends of Muirwood Trilogy

The Wretched of Muirwood

The Blight of Muirwood

The Scourge of Muirwood

Landmoor Series

Landmoor

Silverkin

MASTER
OF THE
ROYAL
SECRET

JEFF WHEELER

To Jane

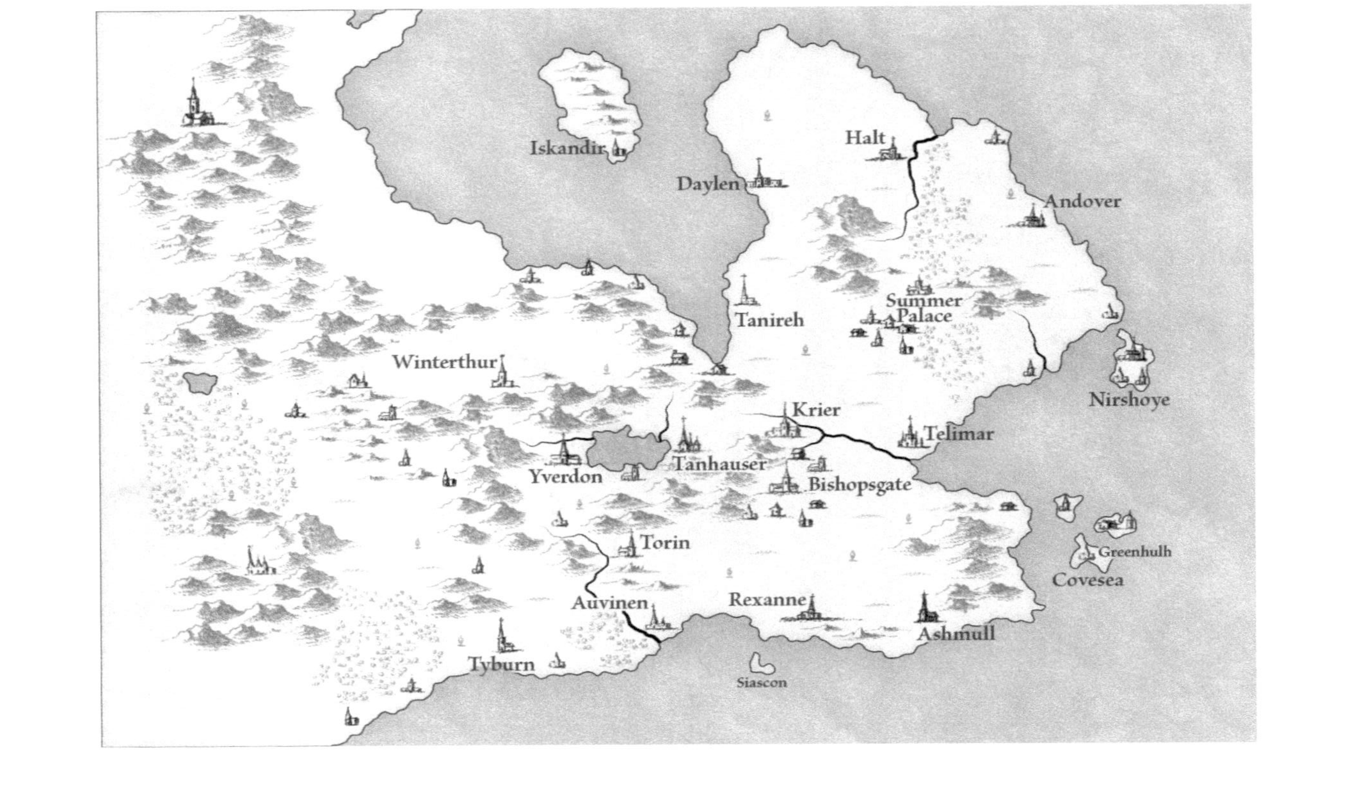

Iskandir
Halt
Daylen
Andover
Tanireh
Summer Palace
Winterthur
Krier
Telimar
Nirshoye
Tanhauser
Yverdon
Bishopsgate
Torin
Greenhulh
Covesea
Auvinen
Rexanne
Ashmull
Tyburn
Siascon

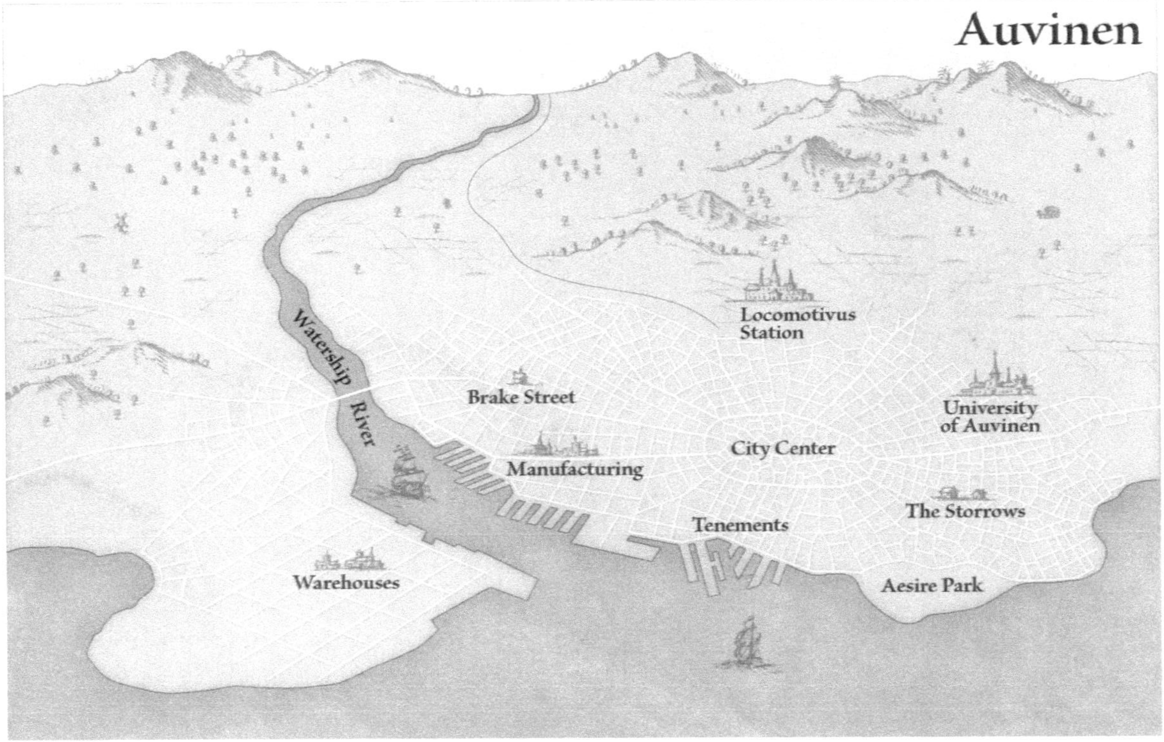
Auvinen
Locomotivus Station
Watership River
Brake Street
University of Auvinen
City Center
Manufacturing
The Storrows
Tenements
Warehouses
Aesire Park

Any citizen of the empire possessing or using any artifact imbued with "intelligence" shall be fined one thousand cuppers for the first offense and sixty days in jail. Brokers of such illegal items shall receive harsher penalties, subject to the magistrate's will within their jurisdiction. Any man or woman who makes a secret "sign" of the order of sorcerers shall be reported and condemned to the fullest extent allowable by law. Membership in the Invisible College is treason.

—Code of Justice, "Laws Against the Use of Sorcery" § 580p, the Marshalcy

Kellin Carrault

PROLOGUE
THE ROGUE SORCERER

The jostling ride came to an end, and Kellin hastily exited the armored wagon, which had parked in front of the Hotel Amboise in downtown Auvinen. He glanced at his pocket watch to observe the time of his arrival—four minutes later than he'd anticipated. He cast a scowl at the driver before meeting his man at the hotel door, where he was standing by a bellman whose uniform had been patched at the left elbow. This hotel was shabbier than most. The walls hadn't even been repainted in years.

"Is he still here?" Kellin demanded in a furtive voice of Arbuckle, his deputy, who had met with the informant to ensure he was a reliable source before getting Kellin involved.

Arbuckle turned to the bellman with an expectant look and an impatient nod.

The bellman was fidgeting. He was obviously hoping to earn some cuppers with his information but perhaps was wondering how valuable it truly was. "Yes, sir. I mean, I believe so, sir. He's not checked out and it's early in the evening still."

"What room is he in?" Kellin asked brusquely. He was eager, for they'd been looking for this rogue sorcerer for quite some time.

"Room four hundred sixteen, sir. Fourth floor," said the bellman. He offered his hand discreetly. His glove had holes in two of the fingers.

Kellin brushed past him with Arbuckle at his side and entered the hotel. The bellman would receive better compensation if the information led to an arrest.

"Did you alert the Marshalcy?" Kellin asked Arbuckle, who was a junior officer in the private security firm but had wealthy and well-connected parents. The cream of Auvinen Society.

"I thought you wouldn't want that, sir," Arbuckle said.

A wise choice. Some junior officers wanted to get in good with the Marshalcy, maybe assuming they could make a bid for a ranked position with them, but Arbuckle was loyal to the firm.

"When did you hear about this?" Kellin asked.

"A little after midnight. The fellow checked in to the hotel after hours. Suspect was about the age we're looking for. Also had a violin case tucked under his arm and no suitcase. That made it stand out."

A violin case! It really could be their man!

They went to the staircase and began to rush up the steps quickly.

Kellin was the head of the firm in Auvinen, a capable investigator who knew most of the tricks sorcerers used to escape detection. Agents of the Trilby weren't bound by the same code of conduct as officers of the Marshalcy, which meant they often got better results. Paying off a man or beating him with a truncheon often produced faster and more useful dividends than mere questions. Better yet—the Marshalcy was usually willing to ignore the odd swollen eye if it meant solving a case sooner.

Kellin was thirty-four himself and had worked for the firm since finishing his studies. He vastly preferred his line of work to the tedium of college life. Cases required imagination. Cleverness. An eye for detail.

When they reached the fourth floor in the stairwell, Kellin opened the door and they marched down the carpeted hall. The carpet was threadbare in places, with some unseemly stains that had never been rubbed out. Shabby indeed.

They reached the marked room—416—promptly. It was the second from the main hallway, with a position near the stairs for a quick getaway. Clever man. But this particular sorcerer had shown himself to be particularly clever. He'd enchanted objects for the ruffians living in the tenements to cause incalescence or generate light—items owned by the landlord who would have to pay the fines if caught, not the tenants. A few even played music, which was an absurd waste of magic. About as useful as listening to the annoying chirp of crickets. The cad had done it all for free, probably thinking it a favor, but magic was illegal and a favor to no one.

Arbuckle pointed to the door and raised his eyebrows inquisitively. His sideburns were cropped to his lower jaw, his cravat and waistcoat more fine than his companion's, although his jacket was humble enough to mask the rest. Kellin preferred to be clean-shaven himself. To dress as inconspicuously as possible.

Kellin reached into his pocket and withdrew the small, hand-held quicksilver bulb. It was glowing, which signaled proximity to magic. Devices such as this one were highly illegal, but Kellin had a writ of permission, signed by the head of the Marshalcy, granting him permission to use it to hunt down and apprehend sorcerers.

Arbuckle gave the bulb an appreciative nod. Such trinkets were expensive on the black market, especially because being caught with one could condemn a man or woman to one of the many debtors' prisons throughout the city. The fines for possessing magic were so steep that incarceration was the likely outcome for all but the wealthy. And most prisoners would languish there until that debt was paid or they died within the prison of natural or unnatural causes.

Kellin nodded and slipped the tube back into his pocket and drew his pistol. Arbuckle did the same.

Kellin carefully reached for the door handle and twisted it.

There was likely a chain bolt in place. But they were frequently broken, and a hotel as decrepit as this one might not even have a functioning one. Another guest was moaning down the hall behind a closed door.

Kellin turned the handle and pushed. The door swung open effortlessly.

The two men stormed inside, pistols raised. It was a squalid little room with a single bed, a dresser with a bowl for washing, a window too tiny to crawl in or out of. The blanket on the bed was still unruffled. Next to the bowl of water, there was a little bronze bell, like the kind from the hotel desk, that was radiating warmth.

Kellin walked over to the dresser and gazed at the bell, scowling fiercely.

"This room hasn't even been used," Arbuckle said, lowering his weapon.

"You're right. I'm afraid it's just a decoy," Kellin said, disappointment throbbing in his stomach. He picked up the little bell and nearly smashed it against the dresser, but he subdued his rage.

Too late, Kellin realized the clever sorcerer's ploy: He had rented this shabby room for a few cuppers, made a show of himself by coming in late, and then had stolen the bell from the front desk, enchanted it, and left it to be found later so it would trigger the quicksilver bulb. He'd probably slipped out the back to avoid being seen and then went to another hotel incognito, to spend the rest of the night untroubled.

"Another miss," Arbuckle said. "From what the bellman said, he could be every man. Didn't even get a decent look at him but noticed the dark, unkempt hair."

"By design, no doubt," Kellin said stiffly. "Well, that was a waste of time."

"I'm sorry, sir. I thought the lead was promising."

Kellin gave him a reassuring gesture, pretending to pat him but not actually touching him. "This is what I pay you for, Arbuckle. You were right to call me in. This rogue sorcerer is proving himself very canny indeed. He knows this city well."

"When the college was shut down, they were easier to catch. Or so I've heard."

"I was a lad myself back then," Kellin said. "You weren't even born."

"The stories I've heard." Arbuckle had a wistful look on his face. "Would have been interesting to see how magic was used everywhere by practically everyone."

"You mean the *lies*," Kellin said in rebuke, and the wistful look vanished.

"Of course, sir."

Kellin yawned and checked his pocket watch again.

"You've had a late night, sir."

"I'm normally abed by now, yes. The play is moving to Bishopsgate in two weeks, and then rehearsals start for the new one opening in Tanhauser."

"You've seen the play every night, sir. Some can't even get tickets. They're sold out."

"They've been sold out for months. Everyone wants to see Miss Kauer perform." A vague smile came to Kellin's mouth. He'd provided security for the company while in Auvinen, which had given him access and privileges that other men would have murdered for.

Miss Kauer was a sensational actress who had captured the imagination and hearts of the citizens of the empire. She'd even been invited to perform before the emperor's family in a gala concert. Her current play was very popular, but her manager had said that the playwright who'd penned it had come up with another one, a play about the Aesir. It would be controversial by design, and her manager knew it would cost a fortune to create—the permits alone to use music would be expensive—but it would reap an even greater fortune in return. Miss Kauer would play the titular role—the Erlking's daughter.

He was eager to see what sort of costume she'd wear.

No one really knew what had become of the Aesir since they'd left the world over twenty years ago, driven out by the military.

The conflict between humans and Aesir had gone on for centuries, but it was over at last. And what an ending. After the citizens learned the Invisible College, which they'd thought was protecting them, had in fact been in league with the enemy, retribution had been fierce. Laws were passed to abolish the sorcery school, and the various quorums, both large and minute, were shut down and vacated. Some properties were still derelict, as it was not clear who had legal ownership of the grounds, and contests were being dragged out through legal auxiliaries. Businesses that had used magical means of production were forced to either shut down or replace their methods with machinery. When recalcitrant sorcerers continued to display magic, they were jailed, and the penalties had become increasingly stiffer to discourage rebellion.

Kellin knew there were still sorcerers among them. Like the cocky violin-playing one who'd been wandering the tenements of Auvinen. But soon they would be no more. The order would be stamped out and eventually forgotten.

"You get to escort Miss Kauer to her hotel every night," Arbuckle said with a tinge of envy in his voice.

"Or her manager," Kellin said, trying not to sound too proud.

"If you ever need help…?" Arbuckle hinted with a twinkle in his eye.

"Oh, I doubt I shall," Kellin retorted.

"Some think she's rather plain. That it's all the costumes and makeup they use for her on stage."

"Oh, she's devastatingly beautiful even without all that," Kellin said, feeling a slight pang in his heart. She *was* astonishingly pretty. But quiet. Guarded. There were secrets in those beautiful eyes. "I'll return to my quarters and get some sleep, I think," Kellin said, stifling another yawn. "I have a meeting with her manager this afternoon."

"I'll pay the bellman," Arbuckle said. "Get some rest, sir."

Kellin gave him a nod and then put the warm bell in his pocket. Who knew how long it would remain enchanted. It all depended on how long the sorcerer had imprisoned the intelligence powering it. Was it just for a night? Or had he cursed the bell permanently? The hotel manager wouldn't want an illegal artifact to be found on his premises. He too could end up in debtors' prison, regardless of whether it was his fault. Those Marshalcy laws regarding magical artifacts were very strict.

Kellin bypassed the bellman without a word and looked up at the driver. "Home," he said curtly.

The smell of manure made him grimace. The streets of Auvinen were caked in refuse. Flies abounded. He had vague memories, from his childhood, of seeing little metallic sweepers scurrying up behind horses and carrying away the dregs.

That job was rarely done anymore with the rampant labor strikes. He climbed into the armored wagon and sat by himself on the back seat, checking his pocket watch again. He should be home in thirty-two minutes.

The driver got him there in thirty-six.

Issac Berrow

CHAPTER ONE
SKRÝMIR

Awakening from the Skrýmir sleep was like being plunged unexpectedly into an iced-over pond. Isaac gasped involuntarily as his every sense recoiled from the drowning sensation and the bitter cold caused by the spell. His heart galloped in his chest, his eyes blinked quickly, and he shivered inside the boxed contraption he'd invented in a much earlier lifetime.

The frigidity in his toes and fingertips began to wane, and his shocked breathing began to settle.

"Hoxta-namorem," he sang softly to summon light into the cramped box where he lay supine. No wisp of light appeared in response to the spell. The darkness was suffocating in its own sense. When he was in the Skrýmir, he didn't breathe at all. But no light meant no intelligences were nearby. He was truly alone.

"Calixspell," he said, invoking the command that would open the metallic box.

Nothing happened for that spell either.

Memories from his various lifetimes began to crowd his consciousness. He reached up to rub his nose, then lowered his arm and lay still, his heart hurting from the memories of all his cumulative losses. The ache was freshest from the loss of McKenna Aurora Foster, a resilient woman from a wealthy barrister's family who had been the latest Semblance of his wife, Eiríka, the Erlking's daughter. They had searched for each other and loved each other in nearly a thousand lifetimes.

But this would be the final time. If they could fall in love and marry just one more time, they'd be fulfilling their bargain with her father. The Aesir would be forced to leave the world and go to another, and the brutal wars between the two species would finally end irrevocably.

A sudden craving for sugared peanuts made his stomach growl. He started to chuckle at the very human need. The blackness within the vault caused an involuntary spasm of fear. What if he were truly trapped there?

The box was hidden in a chamber deep within the bowels of the University of Nirshoye. He'd used it many times to invoke the Skrýmir sleep so he could wait until Eiríka was reborn. The box had never *not* opened before. There was a glamour on it that made anyone looking at it from the outside of the box immediately forget what they'd been doing and retreat. If the glamour had been broken by a more powerful sorcerer, the fail-safe in his device would have awakened him immediately. He reached lower and touched his pocket, but the device was safely nestled inside.

He reached out with his mind to Loyal, the faithful dog intelligence who'd been his companion over many lifetimes.

Where are you, boy?

Silence.

He was in a locked metal box with very little air deep in a chamber buried within the bedrock of the island university. Isaac's heart began to race with fear, but he let out a deep breath and started to think. A memory resurfaced.

Isaac rolled sideways onto his stomach. There was a lever at the top near his head. After groping around a bit, he found it. He dragged it to the side and heard the grinding of gears and wheels, followed by a sigh of air rushing inside. The vents still worked. Good.

Isaac continued to drag the lever until he felt it stop. He

pulled the handle toward himself, recollecting the steps needed to disassemble the box manually.

Another click sounded, and a panel that was level with his head came loose. It took some effort, but he managed to wrangle it sideways and then push it down toward his feet. The next section, at his chest, was released once the first was gone, and he placed it with the other he'd removed. There was an empty void beneath the platform where he'd been lying, about the height of the previous one, which doubled the depth of the space he could move in after he'd cleared away enough of the panels to climb down into the lower portion of the chamber with a few minutes of rigorous work. Once he could sit up, he was able to remove the others more easily.

The lower section of the box had some screwing dials, which he began to turn. They hadn't been oiled in ages, but thankfully they were able to turn with some effort, and soon he'd released the remaining paneling and pushed it away. It was heavy and clanged noisily onto the brick floor beyond. Isaac was about to leave, but he suddenly remembered his violin case and snatched it out with him.

The chamber he entered was full of the pipes, wheels, and dials that controlled the heating and plumbing of the university with ambient light coming in from small windows built high on the wall by the ceiling. They were all cold and still. He reached out and touched one of the pipes and felt no water pressure thrumming against the metal. A memory of having caused an explosion in the university pushed to the forefront of his brain. But surely it had been repaired since then?

The chamber was familiar—he'd designed it, after all—but there was thick dust on the floor. No one had been in this spot in years it seemed. The air was stale and cool. He reached into his pocket and pulled out the device he'd invented. The three Aesir digits in the crystal at the top read: 9-9-9. The philosopher's stone set inside was what kept him youthful and healthy. The inner rings acted like dials that released the sorcerer's ring in the middle.

It had been twenty-three years since he'd last walked the mortal world. It wasn't a random number but a sequence he had researched which predicted when the next Awakening would happen. As always, he was intrigued by what changes he would find. Invariably, he would invent a new life, a new persona to wear as a sort of disguise. In the past, he had learned to glamour himself with the device to numb himself from the haunting memories of losing Eiríka so many times, though he'd included ways to awaken his memories with his device if he didn't find her quickly. But in this life, he wasn't going to forget anything. He didn't know where she was, but he would find her in whatever life the Erlking had chosen for his daughter's final human incarnation. He would find her, and he'd help her remember.

He unlocked the violin case and pulled out the instrument. Lifting it to his chin, he took the bow and played a few notes, wincing at how out of tune it was. Thankfully he had perfect pitch and could tune the instrument without any outside assistance. After a few satisfactory strains, he conjured a quick spell to heat the pipes. But nothing happened.

He realized that all the intelligences that had empowered the boiler room had been set free. The Unseen Powers harnessed willing intelligences to do useful work, but the terms didn't last indefinitely. Once they expired, another intelligence was found to perform the same task. Sorcerers arranged this, using their minds to summon the intelligences, often with a musical form of persuasion.

Intelligences were found in every living creation of the Mind of the Sovereignty. Each had special abilities. A dog's intelligence, for example, might be sent to find something. A horse's, to pull a mechanical tram. There were an abundance of intelligences. Why hadn't those powering these pipes been replaced?

Isaac put away the violin, tucked the case under his arm, and then went to the door. It was locked from the inside. Only a few high-ranking employees of the university even had access to the keys to this space. He unlocked the door and peered back once more at the metal box that looked like part of the boiler room machinery. If all the intelligences were gone, no wonder the spell hadn't worked. Thankfully, he'd had the foresight to create the alternative method of exiting the box.

He started climbing the stairs and heard absolutely nothing except the noise of his own shoes and breathing. The silence was oppressive and unnerving. He'd attended the university as a young man, not realizing he was a Semblance himself. Many lifetimes before he'd become Isaac Berrow, he'd agreed to a covenant to marry Eiríka and begin the effort of finding her over and over. He could not remember those earlier lives, but Eiríka had described them to him. One of the reasons he'd invented the Invisible College in this very university was to assist him in finding and then marrying her. Whoever was the Master of the Royal Secret in this time might even be enlisted to lend him aid.

He reached the top of the stairs and passed through several rooms stuffed with machinery. Everything was dark and still. He knew the university perfectly well, but it had never been this empty before. Dust was everywhere. When he reached the top, he entered a room that was frigid and littered with debris. Windows were broken and pieces of sharp glass lay strewn about the floor. He walked cautiously to the shattered window and gazed outside into the courtyard.

What he beheld was a derelict scene. The courtyard outside was overgrown with weeds. Nearly every window had been broken. Not a soul could be seen. Even the squawk of the seagulls was absent. Confusion and discouragement began to war within his chest. This university had been his safe haven for centuries. But he'd awakened to a tableau that was empty and abandoned. Only slightly over twenty-three years should have passed since he and Eiríka had confronted her father in this very courtyard. What had changed so dramatically?

The door wasn't locked, but the handle was rusty and he struggled to turn it. The hinges creaked as he pulled it open and stepped out into the street. By the overcast sky and the slight chill in the air, he deduced it was late fall. Classes should be in session until the winter. That had always been the case.

Isaac roamed the streets, not finding a single living creature, and it made his stomach knot with worry. Surely the Awakening hadn't happened yet. How tragic it would be if he'd come back to the world after all mortals had been destroyed.

He walked briskly to the main courtyard where the Erlking had confronted the military agents out to kill him. The residue of that conflict was gone, but the windows were all broken. Dead leaves scraped against the barren ground, dragged listlessly by the breeze. He approached the center pavilion that he'd been in, the one with the statue dedicated to Eiríka. He'd had it commissioned long ago, and it was still standing, a mute witness to the desolate place.

He gazed around the courtyard, the past swimming through his memory. He could remember the sulfurous smell of saltpetr hanging in the air after Mr. Stoker and his men tried to murder the Erlking.

As he stood there, reminiscing and wondering, he heard a distinct chord of magic. A Mixolydian chord breaking the silence.

And then the sound of irrupting gunfire came from every direction.

Aimed at him.

Chapter Two
An Unbreakable Magic

The elfshot ricocheted off an invisible web surrounding Isaac. His device had several autonomic defensive spells sensitive to the harmful vibrations of deliberate thoughts of malice against the one who possessed it. It was not perfect in calibrating against all threats, but it had worked in this instance, and the shots struck and cracked against the ground, walls, and other hard structures around him.

"Aóratos," Isaac thought, invoking an aura of invisibility for himself. Plumes of saltpetr billowed from several window frames in the buildings connected to the courtyard. He counted at least six telltale wisps of smoke. He was surrounded. Staying put wasn't the best option, so he broke for the building to the south.

He knew the grounds of the university better than any living man. There were some underground tunnels on that side where he could slip beneath the university.

"Fire!" The order was shouted in a crisp military voice, and another volley of elfshot ripped into the courtyard, aiming at the original place where he'd stood. He had to assume the thought casting worked since they hadn't altered their positions, which implied they couldn't see him. More bullets ricocheted throughout the yard.

As he approached the southern wall of the building, motion in his peripheral vision prompted him to turn and look as a soldier wearing a kappelin leaped out of a window. He heard the subtle tones of magic and watched the soldier float down to the ground, landing softly, holding a large rifle unlike any Isaac had seen before.

The kappelin brought back terrible memories from his life as Robinson Hawksley. Officers from the Brotherhood of Shadows, soldiers trained to hunt and kill Semblances of the Erlking, had attacked the Erlking and his men—who had in turn killed them and reanimated their corpses with Aesir.

The soldier pulled a lever on his rifle, resulting in a clicking noise. He was stalking toward the statue in the center of the courtyard, rifle poised to shoot.

Isaac heard the scuff of his own shoe. The soldier whirled and shot directly at him. Once more, the shell of magic from his device deflected it.

"He's invisible!" shouted the soldier with the rifle. Isacc noted the uniform beneath the kappelin cloak was different in style from what he'd seen when he was Robinson.

Another soldier jumped out a window in the southern building, landing deftly before raising his rifle.

Kalispel, Isaac thought, causing a forced shove which propelled the man into the brick wall behind him. He crumpled and from the dazed look, he'd be down for some time.

"It's him!" another shouted. More bullets launched at him, and Isaac sprinted to the door he'd been heading to. He could hear the rustle of cloaks, the heavy tread of their boots, as they took off after him. He reached the door and saw that the handle had been broken off. No matter. He shoved inside, the hinges groaning from disuse.

Isaac ran as fast as he could, his pulse racing with the thrill of the moment and the fear of being killed. He hadn't died in hundreds of years. If he did, his soul would be sent to another body, and he'd lose all his memories. In that state, he wouldn't even know he was looking for Eiríka. Wouldn't know anything of sorcery or the Invisible College. He might even have to restart life as a child. No, he *had* to get away.

He came to an entry hall with classrooms on each side. Some doors were open, others closed. He raced down the main corridor, the soldiers hot on his heels. Several shots were fired in his direction, but his life was protected by both the device and his invisibility.

He went to the farthest door on the right and quickly plunged inside, only to trip over a chair that had been left in the way. He grunted when he struck the ground, feeling pain shoot through his wrist. Biting his lip to keep from crying out, he scurried to his feet and raced to another door across the room, which led to a dean's office. This part of the building was particularly labyrinthine, with multiple doors in every classroom that led to back hallways and offices, but he remembered the way well. The smell of must was strong and heavy. In a few moments, he'd found the supply closet he'd been looking for and quietly shut the door behind himself. It was risky putting himself there in a dead-end space, but he predicted the soldiers would be confused, and he wanted to lose them before trying to access the tunnels beneath the university.

A door swung open with a bang, and several sets of boots thundered down the narrow corridor. Then they stopped.

"Which door did he take?" someone gasped.

"*Sshh!* Listen!" The curt command cut off any reply.

They stopped, but Isaac could hear them breathing. His own heart was pounding, and he heard a decided gurgle from his stomach. He hadn't eaten in decades, and his bodily functions were starting to awaken after the prolonged slumber. Thirst itched in his throat.

"I don't hear anything," said the first soldier.

"Exactly. He's hiding, not running."

Smart chap.

"I've summoned the others. We'll search room by room. Pull out your quicksilver bulb."

"Yes, sir."

Isaac scowled. It seemed rather unfair for them to use one of his own inventions against him.

He gazed around the supply closet. He'd chosen his hiding place deliberately, and he was rewarded for his quick thinking. While most of the university had been ransacked, there were still chymicals stored on these shelves. Glass bottles covered in dust. He wiped one of the labels clear with his thumb, squinting in the darkness. He couldn't read it, so he pulled it down and gently unstoppered the lid. The smell told him the contents.

There were no intelligences answering his summons, but chymicals always reacted in the same way when mixed properly. He found the two he needed after a brief search. Separately, they were innocuous agents, good for cleaning. Mixed together, they could be dangerous and produce an asphyxiating gas.

"It's glowing stronger that way," said one of the soldiers.

Isaac took a deep breath and began to hold it. He could hold his breath indefinitely since he did not actually need air to breathe because of the philosopher's stone. He'd tested it once and grown bored of holding it after several hours. It wasn't a comfortable sensation, but his body repaired its injuries swiftly. He couldn't starve to death or die of thirst either. But he could still be hungry or thirsty. And he could be killed if he were shot enough times or suffered a fatal injury like a fall from too great a height.

The door to the supply closet was jerked open by one of the soldiers. He was holding a glass lamp, one of the portable kind Isaac had invented as Robinson, with his roommate, Wickens.

Isaac threw both bottles onto the floor, shattering the glass. The vapors were colorless.

The soldier who had opened the door looked confused. Isaac was still invisible, so the man was staring at the floor. The abrupt shattering of glass caused the other soldier to raise an elfshot pistol and aim it into the close space. He fired, and the bullet immediately ricocheted and struck the other man, who grunted in surprise as blood bloomed on the front of his uniform. He instinctively placed his hand on his chest and staggered back, dropping the glowing quicksilver lamp, which also shattered when it struck the ground.

"Tomlinson!" cried the firing soldier in shock, once he realized that he'd essentially shot his own companion.

Isaac felt the sting of the fumes in his nostrils. The other soldier knelt by him, his face twisted with concern. Tomlinson's head sagged against his chest. He'd been shot in the heart. His eyes remained open as he died.

Isaac felt a pang of remorse, even though it hadn't been his fault the man was shot. He watched the soldier's mouth with growing apprehension. A puff of mist came from his lips, like the tendril of fog from someone exhaling on a frigid day. Only it wasn't cold enough for that.

The soldier had been a Semblance.

The other man frowned with frustration but not surprise. His grimace went from sorrowful to furious.

"I know you're still in there," he said angrily. "The others are coming. We'll find you, and we'll kill you."

Isaac saw a glint of white gold on the man's thumb. It was an Aesir ring, the kind that allowed one to communicate by thought. The rings were another of Isaac's inventions.

Both men were Semblances. Isaac imagined that perhaps *all* of the brotherhood had become Semblances. The Erlking had left his lackeys in the mortal world to await Isaac's return. How boring their vigil must have been.

The Erlking was nothing if not extremely patient.

But so was Isaac Berrow. Semblances were still mortal. They still needed to breathe. And as Isaac waited, the man glaring at him became groggy, then confused, and eventually toppled and fell, overcome by the invisible gas Isaac had unleashed.

He stepped over both bodies and left the closet, the door held open by the soldiers' inert forms. His delicate hearing picked up the sound of others running. He walked to another door and opened it, gazing back at the scene. A dead man covered in blood. Another unconscious. Isaac regarded the open door of the supply closet and then thought the command to shove and shatter all the vials and globes within it before he ducked through the door.

It would take hours for all that gas to diffuse. It would knock out anyone who lingered in that space for too long.

Having provided a buffer behind him, he quickly maneuvered through the maze to the private room he'd once used as a professor at the university. It was not Isaac Berrow's office. It was the office of a professor that Isaac had used glamour to become. Having secret past lives did have its advantages.

It had also been ransacked of course. Books once on the shelves littered the floor. The desk chair had been dragged away. The trapdoor was carefully hidden within the flue of a small fireplace that he'd used for experiments, which had been concealed by the debris. He carefully cleared the area. Then on his hands and knees, Isaac found the edges of the door and unlatched the piece that triggered its release. He lifted the trapdoor hatch and gazed down into the darkness. It seemed undisturbed.

He climbed down the little ladder and then shut the trapdoor and heard it click shut. Having more than one way to escape was always preferable. Just like the manual escape hatch he'd built into the apparatus he used for the Skrýmir sleep.

They'd search the island for him. But he'd had a good look at that one soldier's face. The glamour spell Isaac used could make him look like anyone he wished. It seemed only Eiríka was immune to its effects, a condition the Erlking had set so that he couldn't compel her to fall in love with him by making her believe things against her will. But the Semblance soldiers could be deceived.

Isaac pulled the device out of his pocket and quickly turned the combination rings surrounding the philosopher's stone. He loosened the inner ring and then inserted his thumb. A familiar stab of pain struck his temples, making him wince.

So much had clearly changed over twenty-three years, but he hoped one thing had not.

Friendship.

Wickins. Are you there?

He sent the thought out to his old friend and roommate. He would be nearly fifty years old, but a mental thought was all it took to reach out. Of course, Wickins would only be able to respond if he wore a ring of Aesir gold.

Isaac waited in the silence, feeling very much alone. One minute. Two minutes. Six. His heart began to grow heavy. Wickins might be dead, or perhaps he didn't have the ring anymore. It was also possible he'd changed his mind about Isaac after their last conversation. He'd last told the family that he was trying to fulfill an ancient treaty with the Aesir that would expel them from the world forever. He'd told them he might be gone for a long time and that the military would likely hunt for him if they believed he was still alive. In addition, he'd told them that McKenna had been a Semblance of the Erlking's daughter and had died when that intelligence had left her body.

There were many reasons he might be unable or unwilling to respond.

Disappointment filled inside Isaac's chest. He didn't call out again.

Suddenly a surge of relief burst through the disappointment as he heard Wickins's thought scream in his mind.

Dickemore!

Annalise Kauer

Chapter Three
The Cost of Fame

The audience roared in applause, as they typically did at the final curtain. Annalise's temples throbbed with the usual ache caused by the noise. But she smiled her mysterious smile, gave a graceful curtsy, and hooked arms with the other lead actor, the love interest, though she cared nothing for him at all. Kissing him in act 3 was a chore. The audience was on their feet, clapping and cheering loudly. A few shrill whistles sounded as well, worsening her headache.

The scalloped curtain came rushing down, dampening the noise. When it opened again, there would be bouquets of flowers, but she didn't feel she could endure another moment. The heat of the theater and the stage lights were oppressive. She needed some fresh air or she risked fainting.

"That's enough," Annalise said, pulling her arm away from Mr. Beal's. She spun around and left the stage at the back, her voluminous skirts swirling. She wore a Romani costume beneath the more ornate dress she'd quickly donned between scenes. The fussy dress was tight and stifling over the much looser style that she wore in most of the scenes while barefoot. She was grateful that for most of the performance she wore only the simpler costume she preferred rather than these long puffy sleeves, lace collar, and tedious hat, the latter of which she suddenly tugged off and threw to one of the stagehands as she hurried past.

"But the audience—!" Mr. Beal shouted to her in a hushed, urgent voice just as the curtains whipped up again. More thunderous applause came, this time mixed and dulled with confusion since the leading lady was no longer there. But the cast carried on with their bows, knowing they'd earn the ire of Annalise's manager if they didn't act with strict professionalism. Mr. Froman knew all about her bouts of dizziness and her precarious health. She wasn't the precocious sixteen-year-old he'd discovered ten years ago and turned into the star of his theater company, a transformation in luck and fortune that had effectively happened overnight.

"Miss Kauer, can I get you anything?" asked one of the younger stagehands, but she shook her head and sidestepped him, retreating to the changing room where her maid awaited her.

"The applause is still going on," said Maud Jenkins with a quizzical look after she'd burst in.

"Get me out of this costume," Annalise pleaded while tugging off the gloves.

"Where's your hat?"

"I think Johnny has it," Annalise said. Maud hurriedly went to work and helped her untie the costume from behind so that she could shrug out of it.

A knock sounded at the door.

Was it Mr. Froman already? He usually attended her performances unless there were business meetings or guests to entertain. She didn't want to cause him worry. After giving Maud a look indicating she should attend to the visitor, Annalise hurriedly began to remove her fake earrings.

Maud hurried to the door. "What is it?" she asked.

A young man's voice could be heard through the wood. "Miss Kauer dropped her hat."

"Give him a cupper, would you?" Annalise said over her shoulder. The poor wretches who worked at the theater earned so little, and many were sacked for the smallest infringements of the rules, but Annalise knew that without their help, the performances would not be possible, so she tended to be generous.

Moments later, Maud returned with the discarded hat and placed it atop the mannequin in the room and then bent down to pick up the dress off the floor so she could hang that up too, as Annalise gratefully stepped out of it.

There was a pitcher of water on the table and Annalise quickly poured herself a drink, finally feeling less dizzy. Her room was in the farthest corner in the basement of the theater. It was the coolest room in the theater she supposed. Mr. Froman had arranged it so.

Another knock sounded on the door as Annalise fanned herself. It was the distinctive sound of a jewel-tipped cane striking the wood.

Maud looked at her nervously, but Annalise nodded. They'd come to trust and value each other over the last few years of working together. Maud had been a seamstress with the company previously and had earned Mr. Froman's respect through her diligence and discretion. His respect was not easily garnered.

Maud answered the door once again, and this time Mr. Froman stepped inside. He was an austere man, trim and tall and always in a charcoal-gray business suit and bowler hat. The cane he'd used to knock with was of polished walnut embellished with rippled edges and a heavy brass knob at the top housing a round jewel. He had a graying mustache with waxed tips and never a single hair out of place. His eyes were the most piercing, intense eyes Annalise had ever seen, as gray as steel and just as inflexible. He was an intimidating man, wealthy beyond imagining, and his favor had made Annalise wealthy too. She owned two homes, one across the lake from Tanhauser, the other in Bishopsgate, and she'd considered purchasing one in Auvinen because of how long the shows ran there.

She was grateful to him, yet his presence unnerved her, perhaps because she knew his mildness to be a facade. She'd witnessed his flashes of temper firsthand. Even if everyone else in his circle had chosen to forget them.

"You look unwell, Annalise," he said with a probing look, resting his hands on the top of his cane.

"I was nearly about to faint," she answered. "It was hot in the theater tonight."

"You did the right thing," he replied.

Maud clammed up whenever he was around, and she stood demurely to one side after gently shutting the door, as if trying to stay out of his line of sight.

A feeling of unease touched Annalise's mind. Mr. Froman wore a hat because of a disfigurement in his hairline, and no hair grew over the spot, making it stand out even more prominently. It was said the scar had been left by a bullet during a duel. But she had a notion that it hadn't been a duel at all. Whenever he was asked about it, he'd go very quiet and just peer at his interrogator with his icy stare. No one dared ask him about it twice.

"Mr. Carrault will take you back to the hotel," Mr. Froman said. "Once you are changed, of course."

Annalise nodded, knowing it would be highly improper for her to get inside Mr. Carrault's armored carriage wearing the revealing Romani outfit. The skirt went down just past her knees, which exposed her lower legs and ankles and bare feet. The anklets made tinkling noises when she walked or danced. Her hair was still held up and pinned as it had been for that final scene, instead of loose and free like she enjoyed having it, which again would be regarded as rather shocking in Society. Thankfully, successful and wealthy actresses were held in high esteem, despite the outfits.

"I'll be there shortly," Annalise said.

Mr. Froman studied her again, fixing her with his stare. "There are only a few performances left, Annalise. Play them well. We'll begin rehearsing the new project soon."

"I still haven't seen the script," Annalise reminded him, knowing that Mr. Froman had deliberately withheld it from her so as not to take her focus away from her current role.

She was eager to read the play about the Erlking's daughter, modeled after the opera. The titular role was hers, and he'd assured her that with the current investors eager to finance it, it would be an instant success, much like the opera had once been. Operas were no longer performed—live music performances had been banned except by permit because of the machinations of the Invisible College and so the expense of doing a musical performance had become prohibitive. But that didn't stop people from quietly humming the old melodies that had once been so famous in their homes, far away from the listening ears of government officials.

"Good night, Annalise," he said, giving a little nod to her.

Maud opened the door for him and he stepped outside. All sorts of noise infiltrated the room—laughter, complaints, congratulations—all mixing together like the buzzing from a hive of bees. Annalise loved the theater. Loved the people she worked with. But she was not close to many of them. Her work ethic went way beyond theirs. Mr. Froman insisted on perfection, and she was one of the few who consistently put in the work to achieve it.

After she changed out of her Romani costume and into a more modest dress and a simpler arrangement for her hair, Annalise followed Maud through the basement to the rear doors of the massive theater. They found Kellin Carrault waiting by the armored carriage. As soon as he saw Annalise, he produced a friendly smile and a little bow and then gestured for them to enter the conveyance. There was a crowd gathered at the end of the street, but they were held back by some of Kellin's Trilbys.

As soon as the three of them were seated on the padded benches, Kellin shut the door. The horses pulling the carriage were given a command, and it lurched forward. Kellin was checking his pocket watch again. He was always doing that. Keeping track of time was conspicuously important for him.

"I hope the performance went well this evening?" he asked. "You're a few minutes earlier than usual."

"It was stifling tonight," Annalise said, peering out the

window through a slit in the curtain. The crowd parted for the wagon, but she knew the people out there would be vying to get a glimpse of her. She was thankful the curtains were shut to afford her some privacy, but she could hear some of them calling her name. Being a wealthy and famous actress assured no shortage of ardent admirers. Mr. Froman had several Trilbys hired from Kellin's private security agency to keep the mobs at bay, and her hotel was kept a strict secret.

"Mr. Froman said you'll be leaving Auvinen soon," Kellin said. "Is that true?"

"It seems so." She had the sense that he admired her and was proud of his regular contact with her. But he'd never done anything inappropriate or tried to ingratiate himself unpleasantly, the way some men did.

"I almost caught a sorcerer this morning," Kellin said, a little boast in his tone.

That caught her attention.

"Oh?" she asked with genuine interest.

"There's a man who has been haunting the tenements, playing a violin. Conjuring magic in defiance of the prohibition. He checked in to the Hotel Amboise last night. Thought we had him, but he's clever."

"Do you know who he is?"

"No idea," Kellin said. "It is too easy to hide in this city, I'm afraid. Especially in the tenements. The Marshalcy is very intent on bringing him to justice, but with all the crime to deal with, they are short of resources at the moment."

"I've never met a real sorcerer," Annalise said. "Have you?"

"Several actually," Kellin said with another proud smile. He shifted in his seat, glancing at his watch again.

"I was a toddler when the Invisible College was ruined," Annalise mused.

"I was hardly more than a lad myself," Kellin said self-importantly. "But I remember things still. Those mechanical trams pulled by iron horses. Locomotivuses that moved by magic and not by steam. You could get to Bishopsgate from here in a trice back then."

"Do you think all sorcerers are evil, Mr. Carrault?"

"Misguided, Miss Kauer. Misguided. And they defy the law."

When she was younger, she'd dreamed of meeting a sorcerer and learning magic. But as the punishments became increasingly severe, and more and more of the sorcerers ended up in debtors' prison, it was nearly impossible to find someone who'd admit to knowing one. They had their own secret handshakes, she'd heard. A way to tell a friend from a foe. But every now and then, an informer would out one of them, and they'd be arrested and put on trial.

She still *longed* to meet one, truthfully, but even her wealth had not been able to produce an introduction to a real sorcerer. Only charlatans. She had been too young when they'd been abolished to remember anything about them or their magic but had always been so fascinated by stories she'd heard and books she'd read about the past that she was eager to want to know more about what the Invisible College had actually been like. She felt she performed a kind of magic with her acting and words. What would it have been like to sing a spell?

And then Mr. Froman had found out about her efforts. That had put a stop to things.

"Here we are at the hotel," Kellin said. It was quite close to the theater. She was fortunate to be able to stay in such lavish accommodations, whereas most of the cast and crew stayed in the dormitories at the theater. Her costar, Mr. Beal, stayed at a separate hotel. Mr. Froman had made sure to keep them separated out of an abundance of caution. It wasn't uncommon for cast members to develop feelings for each other, especially two romantic leads, but acting on those feelings was strictly forbidden. And punished. Mr. Froman needn't have worried. She wasn't the least bit attracted to her acting partners. It was the craft that she was in love with.

"Thank you for escorting us," Annalise said as the carriage came to a halt.

He gave her a brash smile and opened the door. After climbing out first, he reached up and helped Annalise and Maud step down. They had pulled into the back of the hotel, away from prying eyes. Someone had tried following the carriage once, but Mr. Carrault had arranged for the man to be intercepted—and the intrepid interloper had been given a stern warning never to try again.

Nearly every part of Annalise's life was under the strictest control, especially during performance season. She doubted she would ever marry, because Mr. Froman believed such things would be a distraction from her career. There were would-be suitors aplenty, but none could get past her manager or his minions.

While still holding Kellin's hand after stepping down, she looked him in the eyes. "Well, I hope you find your elusive sorcerer. I would dearly like to meet him before you throw him to the wolves at the Marshalcy."

"You would?" he asked, his eyes twinkling with surprise.

"I'd be most grateful actually." Then she gave him the mysterious smile that had won over audiences all over the empire.

"Of...of course, Miss Kauer," he stammered. She watched his throat bob as he swallowed nervously.

She gave his hand a little squeeze before releasing it. A touch was an innocuous thing. But she'd learned the best performances were subtle ones.

Chapter Four
The Break of Dawn

The carriage wheels clacked loudly against the street paving. Annalise felt the crispness in the morning air, the subtle chill that came with every breath and tingled in her nose. She gazed out the window, watching the city of Auvinen awaken. Men pushed trolleys stuffed with wares to sell. Pigeons pecked at leftover crumbs from the day before. The small cafés hadn't opened yet, and stacks of metal chairs were chained in place to prevent theft. The sliding gates blocking the storefronts were also chained shut, and most were smeared with painted designs slapdashedly done before the culprits were chased away by members of the Marshalcy on patrol.

Her eyes lifted to the brightening sky. Hopefully they wouldn't arrive late to the theater. It wasn't quite sunrise, but it was perilously close, and Mr. Froman did not tolerate tardiness. She'd get her breakfast after the private coaching he routinely gave her. His standards were exacting, but they'd helped her achieve popularity and an income above and beyond expectations.

Still, there were costs...

She'd loved theater life since she was a little child, but it had taken a toll on her health. A toll that Mr. Froman didn't seem to mind collecting from her day by day, week by week. Not many theater girls lasted in the industry beyond their thirties. She was a perishable commodity, and she accepted it.

The carriage lumbered to a halt outside the theater, and Annalise hastily turned the handle and leaped outside before the driver could get down from his box.

"Thank you," she said up to him before dashing toward the front door. All the cheering fans from the night before were probably still abed. Even Maud was allowed to sleep in, but never Annalise.

As she neared the door, it swung open, and Mr. Froman appeared with his cane and immaculate suit. He gazed at his pocket watch, a wrinkle on his brow.

"Cutting it close," he observed before flicking the lid shut. He stepped aside so she could hurry in.

He shut and locked the theater door behind him as she hastened to the stairwell to hurry up the steps. She was gasping for breath by the time she reached the top. It was dark and shadowy still, but she could find her way up there blindfolded. Mr. Froman owned many of the theater houses throughout the empire, and she knew each one by heart. As she reached the top, she rushed across the narrow hall to another door, twisted the handle, and then started up the series of ladders that went to the roof.

When she burst through the final door, panting, she terrified a pigeon, which went winging with a startled sound. From the top of the theater roof, she had an unparalleled view of Auvinen, from the manufacturing sector with its smokestacks to the ironclad ships in the harbor. A few pedestrians were beginning to roam the streets, but most of the thoroughfares were deserted. A whistle sounded shrilly from the distant train yard.

She tried to slow her breathing as she looked toward the eastern sky. The sunrise had already started, but only barely, and she soaked in the sharp light and changing colors spreading over the rooftops. The somber shades of gray from the varying buildings contrasted with the oranges, pinks, and lavender blooming in the sky. The sun was a smudge of brightness that grew increasingly brighter with each panting breath she took. And as she took in the scene of the beautiful if marred city, her galloping pulse eventually started to slow. In that moment, she felt a transcendent feeling. Calm replaced frenzy.

After another minute, the sun was too bright to look at, and she turned and noticed Mr. Froman standing behind her. His gaze was still fixed on the breaking dawn.

"It is beautiful up here," Annalise said, turning to face him. "I never tire of watching the sunrise."

"We do not do it for beauty's sake," Mr. Froman said. "Though the Mind of the Sovereignty has graced it with beauty nonetheless."

The hasty climb up the stairs had refreshed her. Her muscles quivered from usage, and her stomach gave a little gurgle, reminding her that breakfast was still a few hours away.

"Was it Isaac Berrow who discovered that light from the sunrise affects our circadian rhythms?" she asked. Mr. Froman was the most knowledgeable man she knew.

"It was not," he replied with a slightly sardonic lapse in his expression—the constriction of his brow, a look of suspicion in his eyes, and the subtle tug of a frown. Those were all little cues that suggested he despised whomever he was talking about.

"You don't like me mentioning Master Berrow, even though he died centuries ago?" she asked, feeling the urge to prod at his reaction.

"Mention him all you like, but that fact was discovered nearly a century later by an astronomer from the University of Tanireh. John Dortous. He discovered circadian rhythms in plants first. But we mortals are subject to the same eternal laws." He lifted his hand and then slowly lowered it. "A rhythm of nature. A symphony we cannot hear with our ears."

"It is one we see with our eyes," Annalise said.

"Indeed. It requires but a few minutes each day. But look down below. How many perambulating are bothering to look up and notice? They are more concerned about pedestrian matters."

"Can you blame them?" Annalise asked. "When rents are rising every year. People must work harder and harder to earn less and less."

"I did not create the cogs of business," he said with a little shrug.

"But you profit from it," she said, giving him a sidelong look. She glanced back at the sun and found it much too bright for her eyes. "Shall we rehearse?"

"That is why we came, Annalise," he said.

She went back and climbed down the ladder. In a few minutes, they were back on stage. The set pieces had been rearranged during the night to restore things for the opening act. This was a fun comedy about a nobleman's daughter who disguised herself as a Romani girl and teased a young barrister hired to represent the laborers of the village. She provoked him at first and then they fell in love, with him learning her true identity at the end of the play. There was something irresistible about the story that had kept audiences coming back to see the story play out.

"Your performance in act two last night..." Mr. Froman said. "I heard from Sommersby that you improvised some of the lines during the scene of the loom and the tea."

Mr. Sommersby was the director of the play. Of course he'd noticed. And told on her.

"What of it?" Annalise said, walking around the stage, touching different articles and moving them slightly out of place.

"Why?"

She picked up a fake clock, turned it around and set it down backward, then looked at him. He was glaring at her.

"I've performed this play a hundred times," she said. "A little change didn't hurt the outcome."

"One hundred and seventeen times, and you will play it thirteen times more before closing night."

"I don't see how it matters," she said. "They were small changes."

"Tell me why you did it, though."

"Because I felt like it. I wanted to do something..."

"Rebellious?"

He was right, but she didn't want to admit it. "Creative," she responded.

"Does not the playwright deserve your best efforts? Does not the director deserve your loyalty? Do not *I*?" He thumped his cane on the stage as if he were stabbing it with a spear.

"It was a tiny thing. I'm sure no one in the audience realized it."

He stepped closer to her. She was provoking him to anger. That was dangerous. But she still felt like doing it. Why did he have to be so unrelenting and fastidious?

"You can be replaced, Annalise Kauer," he said in an icy tone. "I have not trained you, rehearsed with you, protected you these many years to see you throw it all away in a pique of boredom. Every word, every glance, every gesture must...be...*precise.*" He thumped his cane to punctuate his words. She was weary of his speeches. Of his constant criticism. And yet she knew he was right. If he cast her aside, there were plenty of young women who would prostrate themselves before him and beg for the chance to be his next protégé.

"I understand," she said, feeling a tang of bitterness and shame.

"Perfection is our goal," he said.

She hated when he used sayings and made her repeat them back, and yet she knew what he wanted and gave it to him.

"Excellence will be tolerated," she replied.

He gave her a studying look. "Then we will work on that scene in act two until you are no longer bored with it. Every performance matters, Annalise. For some in the audience, it is their first and only time to see it."

It might not be if you'd lower ticket prices, she felt like saying, but that would only inflame him more.

Every morning, they practiced and perfected another element of the play.

No one else had to do this. Mr. Froman did not spend this amount of time with the other main characters or the understudies. Certainly not with Mr. Beal. Only with her. Was he trying to demonstrate how deeply she was under his control? From the moment the sun came up until the final applause quieted to stillness.

There was no denying he'd helped her achieve success beyond her wildest dreams. But, truthfully, she felt something was missing. She felt it every time she pretended to fall in love with the leading man in one of her plays.

Mr. Froman did not allow anyone to get too close to her, so it was never the same actor twice. He also shielded her from admiring fans, from fortune seekers, from anyone who might distract her. And she resented it.

One of the stage doors opened, and a man in a Marshalcy uniform came striding up to Mr. Froman with a worried look. Disrupting a rehearsal? Was the officer out of his mind? Annalise didn't recognize him, and he spoke in a fervent whisper. But her hearing was exceptionally sharp, and she caught a few of the words.

"Found Professor Wickins. Siaconset."

The accused claims the Aesir ring was an heirloom from a deceased uncle with no knowledge of its magical power. The wearing of Aesir rings, with or without the intent of using them to communicate mental commands, is strictly prohibited and punishable by one year in prison. Sentence upheld. Remand the accused to Mickelgate Prison.

—Winstoffer Case appeal, High Court of Justice, Saint James Park, Bishopsgate

Issac Berrow

CHAPTER FIVE
SIACONSET

The world had changed drastically since Isaac had been asleep. The locomotivuses that had hovered above magnetic tracks had been replaced by ugly iron steam trains that belched coal smoke. They were slower too! He'd watched in fascination and with a bit of reluctance as the gears and levers moved, powered by coal fed into ovens by sooty-faced workers. The streetlamps had all been replaced with foul-smelling oil lamps, lit by urchins on stools with flaming pokers. Detritus littered the streets.

Isaac had found a thousand ways in which useful bits of magic had been done away with. And the noise! Everywhere he went there was a cacophony, and there were no orchestras to pipe out magical defensive spells. Instead, someone had invented a musical contraption that produced tinny, bothersome replications of songs. Brass bands with tiny warbling to accompany it. Nothing that could produce even the most mundane spill of magic. But even the fashions had changed—enough so that Isaac, who could barely care less about such things, noticed. The men wore black suits, the bowler hats he was accustomed to replaced by flat-topped straw hats with fabric or a ribbon around the base above the brim. The women wore dresses still, very tight-fighting and puffing like mushrooms above their elbows, accompanied by an assortment of gaudy, feathered hats with broad brims. Long gloves were all the rage.

He walked along the street from the train yard in Rexanne. It was more populous than it had been the last time he was there, shabbier and more noisy. He had a glamour spell that helped him blend in with the people around him by making it appear he'd adopted their manner of dress. A more advanced glamour could impact who he believed he was and allow him to impersonate someone else, and they would believe it too. The filthy streets stank of manure and the constant noises were distracting. He made his way to the quay, intending to hire a ferry to Siaconset, where he would meet Wickins and Clara.

Wickins had warned him about the dissolution of the Invisible College. The mere act of summoning light could lead to an arrest, so he had also glamoured his violin case to appear as a travel bag.

The ferry station was crowded with people, but he was thankfully able to procure a seat. The bothersome noise of Rexanne was put behind him, replaced by the squawks of an absolute horde of seagulls. At least he had encountered willing intelligences again since leaving the university.

He reached the island and was grateful to see it was still a well-kept community for tourists and guests. The streets were cleanly swept, and he recognized some of the older buildings and shops from the time he'd spent there years before. It had been a popular haunt for the military then, but when he looked around, he saw no uniforms except for those worn by officers of the Marshalcy.

Isaac strode the short distance to Mowbray House. When he saw it, his heart ached from the flood of memories. The white picket fence, the double stairs leading to the front door. The shake shingle siding. A cupola on one of the rooftops. The flowerbeds were tidy and offered a fragrant smell that blended with the scent of the sea.

When he'd been Robinson Dickemore Hawksley, he'd anticipated spending years in this house with his wife, McKenna. Her aunt had left it to her, and indeed, they had spent happy times there together. Yet the whole time, they'd been ignorant of their true identities.

His most important duty was to find Eiríka again. But without any contact from Loyal, he didn't have the help he'd enjoyed in the past. And with magic being forbidden, there wasn't the network of the Invisible College he'd had access to either. This time, things would be much more challenging.

He noticed a Marshalcy officer staring at him and realized he had paused for too long in front of the house. Shaking his head, he continued down the street before taking a footpath to the beach. The wind was gentle, and he walked past the screen of beech trees to reach the water. There was another couple in the distance walking along the edge of the surf, the woman carrying a parasol for shade. Isaac searched the area nearby and found no one present. He summoned the intelligence of seagulls and asked them to patrol the skies and warn him if anyone was coming his way.

Then he dipped his hand into his pocket and produced his sorcerer's ring. After sliding it onto his thumb, which triggered the usual spasm of pain, he contacted Wickins again.

I've arrived. I'm at the beach, approaching Mowbray House from behind.

A few moments later, he felt a reply thought: *I cannot wait to see you, old chap. We'll be there soon.*

Isaac had wondered how best to reveal himself to his friends. They did not know his true identity, nor that McKenna had succumbed to the redoubtable fever and lost her body to Eirika as a little girl, not in a drowning as a young woman.

He hadn't expected it all to unravel so quickly, though.

Isaac clasped his hands behind his back and walked leisurely across the beach. The couple he'd seen earlier had gone the other way and were out of sight. Waves dashed against the shore. A rather plump pelican soared across the waters looking for a meal.

Isaac felt a mental nudge from a seagull intelligence that people were heading his way across the beach.

Within fifteen minutes, he saw Wickins and Clara, arm in arm, on a stroll by the sea. Clara had a parasol, but it was used more as a walking stick. Her hair was done up in an interesting and different style, but he recognized her face instantly. She looked remarkably like Mrs. Foster, who had been like an adoptive mother to Robinson Hawksley. Seeing Clara made him smile, although it caused him some pain to mark her resemblance to McKenna.

He still loved every iteration of Eiríka. They were all different facets of his wife.

Wickins was totally clean-shaven, his hair slicked down with a pomade, but his face—although middle-aged—was totally recognizable, and the effusive grin on his mouth showed he was excited and eager. His suit was not black but a lighter shade of gray, and Isaac noticed the matching tufts of gray at his sideburns. He was still handsome, and his few wrinkles gave him a distinguished look.

As they drew near each other, he dropped his glamour entirely and watched as both Wickins and Clara started in surprise.

Wickins's mouth hung open a moment before he could speak. "You haven't...aged...a day."

Isaac shook his head in agreement. He certainly hadn't. "It's my device that heals. I don't age. I can look older if I use a spell, but I wanted you to see me as I am."

Clara came forward and took his hands in hers, the parasol strap around her wrist. "Robinson," she whispered. Then her eyes brightened with mischief. "You're as skinny as ever! You'd think the device would help with that!"

Robison kissed Clara on the cheek and then gave Wickins a bear hug that brought a surge of warmth to his chest. Usually when he awoke from a long sleep, he had to find new friends, new partners, had to reinvent himself. It was a relief to have shared memories, a common history, and an intimate connection to these people.

"This seems impossible, old chap." Wickins said, brow wrinkling in confusion as he pulled back and gripped Isaac's shoulders.

Isaac drew the device from his pocket. They were both familiar with it. He opened the lid to reveal the marbled brown stone at its center. "This is a philosopher's stone. While I have it with me, I cannot age. A great sorcerer invented it, and it's been passed down to me."

"You'd better keep it hidden, then, old friend," Wickins said, covering the device with his hand and looking both ways.

"We're alone," Isaac said reassuringly. "I know you said the Invisible College has been routed, but I've been in the Skrýmir sleep for many years and don't know what's happened while I was gone."

"Isn't the Skrýmir something only the Aesir do?" Wickins asked in confusion.

"No, it's a magic that anyone who knows the spell can do. I was taught it by the Erlking's daughter. It slows down all bodily functions, and combined with a philosopher's stone, the body can remain in that state indefinitely. But when I awoke, everything had changed. Magic has been outlawed. How?"

"Semblances took over the Brotherhood of Shadows and then the whole military," Wickins said. He glanced at Clara worriedly. "They declared the Aesir war over, saying the Erlking had been shot and killed. The glamoured body they produced was said to prove it. There was a big celebration, and the ice trenches were abandoned."

Isaac gaped in shock.

"Thanks to you, we knew it wasn't true," Clara said, reaching out and touching his arm.

Wickins nodded. "The Invisible College was framed by the military. You, in particular, were accused of conspiring with the *strannik* to turn the world over to the Aesir. It took a few years, but eventually they turned people's opinions against sorcerers.

Quorums were broken into and despoiled. Then laws were passed to limit the use of magic."

"And to punish those who practice it," Clara snapped. She looked incensed.

"Where did all these new inventions come from?" Isaac asked in confusion. "I saw the steam trains."

"The emperor, seeing how unpopular sorcerers had become, began to invest in businesses that could replicate magical effects with nonmagical ones. He assumed more authority and then called on the Marshalcy to stamp out what still remained of the Invisible College. It's as if he saw his opportunity and took it."

"The Aesir threat is far from over," Isaac said in disbelief. "The next Awakening is about to happen, and you're telling me there are no troops in the north to defend the trenches?"

"They've abandoned them all," Wickins said, glancing at Clara in distress. Then his gaze settled back on Isaac. "It's been twenty-three years since you left...the Awakening is this winter?"

Isaac was still in a state of shock. "So there are no more sorcerers," he said in sorrow.

Wickins shook his head. "No, old chap. That's not true. We've just gone underground. It is now fully against the law to practice magic. And there are stiff penalties—fines and imprisonment."

"Is there a Master of the Royal Secret?"

"No," Clara said. "Not anymore. But sorcery is still taught in secret. Person to person. Those of us who were conspicuous members, my family for example, have had to be very discreet and renounce the college. But we still help wherever we can."

"If there is any person leading the college, I don't know who it is," Wickins confessed. "But I've heard rumors from Trudie that there's a rogue sorcerer in Auvinen right now."

"We actually thought it was you," Clara said with a smile.

Isaac was flummoxed. "Me? Why?"

Wickins continued. "They say he plays a violin and helps

people, especially the downtrodden. There's a steep reward for his arrest, but no one has turned him in."

"So you don't know his name. It is a man, though?"

"From what we've heard, yes," Clara answered. "But we think it's more than one man. He's like a ghost who appears and disappears."

"Curious," Isaac said. "And he's in Auvinen. Is Trudie there as well? What about your parents, Clara? Are they still alive?"

"Yes," Clara said. "They're still on Brake Street. The house was rebuilt as promised."

That made Isaac happy. "So you inherited Mowbray House?"

Clara nodded. "Technically it still belongs to you, though."

He shook his head. "Robinson is dead. It's yours."

"There's enough room for all of us, Dickemore," Wickins said. "And Siaconset doesn't have harsh winters, so maybe your parents would enjoy retiring here as well. That way, we could keep an eye on them for their safety."

"None of us will be safe," Isaac said. "Once the Awakening happens, the Aesir will be here within weeks. There is no time to summon an army. Not to mention that the citizens probably don't even believe in the threat anymore."

"Many of us still do," Clara protested.

"The Semblances in the military were waiting for me when I woke up," Isaac said. "They've already tried to kill me."

Clara gasped in surprise.

"That means they'll come looking for me. And anyone I used to be connected with."

"The Marshalcy has been watching us relentlessly," Clara said. "That's why we wanted to meet you here on the beach. They're keeping note of visitors who come to the house."

"You think so?" Wickins asked in surprise.

Clara gave him a sidelong look. "You've kept rather busy with your books, my dear."

Wickins smiled sheepishly.

"They'll be watching Brake Street too, then," Isaac lamented.

"It's been a while since we visited my parents," Clara said, touching Wickins's shoulder. "We could go there and tell them Rob's back."

"Since we haven't traveled there lately, it may seem suspicious if we go there when they know Rob has just come out of hiding. Undoubtedly, our family will be watched even more closely. What reason could we have that wouldn't arouse any extra suspicion?" Wickins said.

"We could say we wanted to see the play," Clara said.

"Tickets are impossible to get," Wickins said brusquely.

"A play?" Isaac asked, confused.

"But my parents own a box seat. The performances have been in the theaters all over the empire," Clara said. "It's all the rage because of the actress starring in it. They stopped doing operas, you know. Because of music's connection to spellcasting, live musical performances are highly restricted and incur exorbitant permit fees, so the operas weren't making enough money to offset the expense. The play is about a man who falls in love with a woman who he thinks is from a lower station, despite the fact that she is actually from a much higher station than him."

"They've just announced that they will be starting rehearsals for a new play about the Erlking's daughter," Wickins said. "Totally reinventing the story. I'm sure it will be rubbish."

Isaac felt a tremor in his psyche. "Who is the actress?" he asked, his mouth going dry.

"She is *so* talented," Clara said. "I saw her in one of her earlier plays."

"Her name is Keer-er, isn't it?" Wickins said. "The owner of the theaters has had a few protégés, but she's been the most successful one by far."

"Annalise Kauer," Clara said.

And at the mention of her name, Isaac heard a barely audible yip in his mind and felt the presence of a very excited entity who had been absent for far too long.

CHAPTER SIX
A Temporary Glamour

The reunion with Loyal had elicited a surge of gratitude and a brightening of hope. Based on the dog intelligence's reaction to the mention of the actress, Isaac didn't have to wonder where to look anymore, and he was confident he'd find a way to meet Eiríka again very soon.

After departing Siaconset, he'd traveled immediately to Auvinen. In this changed world he had entered, it was a relief to see that some things remained the same, and boat travel was one of them. And so were talkative dockworkers, who provided him with some much-needed information on the state of change. Once he left the docks, he was inundated once again with everything transformed. Of all the new inventions that had been made since he'd been gone, Isaac found the electric streetcars to be the most confusing and ugly. Since the iron horses that once pulled the trams no longer functioned, they had adapted the way the cars were carried over the iron tracks laid into grooves on the street. A metal rod jutted from the roof of each vehicle, connecting to a labyrinth of overhead wires. An electric current powered both the cars' iron wheels and the overhead wires, which hummed incessantly with power and provided a source of continual energy to keep the streetcars in motion.

The maze of tracks embedded into the streets went in a variety of directions, with interconnection points at which the cars could change direction. Though there were carriages and horses as well, most people were either hanging off the handles and exterior footrests attached to the repurposed and tarnished tram sections or sitting on the moldering seats inside the cars.

Isaac was sitting on one such, regarding his fellow passengers crammed into the aisle. There was an advertising poster near him revealing the play being performed in Auvinen about a barrister. There was a vague drawing of a woman and a man. It was his first glimpse at what Eiríka might look like now. As soon as his stop was called, he jettisoned from his cramped seat and stepped out onto the street, grateful to Wickins and Clara for providing some updated currency for his journey.

Auvinen was different, yet the streets and several of the buildings were still familiar. The tenements, which had been destroyed by an explosion while he and McKenna had been in Auvinen to prove she was still alive after her kidnapping by the *strannik*, had all been rebuilt into more fashionable apartments. He felt the ugly electrified cables marred the scene, but people seemed entirely accustomed to them. He scratched an itch at the back of his neck, looking up at some familiar buildings that had been there on his last visit.

Before leaving Siaconset, Isaac had settled on a plan with Wickins and Clara, or near enough. Knowing that a Marshalcy officer had made note of his presence when he had paused too long in front of Mowbray House upon his arrival, Isaac erased Clara's and Wickins's memories of his brief visit through a temporary glamour spell, having explained to them that he could easily remove it when they met up again.

As Isaac had expected, the officer had reported the incident to his detective lieutenant, who'd immediately arranged for an interview with Mr. and Mrs. Wickins and arrived on their doorstep soon after they returned home. Isaac, using the invisibility spell once again, had entered the house from the back while the

Marshalcy officers were received at the front door, and lingered nearby in case there was any trouble from the interview, which there was not. Wickins and Clara had argued that they never saw a man outside their door, nor had they had any contact with friends from their past.

As soon as the Marshalcy left, Isaac had thought the glamour reversal spell, which Eiríka had taught him centuries before. They knew it would look more suspect for an unknown man to travel with the couple, so once their memories were restored, they bid Isaac a safe journey before setting their own plans in motion.

They would contact the Fosters to see about joining them in their box at the theater before the play finished its run in Auvinen.

His gaze lingered on the new buildings before he continued with his walk. The explosion had nearly killed Widow Farmer and her children, the family he'd become fond of after meeting them during the Aesir attacks. The entire family had followed Sarah Fuller Fiske and the *strannik* into a new world, opened to them by the Erlking just before the Aesir attack on Nirshoye. What had become of them?

Normally, the Skrýmir was too long to worry about those he had last shared his life with, not to mention that he always glamoured away those recollections, but this time, he had the rare opportunity to still have connections with people from his previous incarnation. Twenty-three years was one of the shortest periods between Awakenings, which was dependent on the random prime numbers that followed in the sequence. Yet still, the world had transformed so much in that little lapse.

Knowing his way around Auvinen helped, and he felt Loyal's presence at his side as he walked down the street to the Storrows, the quorum of the Invisible College that he had joined upon arriving in Auvinen as a would-be professor of elocution.

Turning the next corner, he saw the ruins of that once-proud building. It was at the intersection of two streets. There had been a secret entrance in the tavern across from it, but the walls had been broken open, the windows smashed, and the interior looted.

It was a costly waste of prime real estate to leave such a grand building empty, but showing its ruin sent a symbolic message. As if the Erlking were taunting him. Even the long-lasting Invisible College had succumbed to entropy.

He felt a twist of disappointment at the sight of the broken-down building, but he was grateful there were those who hadn't given up on his vision of sorcerers helping humanity. He'd like to meet that man Wickins had mentioned who was, in all likelihood, inspired by Robinson Dickemore Hawksley.

Take me to Eirika, he thought to Loyal, and he felt a wag of approval and a change in direction. When he neared the city center, he caught the whiff of spiced peanuts in the air. The familiar scent made him salivate. But when he approached the seller, he lost all stomach for the treat. The cart owners in the past had used incalescent stoves, which heated to a precise temperature. This shabby little cart was fed by flaming fuel, and the contents of its blackened kettle looked burnt and unappetizing.

Loyal brought him several streets down to a theater surrounded by a crowd of pedestrians already gathered in the afternoon sun, awaiting entrance to the evening performance. Hawkers outside were trying to sell them food or drinks while they waited for the theater doors to open.

A uniformed man stood in the street, hand on a truncheon, watching the crowd.

It took Isaac a moment to put the pieces together, but he realized that the theater had replaced a building that had previously been part of the Invisible College as a quorum. Preensby had been its name.

It had a triangular roof with ornate statuary in the apex and each side. A dome of sorts was positioned before the vaulted part in the middle, the ornamentation making it look like an emperor's crown. At least seven arches with doors were at the lowest level, columns and balconies presided above that, and there were more sculpted images on the frontage near the lower roofline. The statues on top of the roof had wings, and Isaac surmised they were effigies of Aesir.

It was quite a spectacle to behold.

Annalise was the lead actress who would be performing that night in the theater. When he asked about possibly getting a ticket when he'd arrived at the docks earlier, the worker had laughed at him and said all the rest of the shows were sold out because the play was nearing the end of its run. Miss Kauer's austere manager had another play in the works and the company would be retiring to begin rehearsing it in time for winter performances, which would commence at the Imperial Theater in Tanhauser. Only the very wealthy or well-connected could get tickets to the remaining shows at this point.

Isaac was good at asking questions, especially innocuous ones, and he meandered through the crowd to find out what he could. He learned that Annalise was protected by bodyguards and that her hotel was a great secret. However, this didn't cause Isaac concern, for Loyal would know where she was staying. The dog intelligence had led him to the theater because that was where Annalise was at the moment that he had asked. With his assumption that Annalise Kauer was Eiríka reborn, it was his prevailing theory that her manager, Mr. Froman, was either a glamour or a Semblance of the Erlking himself. It seemed logical that the Erlking would supervise her last life as a human, with the intention of preventing Isaac from marrying her.

The crowd of Annalise's fans had given him many descriptions of her beauty, the humor of her character, the mischievous and enigmatic reputation she had as an actress. All of it made him more eager to meet her in person. To see this version of her. He thought of their final reunion longingly.

"You've been standing there long enough, friend," said the uniformed guard who'd approached him while he gawped at the theater and thought of Eiríka, not realizing the crowd had shifted as people were allowed in, and he was nearly alone now. "Time to move along if you don't have a ticket."

"They're almost impossible to get, I hear," Isaac said in a jovial tone.

The guard nodded. "I'm afraid so. If you've come from far away to see it, you've wasted your time."

Isaac regarded him closely, studying his facial features and the cut of his uniform. The tall boots. Details would help him form a better illusion.

"I live here," Isaac said dismissively and then sighed. "Wish I'd made time to see it sooner. How many times have you seen it?"

"Several," the guard said, rocking on his heels a little, tucking his thumbs in his belt with an aura of self-importance. "Sometimes I guard the street, but we also take turns on the inside." He didn't seem to mind having a conversation. Especially one that made him feel important.

"Oh?" Isaac said brightly.

"I've even escorted Miss Kauer to her carriage on occasion," said the fellow with a wag of his eyebrows.

"You've seen her up close, then?" Isaac asked.

"Indeed, I helped her into the carriage once."

"You don't say. You have an enviable job."

He rocked back on his heels again, looking proud. "I do at that. It's better any day of the week to work in private security rather than for the Marshalcy. Pay's better too."

"Must be," Isaac said. Then he extended his hand in greeting. "I would give up my job in a heartbeat to be you for just one day, Mr...?"

"Puzey. Came from Bishopsgate, you know. Served in the military before they sacked us all. Pension wasn't enough."

"I'm sure it was a meager one," Isaac said, furrowing his brow and nodding in sympathy.

Some people would talk incessantly given any encouragement at all. The guard didn't realize how helpful he was being. He'd confirmed that Isaac could get access to the theater if he looked like him.

A whistled shriek sounded, followed by a colorful burst of

magic that exploded in the air behind the theater. It was a universal cry for assistance recognizable by all sorcerers. And it had gone off in the middle of Auvinen, the first display of magic Isaac had seen since waking from his twenty-three-year sleep. People began to exclaim in fear and concern.

"What on earth was that?" Isaac said, not wanting to seem familiar with the event.

Mr. Puzey scowled and shook his head in anger. "Those awful miscreants," he growled. "Have they no shame?"

"Was it an explosion?" Isaac asked, studying the sparkles of magic dripping from the burning spot in the sky. It was probably only several blocks away.

"No, it's those cursed sorcerers again," said the guard. "Ah, the Marshalcy is already heading to investigate," he said, pointing down the street. A black wagon with gold letters pulled by horses was rattling down the street, picking up speed.

Isaac was intrigued and wanted to investigate it himself. Had it been a cry for help? Or was it perhaps a defiant act meant to infuriate the Marshalcy and those who oppressed sorcerers?

Only one way to find out.

Kellin Carrault

Chapter Seven
Hunting a Ghost

A knock on the door roused Kellin from the paperwork on his desk.

"Come in," he said gruffly, pausing quickly to check the time on his watch. It was early evening. The performance would be starting soon, and he needed to head over to the theater.

Arbuckle opened the door and poked his head in. "We caught one!" he said in an excited tone.

Kellin forgot all about the paperwork. "Who? Do you have a name yet?"

Arbuckle shook his head. "I don't think it's the rogue you've been looking for. No violin case. But he was found with a card in his pocket with a chymical symbol on it and a cipher."

"He's a sorcerer, then," Kellin said, intrigued.

"He set off a flare by the theater," Arbuckle reported. "The Marshalcy came running. We had a chase, but we managed to box him in, in an alley, and got to him first."

"Splendid!" Kellin said, rising from the chair. The paperwork could wait. "Which station is holding him?"

"He's at the Plinth Street station," Arbuckle said. "Detective Inspector Cowdry is working the case."

"Cowdry. Excellent. I'll stop by on my way to the theater."

"Are you going to tell Miss Kauer about this?" Arbuckle asked with a twinkle in his eye.

"If the flare went up by the theater, I'm certain she will ask. Best be prepared to answer."

"I thought you'd want to know right away." The man's expectant smile suggested he was anticipating a romantic development between his employer and the actress.

Kellin gave Arbuckle a scoffing shake of the head and walked around his desk to leave the office. The smell of the other man's pomade lingered in the air.

The firm kept several buildings within Auvinen, mostly nondescript ones that had previously been used in manufacturing. The number of cases and files it handled required vast amounts of storage. It was important to write down little details because a clue that wasn't helpful in one instance might be very helpful in another. Case notes were an important tool in their industry.

He jogged down the stairs to the first floor, which was bustling with men and women coming in for the night shift. The firm had many clients and could afford a large payroll. Kellin felt privileged to have been assigned to Mr. Froman's theater business. It was an unusual arrangement, given their trade, but Mr. Froman had an eccentric's interest in learning when sorcerers had been taken into custody.

After summoning his carriage, Kellin climbed on board and directed the driver to stop by the Plinth Street station. The streets were busy with people heading home after work, so the side journey took longer than usual, but at least the horses managed a steady pace. Once the carriage slowed and stopped in front of the Marshalcy office, Kellin quickly stepped outside.

"Wait for me," he instructed before climbing the steps into the building. The precinct name was carved into the stone with a golden alloy that made the letters stand out.

He asked for directions from a clerk who knew him and was led to an interrogation cell by a Marshalcy officer. Cowdry had his uniform coat off, his shirt sleeves rolled up, and was wiping blood from his knuckles with a rag. He had a thick mustache, an impressive physique, and an air of violence.

A man was bound to a chair, head slumped forward, his face puffy, his eyebrow and nose streaming blood that stained his sweaty shirt. His arms were shackled behind him to the spokes of the chair.

"You look familiar," Cowdry said with a frown. "You're with the firm?"

Kellin nodded. Some Marshalcy officers disdained private security and looked at them as competition. "Kellin Carrault."

"What can I do for you, Mr. Carrault? Do you know this man?"

"Are you using nulling cuffs?" Kellin asked.

"I'm not a simpleton," Cowdry said. "Why are you here?"

"He sent up a flare by the theater," Kellin answered. Some men liked to size other people up based on what rank or authority they had. He could tell Cowdry was like that, and Kellin decided to put him in his place. "Mr. Froman will not be pleased."

His meaning was clear enough. Mr. Froman was one of the wealthiest men in the empire, who also was acquainted with the head of the Marshalcy on familiar terms. One word from Kellin, and Cowdry's career could be in threat.

Cowdry cleared his throat, then said, "It wasn't all that near—"

"It was near enough," Kellin broke in, silencing him. "I'd like a word with your...suspect."

"Take as long as you need," Cowdry said. He grabbed his uniform jacket, slung it over his shoulder, and left the interrogation room.

The man in the chair was breathing hard, groaning slightly from pain. He did not look at Kellin at all. The swollen eye would have made that difficult.

Kellin glanced at his pocket watch again. Time was short. "Rather bold to set off a flare, sorcerer, don't you think?"

The man didn't look at him, just gazed fixedly at the wall. Kellin examined the man's clothes. A dark and shabby suit. His belt had frayed bits by the notches. His jacket looked threadbare.

"I'll keep this simple," Kellin said. "You already know you face years in debtors' prison for what you've done today. I've heard some inmates starve to death because no one will bring them food. I won't guess how long you'll last. I need information that I think you can provide. I'm willing to make a deal. Are you interested?"

The man lifted his chin slightly. He looked apprehensive. There was blood on his lower lip.

Kellin took silence for acquiescence. "I'm looking for the rogue sorcerer. The one who plays the violin."

The man's eyes contracted slightly. That was his only tell.

"You know him," Kellin said eagerly, moving forward.

"I don't know who you're talking about," the man said.

"You *do* know who I'm talking about. I have been at this business a long while. I know when someone is lying. The question at hand isn't whether you know him, but how much money it will take for you to reveal him to me."

Kellin stood erect, hands clasped behind his back, as he gazed across the desk at Mr. Froman in the manager's office at the theater. There were many Aesir artifacts in the room, some of which must have been unimaginably costly. It was against the law for most people to own such things, but Mr. Froman was immune to the law. Extreme wealth had its privileges.

"And what did he reveal to you, Mr. Carrault?"

"He was rather stubborn, as most sorcerers are," Kellin answered. "The man isn't talking...yet."

Mr. Froman said nothing. His eyes were fixed on Kellin's in a manner that was unnerving.

"I thought you'd be interested in the case since it happened so near the theater."

"You judged rightly," said Mr. Froman. Then he fell silent again.

"He had a card with some writing on it," Kellin said. "The Marshalcy is having a code breaker look at it."

"The one you captured was a messenger, then," Froman said.

"That is what I deduced as well. A low-ranking sorcerer who relays messages and panicked when he encountered the Marshalcy, fled on foot but was cornered and tried to summon help."

"So the message wasn't delivered," Froman said with a glimmer in his eye. "Instead, it was intercepted."

"It could contain useful information," Kellin pointed out.

"Good work, Mr. Carrault."

He took it as a dismissal, nodded, and left the office. After shutting the door, he was startled to find Miss Kauer standing nearby.

She approached him and said in an undertone, "I heard a sorcerer was captured this afternoon."

"Indeed, one was," he said. Had she been eavesdropping? Or had someone else told her about the flare?

"Does the Marshalcy have him?"

"He's in custody, yes. They caught him before my men could reach him unfortunately. He was roughed up pretty badly when I got there."

He wasn't sure what reaction he'd been expecting, but he was surprised when she revealed none. Her beautiful face was as inscrutable as ever. She was wearing her Romani costume, her feet bare, the bead necklace and earrings ornamental and cheap. But they twinkled under the stage lights.

"Will he go to debtors' prison, then?"

"Very likely. He's in a great deal of trouble."

"Would you tell me which one when you find out?"

Kellin frowned. "It would be highly inappropriate for you to visit him, Miss Kauer. Not to mention impractical."

"I don't want to visit him," she answered. "I just want to make sure he's fed."

"I could help you arrange it...anonymously," he offered.

The smile she gave him made his heart begin to race. "Thank you, Mr. Carrault. That would ease my mind greatly."

"It would be my pleasure," he said, bowing his head slightly.

When he glanced at her face, she was looking down the hall, her brow furrowing.

Kellin turned and saw one of the theater guards standing at the end of the corridor staring at them.

"Who is that?" Miss Kauer whispered.

"He's one of my guards. Mr. Puzey."

"That is *not* Mr. Puzey," she said forcefully. He heard something in her voice—fear, perhaps? It was difficult to describe. Something was bothering her deeply.

Kellin glanced back, but the guard was gone.

Issac Berrow

CHAPTER EIGHT
THE HOUSE ON BRAKE STREET

Night had fallen over Auvinen. Gas lamps burned behind panes of glass, positioned on the poles that had once held quicksilver lighting. The air had a slight chymical smell, no doubt caused by the burning fuel. Isaac had walked almost the entire way from the theater glamoured as a messenger, his heart heavy with the weight of the decisions he needed to make, his mind crowded with too many thoughts.

And then he saw the Fosters' home on Brake Street just ahead, and the burdens he carried began to ebb. His pace slowed as he took in the familiar sight. The house had been rebuilt after it had been destroyed in a sorcerer's fire, but it matched its predecessor exactly.

There were so many memories connected to this street. Pleasant dinners on Closures. The sound of music from the Broadwood grand or his violin. A snowy night when he'd held McKenna's hand as he guided her over the slippery slush to get her back home safely. The greenhouse where he'd first kissed her.

He stopped and swallowed the sudden thickness in his throat. Though he'd fallen in love with Eiríka across many different lifetimes, that last one had been one of his favorites. One of the most meaningful and extemporaneous. The loss of McKenna still hurt.

In the past, he'd glamoured himself to protect against such pain, but this time he hadn't wanted to risk it. Yes, he'd found her. But getting to know her would be more difficult this time. Eiríka's new life was designed as a trap to catch and kill *him*.

He started toward the house again, trying to sort through the flurry of thoughts and feelings.

When he'd glimpsed Annalise Kauer in the theater, she had seen past the glamour he'd worn of Mr. Puzey. If seeing her hadn't been enough, the fact that she had seen through the glamour and Loyal's excitement would have given him plenty of certitude.

The Erlking had chosen not to hide his daughter in obscurity this time. No, he was pronouncing her identity loudly and boldly. A flame to attract a particular moth.

The bodyguard she'd been with had immediately taken interest in her accusation about Isaac. He'd turned invisible and watched the fellow start to search for him. She'd left the corridor, returning to her dressing room. He'd watched her go, and knowing who she really was had caused him particular torment. But she wouldn't remember him. Only when the host body was close to death did the memories begin to slip free.

To know her and yet not know her...

Eiríka was Annalise Kauer. She had different memories, different experiences. Not to mention she was uncommonly beautiful. It made him feel completely self-conscious. Even though they'd fallen in love hundreds of times, would this time be different? Would her beauty and fame change things?

Isaac was even more certain that her manager, Mr. Froman, was the Erlking himself. Probably a Semblance, otherwise he could not disguise himself from Eiríka once she regained her memories. The fact that he kept his protégé so close was the strongest indicator of his true identity, because he was placed to prevent the covenant from being fulfilled. From what Isaac had gathered, the man was famously wealthy, influential, and had the resources to protect her from outsiders. He needed a way to see her alone. To tell her the truth about herself. About himself.

Because his memories were intact, he felt especially impatient to do so, yet he didn't want to frighten the poor woman half to death. He'd managed the task before, though, just as Eiríka had needed to awaken him to the truth in all those lifetimes before he was born in his current form. He'd been guided by Lydia Brewer. She'd earned his trust and empathy before disclosing her true nature to him. He needed to do the same for her one last time.

The plum trees lining the street were void of leaves and fruit. They were thicker, older looking, with skeletal twigs. He reached the door and knocked on it firmly. He'd sent messages to Brake Street to let them know Wickins and Clara were coming to see the play. And he'd sent messages to Wickins and Clara to invite them. He didn't think they would have arrived so quickly, so this gave him the opportunity to meet up with the Fosters before the company arrived and the Marshalcy would be paying even closer attention.

He heard someone walking briskly to the door. Loyal was at his side, excited. The lock turned, the door opened swiftly, and a woman appeared in the frame. He recognized Trudie, but she was a grown woman.

"You'd better get—" she started to say and then stopped in confusion. It seemed like she'd been expecting someone else.

"I have a message for Mr. Foster," he said as he held a piece of paper out.

"That's my father. Please come in and wait a moment while I get him." She opened the door more widely and let him enter. As soon as he was inside and the door was closed, he let his glamour drop.

Trudie did a double take as her mouth gaped. "Rob!" she said breathlessly. Then she flung herself into his arms and gave him the welcoming hug he'd hoped for.

You're finally here!" she said with wonder and surprise. "We thought you'd been killed after all this time with no word. But you haven't even aged a day!"

"It's so good to see you," he said. "Your parents are here?"

"Yes! They'll be so thrilled." She grasped his hands and gave him the look of an affectionate older sister. She was older than him physically, though not by experience. She had no wedding band on her hand, which surprised him.

"How old are you, Trudie?" he asked.

"You don't expect a woman over thirty to own it, do you?" She laughed. "And I haven't gone by Trudie in *years*. I go by True now."

"That's a lovely nickname," he said.

"Thank you. Father's in the parlor. Come!" She pulled him by the hand and brought him quickly down the familiar corridor. The wallpaper was new and different, but the structure and layout duplicated those of the original home. Even the scents were familiar. There were no servants about. Not a single one.

"Who was at the door this time?" It was Mr. Foster's voice, and he spoke before they reached him.

When they entered the parlor, he was sitting in a stuffed chair in the corner. Not the same one that had burned to ash, but a similar enough replacement that it reminded Isaac of the image he held in his mind. Mr. Foster's hair and beard had gone white. Instead of pince-nez glasses, he had on a larger set of spectacles and held a book open on his lap, which he let fall to the side as they entered. He looked at Isaac in astonishment, and slowly, with a wince of pain, made it to his feet.

"Son!" he declared, and the endearment sent a surge of warmth through Isaac's breast. True held her hands together near her mouth, smiling and crying simultaneously.

Isaac closed the distance and the two men embraced. Footsteps sounded in the hall, and then Mrs. Foster was among them.

"Robinson," she breathed, then joined the embrace. In that moment of bliss and belonging, he felt the deepest yearning for McKenna to be there to experience it. And he thought of a way that she might be, in the future, if all his plans worked out. That was enough for the moment.

"You must not have eaten a good meal in days," Mrs. Foster said in a choked but humorous tone. "Look at you!"

"You're still the age when we last saw you," Mr. Foster said, pulling back and squinting at him. "A philosopher's stone? Is that your secret?"

Isaac nodded but did not elaborate. "I've been away for years, I know. While I haven't aged, I also haven't been aware of all the changes that have happened. But I know that just being here now is a risk to your family. I don't wish to compromise any of you, but I couldn't—"

"You are always welcome in our home," Mrs. Foster said firmly. "Nothing could change that."

"And I am no longer working now," Mr. Foster said. "I do not have the same duties I once held as a judge."

"A judge?" Robinson asked in surprise.

"He was told he had to retire," Mrs. Foster said with contempt. "When the persecutions against sorcerers began, those of us who were active in the Invisible College were targeted and replaced by upstarts."

"I'm sorry to hear that," Isaac said. "I fear Semblances have taken over the government."

"That has been my suspicion as well," Mr. Foster said with a firm nod. "The general told us the *strannik* and his followers took boats at the Nirshoye docks and disappeared without a trace, but we knew the truth from you, that they went to another world. We wondered at one point if you followed them to exact justice, but after several years without word, we feared you had died."

Isaac shook his head. "No, I was here. But through my earlier experience as Master of the Royal Secret, I had learned how to put myself in the Skrýmir sleep and only recently awoke from it. I understand the military has disbanded?"

Mr. Foster looked surprised at this news before answering Isaac's question. "Ah...precisely," he said. "They said the threat is over. The Marshalcy holds the power now."

Mrs. Foster glanced at her husband worriedly. "You told us

before you went into hiding it would be twenty-three years, but it's so much shorter than ever before, we thought you were in error. How do you know that?"

"I deduced the pattern of when the Awakenings happen," Isaac declared. "But there is still a chance to stop the war from coming."

"Without any soldiers at the front, it will be a slaughter," Mr. Foster said worriedly.

"An annihilation," Isaac said. "We'll need sorcerers to help defend the people."

As he said the words, he noticed a look of excitement in True's eyes.

Mrs. Foster held up her hands. "To be honest, no one willingly admits to being a sorcerer anymore," she said. "The consequences are extreme."

"Exorbitant fines that lead to debtors' prison," Mr. Foster said. "Unfortunately, *that* is where you'll find most of our sorcerers nowadays. The rewards offered make it enticing for neighbors to betray one another, and many of our friends have been locked up."

"At least they had the courtesy to round them up for us," Isaac said with a grin.

True looked like she wanted to say something, but she bit her lip and remained silent.

Isaac determined to interrogate True at a more opportune time, then continued. "I went to Mowbray House and visited Clara and Wickins. They say there are people willing to take a stand."

"We have become isolated, but none of that matters with the Aesir threat. Something must be done," said Mr. Foster.

"How can we help?" Mrs. Foster asked, nodding in agreement.

"I'd appreciate a place to spend the night tonight," Isaac said humbly.

Mrs. Foster touched his shoulder. "You can stay every night.

There will be plenty to eat. We only keep one servant now, and she gets the evenings off. We do get visitors on occasion, but nothing to gossip about."

"I can come and go without anyone noticing," Isaac said. "But I can only risk staying one night."

"But you mustn't go," Mrs. Foster objected.

"When I awoke from the Skrýmir, an ambush was waiting for me," he explained. "The Semblances know I'm back, and they'll come looking for me. They'll probably come here, so I can't risk your safety."

"I know a place you can stay!" True suggested with a smile.

"Where?" Mr. Foster asked, his brow wrinkling.

"That is helpful, True," Isaac said. "And your offer of assistance is appreciated. For now, I'll take care of myself. I'd appreciate being able to sleep in a bed tonight. I'll have warning intelligences set up, though. We won't be taken by surprise."

"I'm going to go warm some food," Mrs. Foster said. "We can continue talking in the kitchen. It is so good to see you, Robinson. It means so much that you have come back."

"You've always felt like family," he said, giving tender looks to each of them.

"Losing McKenna was so painful," Mr. Foster said, his voice thick. "Having you back...it brings back good memories, Son."

Isaac felt his own throat thicken.

"I'll let you know when the food is ready," Mrs. Foster said and hurried away.

Isaac walked to the closed curtain and parted it to peer out into the backyard.

There was the greenhouse. Good as new. The memories from his lives began to float and swirl in his mind. He could drown in them if he didn't make the effort to keep them boxed away individually in his skull.

Then he turned and saw True looking at him. She wanted to tell him something, but it was something she did not feel at liberty to say in front of her parents.

"Is McKenna's room still upstairs?" he asked.

True nodded.

Mr. Foster sniffed. "Of course you should stay up there. It's not the same as it was before the fire, but we tried to make it similar."

"Would you show me?" he asked True.

Chapter Nine
Broken Society

The Incurious Mind of Chester Malcolm Weathersby. Isaac examined the title of the dusty leatherbound book before setting it back down on the desk. He had a vague memory of McKenna mentioning the book, but he couldn't remember the details. The scent of her was absent, naturally, but the decorations and setup still felt like hers, felt familiar.

"Should I light a lamp?" True asked, standing near the dresser where he had placed his violin case.

"No," he replied simply, gazing at the bed and curtains. The window was closed. After McKenna had begun to awaken to her Semblance knowledge because of her drowning, the heat had become intolerable to her. She'd always wanted the windows open after that.

There was enough light from the streetlamps outside and the nearly full moon that he could see well enough without any extra. He turned to look at her. "You're a practicing sorcerer. And your parents don't know."

She sighed. "They refused to teach me after the laws changed. So I had to find another teacher."

Down in the parlor, he'd come to some conclusions. She was part of the underground movement.

"You were expecting someone else on your porch tonight," he said. "Who?"

True sighed again. "My husband."

He hadn't been expecting *that* answer. "You don't wear a wedding band."

"Neither of us do. To protect each other."

"I take it your parents don't know about that either?"

"It has been challenging to keep our relationship a secret," True said. "After all we've been through as a family, the theft of your invention, the fire, McKenna's kidnapping, my father being forced into retirement ...I couldn't sit by and let it break entirely."

"So you know other sorcerers, then," Isaac stated.

"Yes. We have to meet in secret. Had to change some of the signs we greet each other with. It's not the same as it was, but the Invisible College is still here. It's just more...invisible."

He couldn't help but feel a surge of relief. "Do you know who is in charge?"

She gave him a tender smile. "Someone who is very much like you. His name is Jacob."

Isaac felt a startled jolt in his chest. "Jacob...?"

"Jacob Hallow Farmer. The widow's son. You told him he could be a sorcerer one day, no matter his beginnings. You helped his family several times, and he never forgot."

Isaac gaped in disbelief. "I thought he was gone. That Sarah had taken them away with the *strannik*."

"He ran away," True said. "He didn't believe what he'd been told, that you were a liar and a villain. He knew you were a good man. And he wanted to be just like you." Her words showed her tender feelings toward him. "He found a used fiddle in a pawn shop and began to teach himself how to play. He worked hard in the factories but never gave up his ambition to become a sorcerer."

"How did you meet him?"

"He came by after the house was rebuilt. Mother invited him to have dinner with us on Closure, just as she did for you. I'm not all that much older than him. I admired his willingness to seek knowledge, even though he could get caught. He *did* get arrested and was sent to debtors' prison a few years ago. I paid his debt. After that, we fell in love and got married in secret."

It was an amazing story. With the hierarchy of the Invisible College destroyed, it would not have been easy for the boy to progress as a sorcerer, especially all alone. His mind flashed back to the moment he'd rescued Jake and his siblings from the rubble left by the *strannik*'s explosion. The doctor had wanted to remove the lad's arm, but Isaac had used the philosopher's stone to heal his fractured limb. It was difficult imagining him as a grown man, but he felt the stirrings of pride for the young man's courage and self-discipline.

"I need to find him," Isaac said. "Does he still come for dinner at Closure?"

True shook her head. "It's too dangerous for him. The Marshalcy is relentless. And there is a private security firm hunting for him as well. He'll play the fiddle from the rooftops just to taunt them."

Isaac chuckled. When he'd helped the Farmers not long after first arriving in Auvinen, he'd had no idea the impact it would have on them. Kindnesses were truly never forgotten. His heart was aglow with warmth.

"Rob?" It was Mrs. Foster's voice calling from downstairs. "Come eat."

"Can you tell me how to find him?" Isaac asked.

"He stays in different places all the time," she said. "Father gave up his sorcerer's ring to the Marshalcy when they were outlawed. And the mold to make more."

"I happen to still have mine," Isaac said, patting his pocket. "And Wickins and Clara have one too."

"They do? They never told me!"

"I can see why. I can contact him since I know who he is."

"He still goes by Jack now. Only I call him Jacob."

"To earn his trust, if I tell him I know you two are married, will he believe me? What message could I give him, from you, that only the two of you would know?"

True thought a moment. "Our first kiss was at the wharf at Kunz. No one else would know about that!"

"I'm going to need his help to rescue all the sorcerers trapped in prison," Isaac said. "I'll need help from both of you."

The wharf at Kunz was busy at all hours, with an endless procession of ships coming and going. Many were large ironclads, crusted with barnacles. One of the reasons Auvinen was such a successful port was because of a feature of the Watership River. If ships remained in the fresh water long enough, the barnacles would drop off on their own. Isaac wondered if such simple knowledge had been forgotten since he saw so many of the creatures clinging to the hull.

It was impossible to pick out a single man amongst so many passersby. But Isaac had said where he'd be standing when he sent his message through the ring. Of course, the man had no way of replying, so Isaac had no notion if he would turn up. It was the hour of meeting, and Isaac stood at a dock post, the smell of fish thick in the air, along with the squawking of thousands of seagulls roaming the planks.

It had felt good to sleep in a bed once more, and Mrs. Foster had provided a lovely breakfast as well. Mr. Foster had kindly given him a wallet full of banknotes, which could be taken to any bank in the city to exchange for coins.

A distant bell rang the hour. Still no sign of him.

A dirty-faced urchin tugged at Isaac's coat.

"'Scuze me, sir, did you drop your coin?" asked the boy, holding out a twenty piece in his palm.

Isaac was about to tell the boy no, but a memory was jogged. Of a night he'd been very hungry and had found a twenty piece in the street. He'd summoned the intelligence of a dog—Loyal, it turned out, although he hadn't fully understood his significance then—to help him find the owner of the coin. It had taken him to Mrs. Farmer and her children.

"I believe I did," Isaac said, realizing this was a test. "Is that a twenty piece?"

"Yes, sir. It's yours. I found it over there." The smudge-faced boy pointed to a building across from them, a taproom. Standing at the corner was a bearded man with a carpet bag tucked under his arm.

Isaac withdrew a banknote worth five crowns and handed it to the urchin. "Thank you."

The boy's eyes lit with wonder when he touched the paper currency. His expression exploded into a smile as he dashed away. Isaac saw the bearded man shake his head, grinning, and he crossed over to him.

Isaac wouldn't have recognized the man as the boy except for maybe the sad eyes. He had dark thick hair, a neatly trimmed beard, and a harried expression that had ceded to his grin. The two men embraced each other with fondness.

"Professor," Jacob Farmer said. He had grown to be a bigger man than Isaac. His clothes were simple, inconspicuous. The carpet bag was battered and scarred.

Isaac felt Loyal's tail wagging fiercely. He offered the coin back, and Jack took it, gazing at him in disbelief.

"You look just as you did," Jack said, struggling with his emotions. Tears thickened on his lashes.

"You've changed enough for both of us," Isaac said, feeling overjoyed and proud simultaneously. He looked a little older than Isaac, probably thirty years old.

"Do you know what happened to my mum? My siblings? I haven't seen them since that day our ears shattered."

"I haven't seen them," Isaac said sorrowfully. "But I haven't stopped thinking about them. Or you. I thought you'd left with them."

Jack rubbed his bearded mouth and then shook his head. "I

couldn't. I didn't believe what they said about you. I've done what I could to keep the college going. Lost another good man yesterday to the prisons." His cheek twitched with anger.

Isaac reached out and gripped his shoulder. "We'll get him back."

"How?" Jack asked in a hopeless tone. "I know what it's like to be in there."

"True says she bought your freedom."

Jack wiped his eyes and nodded. "There are so many still in there. Been there for *years*."

A throb of warning came from Loyal. Isaac's senses sharpened, and he hummed a defensive spell. Jack's eyes widened with surprise when he caught the tone.

"What's wrong?" Jack said in a hushed voice. He opened the carpet bag, revealing a violin case within.

An inaudible growl came next.

"Someone is watching us," Isaac said.

"Follow me," Jack said curtly and took him down the alley next to the taphouse. They both walked swiftly, easily keeping pace. Isaac heard the crunch of boots coming from behind them. He didn't look back.

A pistol sounded, and a bullet deflected off his invisible shield.

"Run!" Jack bellowed. They darted around the next opening between buildings. They'd gone around yet another when Jack grabbed Isaac by the collar and shoved him against the wall, then pushed the carpet bag in his hands.

"What are you—"

Jack shook his head and charged around the corner. Isaac, startled, turned the corner and watched as Jack punched the Marshalcy officer in the jaw so hard that the man left his feet and landed on his back. When his pistol clattered on the ground, Jack kicked it away. The officer had been knocked out cold.

Jack massaged his knuckles and gazed down at the man in contempt.

Isaac stepped into sight and came up to the man lying on the ground. He watched in surprise as a little puff of smoke issued from the officer's mouth. But the man hadn't stopped breathing.

Jack's eyes darkened. "Another one," he muttered darkly.

"He was a Semblance," Isaac said. He'd only seen the puff of mist leave their mouth when the host died. Did that mean more than one Aesir had infested the man's body? Was such a thing possible?

"It's going to warn another officer," Jack said. "But there's more than one in this fellow. He'll be on his feet soon. We need to hide. Come with me. I know where we can go."

The whistle of a Marshalcy officer sounded shrilly in the distance. It was followed by another. And another.

"They'll try and box us in," Jack said. "We can't stay here."

He looked feverish with worry, but Isaac could see he was used to running away.

He handed the carpet bag back to Jack and put his hand on his shoulder. "We don't need to run. You just need to learn a new spell. It is one you can cast in your mind with your thoughts. Listen carefully. *Aóratos*."

Jack's eyes widened with surprise when Isaac disappeared right in front of him. But Isaac squeezed his shoulder to show he was still there.

"Think it for yourself. *Aóratos*."

And Jack vanished a moment before more Marshalcy officers appeared around the corner.

Lieutenant Graff reports no survivors in the village of Meacham. Village population is estimated to be two hundred and six souls, according to the last census, and located on the northern borders of Winterthur, near the vestiges of the abandoned ice trenches. No evidence of the marauders who did this fell deed. Lieutenant Graff claims it was done by the Aesir, but there is no evidence. Recommendation—mass burial and claim an infestation of virulent measles.

—Signals Intelligences, Gresham College, Bishopsgate

Annalise Kauer

Chapter Ten
Familiar Faces

She was drowning in the sea.

Annalise knew it was a dream. She'd had it before, but it was so vivid she could taste the salt water in her mouth, feel the sodden dress clinging to her body. She could see the roaring waters but not hear them. She could see the shore in the distance, but no matter how hard she tried swimming, she couldn't reach it. She was underwater, her legs kicking lethargically against the pull of the deep.

She awoke with a shuddering start, sitting up in bed, trying to quell the panic and desperation that mixed with the dread of drowning.

The memory of the distant shore began to fade. Her racing heart began to quiet. It was one of many recurring dreams she'd had since becoming an actress. She still remembered one she'd awoken screaming from. Her mother had come to soothe her. She'd brought her some rice pudding and had to spoon feed her some because the awful taste of the salt water had filled her mouth. There were other dreams too, dreams so vivid and startlingly different that she was almost convinced that reincarnation was possible and that she had lived multiple lives.

Or maybe that was just the natural consequence of being a child actress and having played so many different roles.

Annalise knew she wouldn't be able to fall asleep again. The terror of the nightmare had thoroughly roused her, so she slipped out of the comfortable sheets. It was still another hour until dawn when she'd be expected at the theater to watch the sunrise.

Seeing Maud fast asleep gave her a little pang of jealousy, but she brushed it aside and began to dress. When she was at her estate, Caddam House, which bordered a vast lake, she'd started taking early-morning swims to conquer her fear of drowning. But taking a dip in the Watership River wasn't a prudent option—it was filthy—though, at least she could walk to the theater. The crisp morning air and exercise would both do her some good, and there wouldn't be many people about this early.

After dressing, tying back her hair, and putting on a walking cape, she gazed once more at Maud's sleeping countenance, took a little purse of coins, and left the room, locking it behind her. She tramped quickly down the stairs to the main floor of the prestigious hotel and hurried to the front desk.

"Miss Kauer!" said the bearded man in astonishment. "Your carriage won't arrive for another hour."

"I know," she answered. "Would you tell the driver that I walked to the theater this morning?"

"I can order a conveyance for you, Miss Kauer. It would be no trouble at all."

"That won't be necessary. I'd prefer to walk today. If you'd deliver the message for me?"

"I will without fail," replied the manager, nodding vigorously. She noticed a little child on the floor rubbing his eyes behind the desk counter. Poor thing should have been in bed still.

She thanked him again and then hastened to the hotel door. A bellman opened it for her and made a little bow as she left.

The early smudges of dawn were coming, and she felt a delicious shiver, similar to the way her body felt when she finished a swim and stepped into the chill of the morning air.

Auvinen was a special place. She'd been there for several months, and had visited previously, but the connection she felt to it could not be altogether explained by that. As she passed by a little park on her route, it reminded her of another near the shore, which the locals called Aesir Park, where a boulder had once hovered in the air. After the Aesir disappeared, the boulder had fallen and broken to pieces, and later it had been carted off. She'd gone to that park on a Closure day and taken a stroll there, and it had felt so familiar to her, although she couldn't remember having been there before.

Walking briskly down the street, she looked around at the businesses coming awake. From the corner of her eye, she noticed a lanky man following her at a discreet distance. He wore a nondescript suit and no hat. She didn't turn fully to study his face, just enough to note his presence and that he was another soul out for a walk.

Annalise wondered if he were following her, so she adjusted her route and took another way that would lead her near a prestigious shopping district. The shops weren't open yet, but they boasted rows of beautiful clean windows displaying their wares. She slowed and pretended to admire something in one of the tableaus, wanting to see if the man behind her did the same. A surreptitious glance revealed that he had indeed stopped. He was gazing down the street in another direction while she perused the windows.

Had Mr. Froman assigned someone to trail her in case she ever left the hotel early? Was he protecting his asset? It seemed an extravagant expense to employ others in such a way. She paused at another window, looking through the glass and thinking about what to do. Should she try to elude him? Should she confront her manager and inform him that he was being too intrusive? Or maybe she had it wrong, and this man was someone with ill intentions...

She started walking again along the row of windows and increased her pace before crossing the street at the next intersection and rejoining her original path to the theater. Sure enough, the man persisted in following her. She would have normally enjoyed the row of silver linden trees that were elegantly pruned, with their bare trunks and thick upper foliage, providing a shady canopy for those walking the streets, but she couldn't...because of him.

He was becoming irksome to her. Her pique had been roused, and so she walked even faster, which forced him to compensate and increase his speed as well. They had reached the city center, so the tall buildings with beautiful frontages were pleasant looking, but the joy of having a solitary walk had been upended by the buffoon trailing her. She decided to confront the man.

When she reached the intersection, she turned the corner and then waited, pressing her back against the wall. The sun would be coming up very soon, and she needed to be on the rooftop, but she felt compelled to scold the pursuer and warn him that if he ever did it again, she would be very disappointed and have him sent away from her detail. There were other people about, so she felt safe if he tried to accost her.

He made no effort to hide his approach, his footfalls steadily approaching the corner where she waited.

Just as he reached the edge, she stepped away from the wall, turned, and faced the intruder, ready to teach him a lesson with a sound scolding.

But the moment Annalise saw his face, she had the uncanny feeling she recognized him. That stopped her from uttering the rebuke she'd intended, though she couldn't remember where she'd met him before. He was tall, a little gaunt, with untamed dark hair and a warm look of fondness on his face. Why did he look so familiar?

"You were following me," she said, her words not as harsh as she'd originally intended them. She stated it as a fact, not a question.

"I was, Miss Kauer." Even his voice sounded familiar to her.

Had they been in a play together early in her career? Was he part of the crew? He didn't look like one of the Trilbys who were in service to Mr. Froman. He knew her name, so there was no mistaking the deliberateness of his actions.

"Do you work for Mr. Froman? There really is no need—"

"I don't," he said, cutting her off. His eyes were full of baffling warmth. She'd never had any real beaus, but she was reminded of a young man who had taken some liberties in trying to make himself into an escort of sorts, opening doors and lavishing attention on her, though she'd given him no encouragement. It had become so awkward that her mother had to chase him away, telling him he was wasting his time and that her daughter had no thought of dalliances with young men or marrying. He finally left once Mr. Froman "found" her and took over the task of dissuading suitors as his self-appointed duty. That man had made her uncomfortable with his adoring looks, but not this familiar stranger before her. She felt a flush of warmth.

"Will you tell me why you're following me, then?" she asked, giving him an arch look that seemed to cause him some pain.

He looked like he was about to speak, but his gaze shifted above her head to something behind her.

Annalise turned and saw Mr. Froman standing on the rooftop of the theater, gazing down at them. That was unfortunate. She didn't want to give her manager the impression that she was encouraging suitors.

"You'd better go," she told him with a slight warning tone as she turned back to face him.

His eyes were still fixed on her manager on the rooftop. His expression had altered to one of wariness and animosity. That was entirely natural since Mr. Froman could be severe, but the look had a certain familiarity to it—as if the two were acquainted with each other and bore a mutual dislike.

The familiar man looked down at her again. "When can I see you?" he asked her softly, which was incredibly forward of him.

Then she remembered his face. She'd seen him outside Mr. Froman's office. He was the man whom Mr. Carrault had mistaken for Mr. Puzey. He was wearing a different suit, so that had slightly altered his appearance, but the quick glimpse she'd had of him then matched what she saw before her. And yet...she had the feeling she'd met him even before that. Knew him well, in fact.

And then there was the bewildering question he'd asked. It was overly presumptuous, to say the least.

"That's quite impossible," she said firmly, and then turned and began to walk toward the theater.

She found the door open, as she'd expected, but stopped to glance back. The man was still standing there, gazing at her helplessly, his expression full of anguish. Had she been too abrupt in her dismissal? She felt for him, but it was likely for the best, given the situation. She wouldn't want to give him false hope.

Annalise hurried up the stairs, arriving breathless at the top. The sun had already peeked over the sloping rooftops. She was late but only by a few minutes.

Mr. Froman stood with his back to her, gripping his cane tightly in one hand. His shoulders looked tense and hunched.

"I apologize for being late," she said, coming to stand by him and gazing at the sunrise. "I was hounded by that man down below. Do you know him? He wasn't one of yours, was he?"

"He's a man of little significance," said Mr. Froman, his voice throbbing with resentment.

From his tone, she interpreted the opposite.

"Who is he?" she asked. She gazed down, and to her surprise, he was still there, peering up at them.

"You could say he's an actor too," said Mr. Froman with a dark chuckle. "Of a sort. The ambitious kind. The dangerous kind."

"Has he been in one of your plays, then?" she asked, genuinely curious.

"Not the kind of play you are thinking," Mr. Froman said cryptically. Then he turned and gave her a savage look. "Now you've made things more difficult for me. I'll have to move you to another hotel. I'll have Maud pack your things while you rehearse."

Chapter Eleven
Voices of Magic

"You were off your mark, Annalise," Mr. Froman said with a stern tone. "Again!"

The rehearsal had been, so far, an unmitigated disaster in her manager's scrutinizing eyes. His standards had always been exacting, but there was something different about him this time. A feeling of urgency. His criticisms were more frequent and sharper, tinged with impatience.

"I'm sorry," Annalise said, stepping back to the previous movement. She wore her Romani costume beneath the cloak.

Mr. Froman stood opposite her in place of her stage partner. He knew every line of every character in the entire play. "On the hill and in the square, you spoke as broadly as any woman in the slums. Now you fling a cloak over your shoulders and become a fine lady. Perhaps it was the cloak that bewitched me."

Annalise tossed aside a fold of the fabric and performed a little swaying motion, making sure her bare foot hit the mark on the floor precisely. "Aye, it was only the cloak. I'm just a pure, ignorant lass again." She turned the opposite way, stepping around him, the motion making the hem of the cloak twirl a bit. She gave him a teasing, playful smile. "But certainly clothes *do* make a difference to a woman."

"You are flirtatious!" he said in response.

Annalise bowed with an acknowledging smile. "Goodbye, good sir, if you're not about to give me up."

"I'm not an officer of the law."

"Surely we part as friends, then?" Annalise gave him a hopeful smile. She'd performed this scene hundreds of times.

"Your timing was off," Mr. Froman snarled. "A little pause before 'friends.' It's a suggestion. You are manipulating your lover with those words. Turning the stranger to friend and getting him to accept it."

Annalise resisted the urge to scowl at his correction. The audience never failed to react to her character's antics. She could tell from their laughter and applause that she was affecting them. But her performance never seemed quite to Mr. Froman's liking.

She bowed again. "Surely we part as...friends, then?"

"No. I hope never to see your face again."

"I can't help you not liking it." It was said in such an ironic tone. The audience admired Annalise's beauty. Sometimes she could see members of the audience, the young men, squirm in their seats as they watched her perform this role of the Romani girl wooing the young barrister.

She reached out and playfully swiped at his cheek. "There's a splotch on your own. Must have come off a divot you flung at the cap'n." Mr. Beal would always put his hand to his cheek at this point in the play, as if her touch entranced him.

She turned suddenly, adopting a worried and anxious expression. She focused on the frenzied little walk—two steps this way, turn, two steps the other, growing more anxious. "There are soldiers at the top of that hill. Can't escape that way. There's no other way!" She turned and reached for him. "Won't you help me again?"

"Why would I do that? I'm in trouble enough because of you." Mr. Froman said the lines, but he wasn't trying to act them. He stood with his cane in a fixed spot, his probing eyes continuously judging her performance.

"Why not?"

Mr. Froman said, "She'll see us."

"'She'? Oh...your—"

"My mother. If you're caught, they'll learn that I helped you escape."

"You'd say you didn't help me," Annalise said, hands on her hips and giving him a jaunty look.

"There would be consequences if they learned I'd let you... pass yourself off...as my wife."

"I'm sorry," she said with a deliberate pout.

"It's not the punishment from them I fear. No, it's from my conscience."

"You have a conscience?" she said with a smirk.

He scowled at her again. "More subtle. Be more subtle!"

Was it her look or tone that had offended him?

"You have a conscience?" she repeated, less ironically that time.

"My mother has had trials you couldn't imagine. My job has brought her peace, and now you might destroy her happiness. You have her life in your hands."

Annalise turned abruptly and began to walk away.

"Where are you going?" he said.

"To give myself up."

"Stop! Why don't you hide in the manse garden? Nobody would think to look for you there."

She sauntered up to him. "You're a good man. I like you."

"Too provoking," Mr. Froman snapped.

She sighed, unable to help herself. This wasn't even the more taxing part of the play, and he was treating each moment as if it were challenging. She changed her tone, just slightly. "You're a good man. I like you."

"Do not say that."

She lightly touched his arm. "Listen...I believe you've liked me all this time."

"Can a man like a woman against his will? Against reason?"

"Of course he *can*," she said with a little spin and bow, facing the audience seats. "That's the very nicest *way* to be liked."

When she delivered that line, it never failed to cause the audience to erupt in applause. But there was only silence from the empty seats.

The play, *The Little Barrister*, had been a delightful hit. It was about a nobleman's daughter pretending to be a Romani girl to help a local village, who falls in love with a young barrister when he returns home to aid his ailing mother and the workers of the village. He fell in love with this girl from a lower station, even though in reality she was higher than he was. It was a comedy, a romance, and a drama about a young woman's mistaken identity.

She rose and turned to face him, arching an eyebrow to see if her delivery, which she felt she'd perfected, had been acceptable.

"Tolerable," he said without enthusiasm.

Her shoulders slumped. "I don't understand what has gotten into you today."

"All the applause has dulled your professionalism," he countered. "You've gotten increasingly lazy in your performances of late."

"You think I'm lazy?" she said, feeling a surge of heat. She was at the theater at sunrise. She worked for hours before any of the other cast showed up. She had afternoons off, thankfully, but her work ethic had always been prodigious. That was a word she especially liked. She was proud of her vocabulary.

He stepped closer, his eyes flashing with anger. "Don't be contemptible, Annalise," he said bitingly.

"I have performed my role to your standards, have I not? The rest of the shows are sold out, are they not?"

"It's not this play that concerns me," he chided with an uncaring toss of his head. "I thought you might be the ideal actress to play the Erlking's daughter in the next production. But maybe you'd prefer to do...comedies for the rest of your career"—this was said in a tone of disdain—"instead of a role with more depth."

"You know I want that role," she said, feeling a shiver of fear in her chest. Was he threatening to replace her? Was there another ingenue he had in mind that she wasn't aware of? She had been that discovery once. She knew that as an actress, her opportunities would shrink as she aged. So she'd prepared for her eventual retirement. Why, she'd planted walnut trees on her estate that would be worth a small fortune once they grew and matured and could provide an easy living for the rest of her life. But at twenty-six, she was still young and lively. She wasn't even at the peak of her career yet!

"But do you want it *enough*, Annalise?" he asked with a look of condemnation.

"You haven't even let me read the script yet," she said, her stomach twisting into knots.

"I didn't want to distract you from your performance in this play. What we read permeates our thoughts. Intrudes on our feelings. And I need an actress who can *sing*."

She gave a small gasp. Singing in front of an audience! Her heart raced as she noted the challenging look in Mr. Froman's eyes. "I can sing!" she said defensively, feeling deeply unsettled at the thought of missing out on such a rare opportunity.

"But can you sing with the purity and clarity of an Aesir?" he said, his eyes challenging her. "Your voice must fill every inch of a much grander hall than this dingy one. You will sing before rulers and nobles. The Volksoper at Tanhauser is one of the finest. Are you ready for that stage?"

"I know I will be," she said with fixed determination. "I have done everything you've asked of me."

"Have you?"

"I have! I've surrendered my life to your tutelage. I would be nothing without you."

"Actresses. There are hundreds, and you're all the same. I thought you were different. Special."

"I have done everything you've asked of me," she repeated, frustrated.

"You've tried your best. But are you capable of true greatness?"

She felt like he was about to cast her off. "Give me a chance to prove myself."

He gave her a cold look and then chuckled. "Would you like to hear an aria from it?"

"Yes," she begged, sensing a mercurial shift in his mood. Sometimes he toyed with her like this. To make her desperate to please him. She hated when he did that, but she knew that if she did not submit, he would cast her off.

He tapped his cane against the stage floor and the sound reverberated. "Imagine a domed theater twice this size. Every seat filled with anticipating listeners. This is unlike any play you've done thus far, Annalise. The costumes will be like the classics of old. It hearkens to the days of Shopenhauer. To Tigivanny."

She watched in fascination as his countenance changed, as if he were assuming a new role himself. His back straightened. He held his head up proudly. He lifted the cane, and then he began to sing. It was not a language she recognized. Was it Iskandir? But the melody...

It was unearthly in its beauty, and the song captured feelings that stirred her heart and unleashed thoughts of palaces made of ice and choirs of otherworldly beings who had reached the pinnacle of perfection. It was the most devastatingly beautiful thing she had ever heard, and it sounded *familiar*. She watched him sing, mesmerized by the vocal aptitude Mr. Froman possessed. He didn't just demand perfection. He was capable of it.

The tone of his tenor voice along with the piercing mood of the piece touched her heart and tugged tears from her eyes. It was a mournful song, a haunting melody that gutted her. It was the most amazing piece of music she had ever experienced. And it was only...one...song.

The final notes faded into silence. Mr. Froman had his cane poised in the air, but he slowly brought it down, breaking the fascination the music had caused. He tapped it on the stage floor again.

"What is that music?" she whispered huskily. "Did *you* write it?"

"It is my own," Mr. Froman said. "That aria is called 'The Erlking's Lament.' It is about the unfailing love between a father and his daughter. It is a song about choosing loyalty over romantic love."

"It was...beautiful," she said thickly.

"We finish this play on time. Per our schedule. Then we head north and begin rehearsals."

"Rehearsals? What about the auditions?" she asked in confusion.

"You think I am idle while you are at your ease and resting? The auditions are finished. The cast has been chosen."

"Is there another competing for the role of the Erlking's daughter?" Annalise asked, her heart surging with fear.

"There is always an understudy," he said mockingly. "There will always be another willing to be what I need her to be."

And Annalise felt, deep in her soul, that if Mr. Froman cast her away, she would lose everything she'd worked so hard to build for herself.

Issac Berrow

Chapter Twelve
The Little Barrister

Isaac stood at the intersection by the theater as a swelling crowd of patrons of that evening's performance of the play passed him on their way to the entrance. Many were dressed formally in dark suits, black shirts, and silken bow ties, but not all. Some had come more informally, the men wearing straw hats while the women and children had their hair done up with ribbons or simple hats. Wearing a glamour so as not to be noticed, he gazed at the flow of people parting to enter through different doors, the wealthy allowed to pass immediately, while the others waited in a queue to see if there would be seats left for them.

He recognized Mr. Foster's carriage as it approached. Isaac stepped away from his spot and watched as the carriage disgorged Mr. and Mrs. Foster, Clara, Wickins, and True.

A little throb of warmth came into his chest, but it did little to temper the anxiety inside him. After following Annalise to the theater that morning, and even having met her briefly, he had quickly realized that getting her alone would be exceptionally difficult. When she left the theater for an afternoon break, there were fans and smitten men swirling around her and her bodyguard, trying to gain her attention. They were ignored, and her carriage quickly vanished in a series of turns through city streets.

Loyal had led him to her hotel, but there were always guards on the periphery, watching her closely.

This was the last performance before Closure, so Annalise would have a day off the following day. From what he'd gathered from hotel staff he'd discreetly interviewed, her plans varied, but she usually spent her days off in solitude. Sometimes she'd go for a carriage ride. Sometimes for walks in parks. Sometimes shopping at a bookstore. And she spent a great deal of time in her room resting.

Closure would be an ideal time to try to speak to her alone. But how did one tell a famous actress that she was really a being of immense wisdom and power whose memories from former lives were locked away by a spell? Not only that, but she was an incredibly attractive woman who was on her guard against potential wooers.

Isaac fell in behind the family as they walked toward the upper theater doors. He remained behind them with several strangers in between so his presence would not be easily noticed in case anyone were watching them. The play had been the pretext for Wickins and Clara to come to Auvinen, knowing the Fosters held box seats where they could watch the play together and Isaac could slip in after them without being seen.

They were chatting amongst themselves, excited to be reunited after a long stretch, unaware of his own return and presence—they'd agreed it was safest for him to use a glamour on them so they wouldn't remember his visits unless needed. But all it would take was a word.

There were theater employees at the doors checking tickets, but a private entrance for those with box seats was off to the side.

"Box six," said the attendant, recognizing the family. "Enjoy the play."

Mr. Foster inclined his head, and the family entered the majestic theater. The bright lighting wasn't made of flame but of glowing incandescent bulbs similar to the magical ones of an earlier time, except that they were powered by electricity. Isaac heard the hum as he passed. The butter-colored marble with darker striations appeared in the double columns, supporting arches, and decorated scenes in the stone. There was a wide staircase that forked to the right and left to reach the highest floors, and the family joined the flow of people going there. Isaac released the glamour.

"You look nervous," True commented without shifting her gaze to him.

He *was* nervous and not just about seeing Annalise again. Anyone in the crowd could be a Semblance working for the Erlking. In his previous lives, Semblances had often sought him out to attempt to kill him. He couldn't sense Loyal's presence, but he'd instructed the dog intelligence to stay close to Annalise and warn him if she were in any danger.

"There is a lot riding on this night, I suppose," he answered. True knew the rest of the plan, that Jack was going to rescue sorcerers from one of the debtors' prisons that very night. Isaac had spent hours with the young man over the past couple of days, teaching him spells to help him achieve the liberation of the incarcerated men and women. They'd hide in the tenements and in warehouses.

Another sorcerer had been sent ahead to Bishopsgate to begin making preparations to bring some of the rescued sorcerers north. Going to the play was also an alibi for the Fosters and Wickinses, so there could be no suspicion of their involvement.

True gave him a private smile as they reached the upper floor and headed to their box. The noise from the floor seats was abundant as people were eager to see the play. Though many of the wealthy had already seen it, most of the people who bought tickets were there to enjoy it for the first time.

There were six seats in their box, the chairs padded with armrests. The décor inside was opulent, the craftsmanship of its embellishments exquisite and containing symbols of Aesir runes.

Isaac sat in the farthest seat on the left, with True next to him, the Fosters in the middle, and Clara and Wickins at the end. It was noisy enough in the theater that he could barely hear a comment Mrs. Foster made to her husband.

"What do you know of Miss Kauer?" he asked True in an undertone.

"Mostly rumors," she replied. "She's been working for her manager since she was around sixteen. Some believe they are secretly married and he's jealous of her and always replaces the lead men in the plays so she can't become attached to any one of them."

"People like to come up with shocking stories, but I'd imagine her manager would discourage suitors to keep her under his control for financial reasons," Isaac said absently. He was watching the thick scalloped curtains, anxious for the play to get started.

I'm inside Mickelgate.

The thought came to his mind from Jack.

One of the first things Isaac had done after his reunion with the Farmer boy was buy a cuttlefish bone and make a mold for another sorcerer's ring. Thankfully some of the sorcerers in Auvinen kept an alchemy underground where they mixed reagents and practiced spellwork from the books they'd managed to save. Isaac had made six rings and taught them how to make more so Jack's band of rogue sorcerers could easily communicate at a distance.

Isaac fished his hand into his pocket and slipped his ring onto his thumb. The expected jolt of pain in his temple followed.

I'm at the theater.

Tell True I miss her.

Tell her yourself. Isaac thought back with a smile.

He watched as True's expression changed and a delighted smile creased her mouth. She patted Isaac's leg. The small orchestra had just begun to play a wheezy song with a sluggish tempo and a faintly comical air.

Fortune go with you, my friend, Isaac thought to Jack.

His task was not an easy one, but Isaac rather thought he was up to it.

People were admitted to see the inmates of the debtors' prisons during the day, to bring food and provide company, but at sunset, the gate was locked and anyone still inside would have to stay there until dawn. The prisoners were never allowed to leave until all their debts had been paid. Jack had infiltrated the prison before sunset and was staying there during the night to launch their plan. A locked gate was nothing a sorcerer couldn't handle in ordinary circumstances. But the prison gate had nullified locks, which prevented spells from opening them.

Unless one was working with the Master of the Royal Secret, who had access to a unique thought spell to override nullification wards, which could be transmitted through the sorcerer's rings.

The curtains pulled open, revealing the scene, made to resemble the woods outside a village. He knew the gist of the play from Clara's description, but knowing the true story, he could see it wasn't subtle at all. Especially the part about the daughter tricking her father, the local lord, into allowing her to marry the young barrister.

Annalise lightly touched the lead actor's arm. "Listen...I believe you've liked me all this time."

"Can a man like a woman against his will? Against reason?"

Isaac felt a blush forming on his cheeks and shifted uncomfortably in his seat. True noticed and gave him a questioning look. It wasn't the right moment to explain he was falling in love with Eiríka all over again and agitated that he was watching a version of *their* story play out on a stage for all the world to see. And the actor was too handsome. Entirely too handsome.

He could feel the Erlking gloating about what he'd done. He'd made a comedy of their story. To mock it? To make it seem too simple? Too naive?

"Of course he *can*," Annalise said with a little spin and bow, turning to the audience. She was facing his direction. He leaned forward with his hands gripping the balcony railing. "That's the very nicest *way* to be liked."

The audience burst into applause, some cheering rather obnoxiously.

And then Annalise seemed to notice Isaac. Her pretty smile faded; her eyes enlarged with surprise. She held her little bow, but her eyes were fixed on his. The Fosters were clapping. So was True. His peripheral vision revealed that, but Isaac's eyes were locked on hers, and he knew she remembered him from that morning.

Annalise's face went white with fear. She straightened and then bowed again, which Isaac felt wasn't part of her regular performance. She was flustered. He'd flustered her.

"What's wrong, Rob?" True asked, her voice low but concerned.

"I need to leave," he said, standing from his chair. He squeezed around it to go to the back of the box but turned and looked at the stage again. She was still standing there, gazing at him in fear. But then she delivered her next line and the curtain began to fall.

"Eshi omorfi matia," he whisper-sang, casting the glamour spell again so the Fosters wouldn't remember he was there with them. It was the kind of magic that hurt, but he knew it was for their own protection.

His heart hammered in his chest as he left the box, opening the door and promptly shutting it. The corridor was darkened for the performance, and he could hear muffled applause through the doors lining it. He quickly strode down the hall to the steps leading to the lower floor, taking them two at a time.

The main staircase was empty still, the glistening marble hall full of splendor. When he reached the bottom step, a man's voice accosted him.

"Are we not enjoying the play tonight?"

Isaac recognized the voice and the man. Not Mr. Froman, but

the bodyguard Isaac had seen outside the manager's door with Annalise. He had positioned himself in the lower hall behind the stairs so he wouldn't be seen when Isaac came down.

"I need some fresh air," Isaac said, hastening toward the doors.

Several men appeared from the sides and blocked his way.

"Miss Kauer would like to speak with you," the man said smugly. "She thinks you're a sorcerer."

Chapter Thirteen
A Familiar Voice

"The play is still going on," Isaac said, feeling his apprehension warring with the opportunity that had suddenly presented itself. He did not trust this man. He had no reason to.

"I don't mean *now*," the fellow said, coming a few steps closer. "At the end of the play. She asked me to bring you to her carriage for a brief interview."

"Do you know who I am?" Isaac asked the man, his distrust continuing to swell.

"I know you're a sorcerer. She has a fancy to meet one."

"I wouldn't want to disappoint her," Isaac said, his body tense.

"Come with me. We can enjoy the rest of the performance from a private box."

Isaac turned. The men by the doors hadn't moved, but they'd assumed postures of authority and readiness. Arms folded crossly. Looks of contempt on their faces.

The man gestured with his palm, indicating he would like to be followed, and Isaac decided to take the opportunity a little further. He wasn't sure whether they were truly acting on Miss Kauer's request, but it would be easy enough to find out. He worried about a confrontation with the Erlking, who knew sorcery better than anyone, but this bodyguard's mind could easily be muddled with a glamour.

Isaac was escorted to a polished door on the right side of the theater house. They passed beneath an ornate archway before the door, which opened to reveal a narrow corridor. The performance could be heard, although the words were muffled because of the walls. The man held the door open for him to enter first.

As soon as he passed the fellow, he felt something clamp around his wrist. A metal nulling cuff.

The man grinned in satisfaction and then clamped the other end around his own wrist, binding the two of them together.

"I said I would introduce you. But I must ensure she is safe from the likes of you."

Isaac gazed down at the nulling cuff on his left arm. The fellow looked rather proud of himself, but Isaac had been practicing magic for many lifetimes. He knew the command that would release it. That was a secret he suspected even the Erlking didn't know.

"Are we really going to see her?" Isaac asked, watching the smug face for any signs of trickery.

"I wouldn't dare disappoint her. But I'm not letting you out of my grasp this time, sorcerer. We'll have an interview with the Marshalcy next."

Isaac was still wearing his sorcerer's ring on the thumb of his left hand. Had the bodyguard noticed it? Would the cuffs deflect the thought magic?

Jack—can you hear me?

The response was nearly instantaneous. *I'm here. I was going to wait until midnight when things quiet down more.*

Start now.

So the nulling cuffs couldn't prevent thoughts from transferring. They were designed to disrupt musical pitches. Not the alchemy of thought.

"Shall we?" Isaac asked brightly, feigning unconcern.

The man looked shocked by Isaac's indifference, but he led the way down the tight corridor. After passing through several doors, they ended up backstage, behind a thick set of curtains. There were other actors waiting to go on—dressed in attire that reminded Isaac of a previous life more than a century earlier. Across the stage, on the opposite side, he saw Mr. Froman sitting in an ornate chair with a perfect view of the performance. He had a special cane settled across his lap as his eyes were fixed on the play.

Isaac's escort took him to a private box on the main stage with only two seats, both unoccupied. The two sat down together. It wasn't at all comfortable, but he had no choice if he wished for his audience with Annalise.

As Isaac watched the scene, he decided to test the powers of the ring once more. It hadn't worked with Eiríka for several lifetimes, for the Erlking had discovered its powers and intervened to prevent them from communicating so easily. Isaac wasn't sure how this was accomplished, but it was why the ring had never worked with McKenna, not because she'd been deaf.

Isaac gazed at her on the stage and sent a thought. *Miss Kauer. This is the sorcerer you wished to meet. If you can hear this thought, look at the private box.*

He carefully watched her face, but there was no sign of any abnormal reaction from her at all. She continued with the performance.

We're breaking out now. The main guard just opened the gate for us.

Isaac felt a surge of victory in his chest. *How many did you find?*

About three dozen willing. We're leaving the gate open so anyone else can leave who wants to.

Three dozen sorcerers freed. The numbers would begin to multiply. They would need more. Many, many more.

Do me a favor. Send up a warning flare from the prison. Draw attention to it.

I'd like more time to get farther away. But I'll do it because you say so.

Thank you, Jack.

It took about half an hour before the news of the escape reached the theater. A man came barging into the box, his eyes wide with disbelief, and bent his head to whisper in the ear of Isaac's captor.

Isaac's hearing had always been sharp and he took in every word.

"Mickelgate Prison's breached! About a hundred sorcerers have escaped!"

The man bound to Isaac stiffened, his eyes wide with shock. "When?"

"I just heard. I don't know when it happened, but it was recently. The braggarts sent up a flare to announce it. What should we do?"

"I need to tell Froman," the other said. He gave Isaac an accusing look.

"Is something amiss?" Isaac asked with an innocent expression.

"You'll stay here," said the bodyguard. He fussed with the cuff on his own wrist and then rose from the seat. "Sit here, Arbuckle. Take my place. Stay—right—here." His voice was very insistent. Arbuckle gamely swapped places with him and didn't resist being bound to Isaac with the cuff. The play was nearing the end. Events were happening quickly on stage.

The other fellow departed the box without a backward look.

Isaac thought the command to release the cuff, and it instantly opened. Arbuckle turned in surprise at the noise, his mouth gaping.

"Eshi omorfi matia," Isaac sang in a whisper while he locked the open cuff to the armrest of his chair. He put the thought in the man's mind that Isaac was sitting passively next to him and that he should continue to obey the command he was given to stay put. Then, after cloaking himself with invisibility, Isaac

slipped away from the box seat and began to wander through the backstage area.

The Marshalcy is gathering in force. Isaac could hear the laughter in Jack's thoughts. *I've never seen so many gathered in one place before.*

You did well, Jack. The flare helped me get out of a predicament. Thank you.

I taught everyone the new handshake. Told them about the Awakening.

Good. I have one more thing to do here tonight, then I'll meet you at the culvert.

We all feel a flicker of hope, Professor. It's been a while since we've had any.

Isaac smiled to himself and thanked Jack again for his cooperation. A burly, bearded man carrying a chest came barreling through the thin aisle and nearly collided with the unseen sorcerer. Isaac began to search for the rooms backstage and took a while to find Miss Kauer's, which was tucked away on a lower floor. The door was locked, but a quick spell solved that.

"Annixe," he sang, and the door yielded to his hand. He pushed it open and hurriedly shut it and locked it again. The room was dark.

"Hoxta-namorem."

The noise of applause from the audience rose to a thunder out in the theater. The will-o'-the-wisp of light hovered by him as he examined the area. There were other versions of her costumes hanging from racks, a vanity mirror surrounded by electric bulbs, and a tidy desk with stage makeup and several books nearby. She'd always loved reading. The dress she'd been wearing that morning hung from the rack as well.

The noise grew even louder as the applause rose to a crescendo. That meant Annalise Kauer was taking her bows. His mouth was suddenly dry. He began to pace nervously. If only he could snap his fingers and restore the memories from their past lives in an instant. They could find a magistrate in the morning, proclaim their vows, and the Aesir threat would end. If the Aesir left, Eiríka's intelligence would be bound in a mortal body since all the Aesir were required to leave.

Falling in love could take time. Not on his part, his heart was already entangled, but it would be new for this version of Eiríka.

The sound of footsteps came toward the door. He extinguished the light, feeling his pulse race with worry. Then he felt the presence of Loyal in the room, full of excitement and eagerness.

The applause was still underway. Confusion rattled him as the door was unlocked and opened.

But it was her, he knew instantly. He saw her silhouette in the doorframe before she reached over and flicked a switch by the door. The vanity lights flashed, momentarily blinding him.

She froze, her hand seemingly stuck on the switch. He was still invisible, but she seemed to be sensing something preternaturally. She wore the fancy dress from the last scene, looking both beautiful and anxious. Then she whirled and shut the door, locking it again.

Isaac released the invisibility spell.

"Miss Kauer," he said softly, watching as she bowed her head against the door, her forehead pressed to it as if she were in pain.

She didn't jerk in surprise. Loyal was wagging his ephemeral tail fiercely, thrilled that the two were together again in the same room at the same time.

Easy there, he thought to his faithful friend.

"How did you get in my room?" she demanded, finally turning around to face him. "Did Mr. Carrault let you in?"

Isaac shook his head no. "I unlocked it with a spell. He told me you wanted to see me."

"I told him to bring you to my *carriage*," she said forcefully. She looked fearful, yet interested.

"I know," Isaac said. "But then he was going to bring me to the Marshalcy, and I didn't think that would be wise."

"He told you that?" she said, blinking. "That's not what I—"

"Why did you want to see me?"

She looked down, as if she were embarrassed. Then she lifted her head. "There are many ways to open doors. Can you prove you're a sorcerer?"

"Hoxta-namorem," he sang softly. Five simple musical notes. Even a child could cast that spell to drive away the dark. The will-o'-the-wisp returned, and Miss Kauer gasped, her expression full of wonder as she gazed at the pulsing whorl of light.

"Can you...can you teach me to do that?" she asked.

"I just did. You only need to sing the words, Miss Kauer." He made the light disappear again.

"Hoxta-namorem?" she asked, but without singing them. Her memory was quick, but that was to be expected from an actress.

Isaac nodded to her.

There was eagerness in her eyes. She'd been wanting this for a long time. She'd been hungering to learn magic. McKenna had been desperate for magic too. In that life, she'd originally been blocked from it because of her deafness. In this incarnation, she'd been blocked because it was illegal.

"Hoxta-namorem," she sang, and her pitch was so perfect and lovely it made his heart stutter.

A will-o'-the-wisp appeared. Much brighter and stronger than the one he'd summoned. It sent a jolt of electricity into the room and made the lightbulbs hum. Their light increased too.

The sound of footsteps came toward the door. Isaac listened keenly for the telltale sound of a cane, but it was only the tread of shoes coming to her door.

"Someone's—"

"—coming."

They'd spoken the words at the same time. The will-o'-the-wisp vanished.

"Tomorrow is Closure," he said softly. "When can I see you?"

"Mr. Froman's moved my hotel," she said with a regretful sigh. "I don't know where it is yet."

He didn't want to alarm her by stating that he'd be able to

find it without her help. "Meet me tomorrow at Aesir Park," he suggested.

"The one that used to have the floating boulder?"

"That's the one," he replied.

"I'll be there at sunrise," she said.

A loud knock sounded at the door. It was an urgent pounding.

Miss Kauer looked at him worriedly. "If they find you here..."

"They won't."

Aóratos.

He vanished before her eyes, and she looked mystified by it. Then she turned and unlocked the door.

The man who had apprehended Isaac earlier stood in the opening. "Miss Kauer," he said breathlessly. "I'm so glad I found you."

"I need to change, Mr. Carrault. Did you find the man?"

He looked conflicted and then he frowned. "He's gone. Left Arbuckle shackled to the theater seat."

Isaac grinned. Miss Kauer kept her composure. "See if you can find him."

"I will, but he's probably long gone. There was a...break-in at one of the debtors' prisons. Mickelgate. It's a disaster. The company is calling on every available man to help search for the sorcerers who escaped."

"It happened this very evening?" Miss Kauer asked incredulously.

"I'll take you to your hotel, as usual, but we'll be working all night to find them. I can't...I have to help look for them."

"I see," she said flatly. "Well, let me change so we can be on our way."

"I apologize, Miss Kauer. I failed to fulfill your request."

"It was probably a foolish fancy on my part anyway," she said. "Thank you for trying."

She shut the door and locked it again. Slowly turning, she gazed around the room. "Are you still here?" she whispered.

"When you come to the park tomorrow, I'll be there even if you can't see me. I know you are being watched."

"Why did you come to the performance tonight? I knew you were there from the start, even though I didn't see you until I glimpsed you in box six."

He appeared again. "That's one of the things about magic, Miss Kauer. It connects people. It brought me to you."

She was watching his face as he spoke. The fear was gone. "I don't even know your name. But you seem...familiar to me. Have we met before?"

He felt tears sting his eyes.

"What is your name?" she urged.

"My name is Isaac Berrow."

"You were named after the famous inventor?" she asked, her brow wrinkling as a pretty smile came to her mouth.

"I didn't choose my name," he answered, feeling his heart would burst. "Tomorrow, then?"

"Aesir Park," she avowed. "I look forward to it, Mr. Berrow."

"Please. Call me Isaac."

Chapter Fourteen
Rising of the Invisible College

All the windows in the Napier warehouse were dark. Judging by the stars and position of the constellations, it was an hour or so after midnight. The moon hadn't risen yet, but Isaac and Jack maneuvered through the alley alongside the warehouse easily enough. A lone cat gave off a low-throated growl, a mouse clutched in its teeth as it padded out of their way.

"The Marshalcy are still banging on doors near Mickelgate," Jack said, stifling a chuckle. "They are frantic."

"Who told you that?" Isaac asked.

"True did. Their carriage was stopped before reaching Brake Street. But you weren't on board, were you?"

Isaac couldn't suppress a grin himself. Annalise's bodyguard, one Kellin Carrault, hadn't been too difficult to outsmart. They'd all be chasing their tails for a while.

Jack reached a bulkhead door and paused, looking back the way they'd come.

"We've not been followed," Isaac said reassuringly. He'd summoned intelligences to trail them and warn him of danger ahead and behind. The Unseen Powers were easily entreated and willing to help him in his mission. He hoped he'd get at least a few hours of rest before going to Aesir Park to meet Annalise, although he wasn't sure he'd be able to sleep. Insomnia had been a scourge in his life for a very long time.

"Annixe." Jack cast the simple spell to unlock the padlock connected to the chains. Then they worked together to quickly unfasten them, and each pulled one of the angled doors, revealing steep steps leading into the underground space beneath the warehouse. It smelled of iron and grease. They stepped over the lip at the top and pulled the doors shut behind them.

Jack set the chains and lock on the top step, and they both went down into the gloomy space.

"Hoxta-namorem," sang Isaac's companion, and a beautiful will-o'-the-wisp appeared.

They hadn't yet reached the bottom of the stairs when a dozen other lights appeared, revealing the sorcerers hiding below. A quick perusal suggested there were over fifty people. A man and a woman strode up to them, holding hands, followed by their own floating light. This must be the couple Jack had mentioned when he'd been training with Isaac and asked him to meet up and discuss next steps.

"You made it, Jack," said Mr. Turner, and shook his hand heartily.

Mrs. Turner gave Isaac a suspicious look. She and her husband were in their early forties by Isaac's estimation.

"Nathan, Paige, this is Professor Hawksley." Jack made the formal introduction.

Nathan was quick to shake Isaac's hand, but Paige still looked wary.

"Brilliant to meet you, Professor," Nathan said eagerly. "I saw you before. When I was a lad. You haven't aged a day. Jack said you're the only sorcerer who knows how to make a philosopher's stone!"

"Mrs. Turner," Isaac said, offering his hand. She took it, but her distrustful expression remained, and she didn't say anything after shaking his hand.

"How many from Mickelgate are here?" Jack asked.

"About twenty," Mrs. Turner said. "We've fed 'em and helped change their clothes. Some had been in prison for nearly twenty year." Her accent and grammar suggested she was from the slums. Isaac noted the way she hadn't pluralized "year" as a telltale sign.

"That's a long time to be trapped in a cage," Jack said. "We'll start moving them for the next stage when the steam trains begin their runs."

"We already have the tickets," Nathan said. He tapped the edge of his nose. "The Marshalcy will be looking for those without 'em, I think."

"The dunderheads," Paige said under her breath.

"I'll bet they were hungry," Isaac said to her, offering an appreciative smile.

She brightened for a moment, then scowled. "It's not right what they done."

"I agree," Isaac said.

He turned and looked at the others, many of whom were standing and coming forward to meet them. His heart ached at the fervor in their eyes.

Soon he was clasping hands and making his way through the group of impoverished sorcerers.

"Good to meet you, Professor!"

"Thought you were dead, sir!"

After he'd greeted each of them in turn, their voices fell silent and they looked at him as if he were some kind of politician and they were expecting a speech. He hadn't anticipated that, but he felt it only right to be accommodating.

"I am sorry that so many of you have suffered because you were part of the Invisible College. You might not believe me, but this isn't the first time sorcerers have been persecuted or hunted. It will take time, but I intend to make sure that every sorcerer is freed."

He heard some rumbles of enthusiasm from the group but held up his hands to quiet them. "I hope the laws will be changed. But whether they are or not, we're on borrowed time. The Awakening has already started. The Aesir have begun to attack. An entire village in the north was wiped out because there were no sorcerers there to sing the shield songs."

He'd learned this from Wickins, who had met up with a military friend upon arriving in Auvinen. Being able to communicate by the sorcerer's rings had been so useful—and it would become more so as additional rings were made.

He shifted his posture, his heart yearning to help these people, to give them hope. There was no way to hold off the onslaught of the Aesir. The military seemed completely unconcerned, although that was mostly due to the number of Semblances in their ranks. The new generation had not been trained to defend the empire from their ancient enemy.

"We must do what we can," Isaac said, feeling the anguish of knowing that many could die before the terms of the covenant with the Erlking were fulfilled. "I have found a way to stop the war. But I need time. And even if we cannot do much, we can at least use our magic to protect the innocent. We can even use it to defend those who have hunted and abused us."

"Why should we?" asked an older man with an angry frown. "I just want to go home!"

"Do you remember when the *strannik* caused that explosion in the city?" Jack said, coming to stand by Isaac. "I was in the tenements when it happened. Covered in rubble. My arm and leg were broken. And this man came for me, even when everyone said it was hopeless. He dug me out with his bare hands. He didn't need to. He'd already done enough for my family." He looked at Isaac, tears in his eyes. Isaac felt his own throat thicken.

Jack pointed at him, trying to master his emotions. "And he did more. When the Aesir bombarded Auvinen, he played his violin over our buildings when the other sorcerers were busy protecting the factories. He cares about everyone. And it was his idea to rescue you all tonight."

"It was *your* idea, Jack." Isaac shook his head. "There are others willing to stand up and help. I understand about wanting to go home. I really do. But if we don't act now, there will be no more homes to return to. The Aesir are coming to destroy us. When the snows come, so will they."

"How do you know this, Professor?" a woman asked.

"Hush! He knows!" said a man.

Even if he had the rest of the night, he wouldn't be able to answer all their questions, so he decided to start with the biggest. "Because I am the last Master of the Royal Secret," he said. "I hold the highest rank in the Invisible College. I know things I can't share with you, but I came back to help. I'll do whatever I can at whatever the cost. It won't be easy. It may not even be possible to..."

He couldn't finish the thought. His mind was buzzing with warnings. The intelligences had found a threat approaching the warehouse.

"What's wrong?" Jack asked worriedly.

"Can I borrow your violin?" Isaac asked, pointing to the instrument dangling from a strap around the other man's shoulder. He'd left his own instrument in McKenna's room at the Foster's home.

Jack unslung it and handed it over without hesitation.

"Are they come for us already?" Mrs. Turner asked worriedly.

Her husband grasped her hand, his own face troubled.

"I'll lead them away," Isaac said to her. "You'll be safe. I promise."

Then he slung the strap over his own shoulder and nodded to Jack. He was the person they knew and trusted. He was the right person to lead them to safety. Besides, Isaac knew magic that none of them did. He marched back to the steps leading to the double doors and hurriedly went up. He took the chains from the top step and used them to lock the doors behind him. There were other ways out of the warehouse Jack could use to help them escape.

Isaac communed with the intelligences and discovered a single man was coming. Someone with weapons. Someone with anger in his heart.

Isaac hummed a shield spell and then unlatched the violin case and drew out the instrument. He grazed the bow over the strings and quickly adjusted the pegs to tune it. He could hear footsteps getting closer. The warehouse windows were high on its brick walls. Isaac strummed a few notes, channeling magic to strengthen the chains and the wooden cargo doors. Imbuing them with shield spells.

The footsteps fell silent.

Isaac walked away from the doors, continuing to play spells as he walked. He sent the magic down the streets, protecting windows on both sides of the dark alley. At the corner of the warehouse, he turned and walked along that side, expanding the net of defensive magic.

A shot was fired. He saw the muzzle flash, heard the bullet whistle and then ricochet off his personal shield. The shot had come from the rooftop. He saw the ripple of an Aesir cloak as the fellow leaped from the roof, launching himself at him with a glowing harrosheth blade in his hand.

Isaac changed the chord to a minor one, his fingers unleashing a shivering convulsion of notes, faster and faster. The man's boots had been spelled with the intelligences of grasshoppers—allowing him to perform inhuman feats, but Isaac's magic freed them.

The fellow plummeted to the stone street, breaking both legs on impact, and landed in a heap. The harrosheth blade spun away from him on the ground, yanked back by Isaac's next tune. He worked the strings relentlessly, encasing the man in the shield he'd invented to entrap Joseph Crossthwait and the Semblance at the Great Exhibition. If the man was a Semblance, as Isaac suspected, he would not be able to abandon his body for another.

Isaac stood over the man's crumpled body, playing wave after wave of music, increasing the tempo into a frenzy before slowing it down to a delicate, tremulous tension of notes, all while the man gasped in agony from his injuries.

And then he cast another spell that put the man to sleep, a sleep suffused with magic.

Isaac finished the spell and tucked the violin back into the case.

By the time the Semblance awoke, all the sorcerers in Napier warehouse would be gone. Even after Isaac stopped playing, he could still hear the music lingering in the air, as if entombed by the bricks.

Any citizen uttering or singing magical incantations shall be fined three thousand cuppers and spend up to fifty days in jail unless they cooperate and name the identity of the person or persons who taught them the magical phrases. For doing so, lenience may be permitted by the magistrate. No respect to age or infirmity will be permitted, nor will it be considered sufficient excuse. Those exempt from these harsh penalties are the ones seeking to infiltrate the vestiges of this pernicious cult and reveal the ringleaders. Proper care should be taken to conceal the identity of these informants, and they alone will be fully immune from prosecution.

—Code of Justice, "Laws Against the Use of Sorcery" § 423p, the Marshalcy

Annalise Kauer

Chapter Fifteen
A Charming Man

Annalise would ordinarily have been in bed on Closure so early in the morning. Usually, such days were spent leisurely, with a late social breakfast, followed by several delightfully calm hours. She predicted that meeting the enigmatic sorcerer at daybreak, as planned, would give them the most uninterrupted time possible.

That was something she desperately wanted. Indeed, sleep had come in fits and starts the previous night because she was so eager to meet this man again. Something about him had seized her interest and not just because he was the first sorcerer she had met, though he'd surprised her with his willingness to share information about spells when the consequences for doing so were dire indeed. She'd also been shocked, and pleased, by how easily she herself had learned the spell for summoning light. Could she learn other spells as simply?

The hotel had provided a carriage and she'd reached the park early. She paid a few cuppers to the yawning driver, who had vowed to remain until she was ready to return.

She wore a black-and-white dress with a ruffle-edged jacket and a matching white hat with black feathers. It was fancier than the occasion required, but she felt formality would help maintain some distance between them. It wouldn't do for him to know she was interested in him. Self-preservation required her to be on her guard, especially since she was behaving a little recklessly. She could, of course, afford any fine the Marshalcy chose to impose, and she believed her fame and Mr. Froman's status in Society would shield her from any serious scandal. And yet...

She felt the danger. She felt the *excitement*.

There was a little mist hanging over the park's greenery. But the view of the river was exquisite and she walked along the path circumnavigating the park, shielded by poplar trees along the fringes. She liked that word—"circumnavigating." One of the things she respected about Mr. Froman was his taste in language and how he would command the scriptwriters to make alterations that always improved how lines were delivered.

She'd made it halfway around the park and was near the spot where the ancient boulder had once hung in the air. Only a few lumps of stone had been left on the lawn. A frisson of tension went down her spine. The sorcerer was invisible, surely, as he said he'd be. Was he there already?

"Miss Kauer."

She did not start at being addressed in such a way. She turned her head and found him standing to the side, leaning against one of the trees. The carriage was a good distance away, too far for the driver to see.

"Mr. Berrow." She inclined her head.

"I thought we might walk along the waterfront."

He was rather thin of frame and looked as if he too hadn't slept much the previous night either. There was a decided lack of care in his manner of dress. She noticed it not because it bothered her but because she tended to notice things about people, especially when seeking to learn more about them. Still, there was something hauntingly familiar about him. The feeling of déjà vu hung heavily in the air between them.

She nodded and abandoned the footpath to cross the lawn.

They walked down a little slope of turf before reaching a dirt path along the river's edge. She could see no one else in the park.

"I do want to say, Mr. Berrow—"

"Isaac if you please."

"We've only just met, Mr. Berrow. I think it wise to be formal."

"As you wish."

The way he said it was tender. He wasn't acting like a stranger. His eyes were studying her face, paying her a great deal of focused attention.

"I'm sorry for interrupting you," he said. "Go on."

"What I wanted to say, Mr. Berrow, is that I understand the risk you took in showing me what you did last night. If you are ever caught by the Marshalcy and put in debtors' prison, I will pay for your immediate release."

"Thank you, Miss Kauer. How would I go about contacting you?"

"Send a message to my maid, Maud Jenkins. She will inform me, and I will see to it that you're released. Any messages sent to me directly never reach me, you see. You have to send them through Maud. I'm deeply alarmed that the punishments are so strict, especially since no one will explain why. I was hoping you could educate me. The explanations I've been given thus far are wholly inadequate."

"You have a way with words," he said with a gleam in his eyes. He clasped his hands behind his back as they walked languidly along the river's edge.

"I've always been fascinated by language," she said.

"To answer your question...twenty-three years ago, there was a confrontation between several factions: the Aesir, who condemn mortals for violating an ancient treaty between our people; the Invisible College, which was a society of sorcerers seeking to protect humanity from destruction; and finally, there was a faction led by a *strannik*. Do you know that term?"

Annalise thought a moment and then shook her head.

"That's the title of a religious pilgrim of sorts. This particular man, Gregor Skoye, made an alliance with the Aesir, and in return for his help, he and his followers were permitted to leave this world for another one."

"What do you mean 'for another one'?" she asked. This was all new information to her, although parts of it sounded vaguely familiar.

"The Aesir came to this world because it was cold, like their dying planet was. But the climate began to alter and the glaciers receded. Mortals violated the Aesir's homeland and took possession of their fortresses. This city, Auvinen, used to be one of them."

"Indeed? This isn't common knowledge."

"Not anymore. The difficulty is that the Aesir are immortal. They can live for tens of thousands of years. Even hundreds of thousands."

"But they can be killed? I've seen the effigies of them laid to rest."

"They can, although they do not age and are not susceptible to disease. They are quicker than us, more intelligent, and have magical abilities we cannot replicate. Because of the *strannik*'s duplicity during the last Awakening, the Invisible College was overrun by Semblances who tried to dismantle it from within. These imposters helped foster the laws that made magic illegal."

"By the Awakening, you mean when the Aesir used to attack us?" she asked. Every time she had tried to ask about such things, she'd found the answers entirely incomprehensible. This man, named after the famous founder of the Invisible College, was providing details no one else had been willing or able to. "I thought they were gone for good."

"They have always come back. Because of their longevity, the Aesir must enter a state of rest called the Skrýmir. It goes on for decades, sometimes centuries. Then they awaken and seek to reclaim the edges of their world they lost while they slept."

"So they are not gone?" she said, her brow wrinkling with concern.

He shook his head. "They are not. The Awakening is happening now. They will attack us again this winter, for only in the cold can they thrive."

"But that's ridiculous," Annalise said. He seemed so sincere. Either he was a fantastic actor or he believed what he told her to be the truth. If it *was* true, it meant the world was in terrible danger, even though no one was acting as if anything were amiss. No one had mentioned the Awakening to her. Not once.

"Improbable. Unlikely. Uncertain. But what I said is true nonetheless."

She liked his choice of words—and even the sound of his voice saying them. That thought made her flinch within herself. She was not interested in getting to know men socially or in any way other than professionally. Romantic attachments would be nothing but an impediment to her career.

"How do you know this, Mr. Berrow? Is there some secret ledger chronicling when these Awakenings will happen?"

"No, the answer is far more prosaic."

When he didn't elaborate, she gave him an inquisitive arch of her eyebrows.

"I did the arithmetic," he said simply. "It is a complex equation regarding the ratio of a circle to its radius. It takes a dreadfully long time to calculate by hand, but it has reliably predicted the Awakenings for the last several hundred years. The numbers seem random—fifty-nine, twenty-six, fifty-three, fifty-eight, ninety-seven, ninety-three, twenty-three. But the sequence of numbers is calculable. It has been twenty-three years since the last Awakening."

"But why would the military or the Marshalcy seek to hide this knowledge?" she asked. "If what you say is true and the Aesir will imminently attack us, why doesn't anyone know about it?"

"The imposters I mentioned earlier." They reached a segment on the path that had a bench and he gestured for her to sit with a little shrug to indicate that it was her decision. She preferred to keep walking. She gazed around, but there was still no one else to be seen.

"What about the imposters?" she asked. "How do the Aesir walk among us when it isn't cold?"

"The Aesir have a magic that allow them to hide undetected. Their intelligence, their *soul*, can be put inside a human. These are the Semblances I mentioned earlier." He said the word in a very pointed way and seemed to be studying her face for a reaction.

"'Semblances'?" she replied with a shrug.

A flash of disappointment came and went from his eyes.

"It's my understanding that even talking about them is illegal," Mr. Berrow said. "Before the Aesir went to sleep the last time, they sent Semblances to infiltrate the military. Then the Marshalcy. The hierarchy of the Invisible College were lured to the University of Nirshoye, where they were all killed."

"How did the knowledge get passed down, then?" she asked, feeling a bit incredulous. "You must have been a child." Surely if the threat were real, people would know about it. She needed to validate his words somehow. But how could she hope to do so when even talking about the Invisible College was illegal?

"Because I was there, Miss Kauer. I witnessed it." He reached into his vest and pulled out a pocket watch. That was an odd thing to do after such a ridiculous pronouncement. He opened the lid, and instead of a face and hands telling the time, she saw a multicolored stone set inside an intricate series of rings.

"What is that?" she asked.

"This stone is a philosopher's stone. As long as it is near me, I cannot age. I was *there*, Annalise. I saw it all happen. I've seen so many things happen."

Impossible. Preposterous. Intriguing.

"May I hold it?" she asked.

"By all means," he answered and handed it to her. It had a brass or bronze finish. In addition to the inner rings and stone, there was a little sliver of glass with numbered runes on it. Aesir runes. She knew the numerical alphabet because Mr. Froman used it in his correspondence and to number the scenes and acts in the plays.

"Those are numbers," she said. "The number nine, three times."

"That is correct," he said, his voice becoming more earnest.

"What is their significance?" she asked, handing the device back to him. Their fingers touched and she was grateful she was wearing gloves because that slight brush had caused an arresting feeling to surge up her arm. In her years on the stage, she'd learned the importance of physical touch between actors to make an audience feel something. In a play, every gesture and caress was contrived. Staged.

This was...different. She'd felt something very tangible with that brief contact.

Mr. Berrow clicked the lid shut and slid it back into his pocket. He seemed to be wrestling with whether he should answer her last question.

Some birds started squawking over a twig or something, drawing her attention to them for a moment.

"There are some secrets I cannot share with you until you are ready," he finally said enigmatically.

"Is that part of the rules of the Invisible College? Are the members allowed access to these secrets?"

"Precisely so," he said. "They gain knowledge as they rise in the ranks." But she felt there was something else he wasn't saying.

"How does one join the Invisible College?" she asked. "Is there an initiation of sorts?"

"You wish to join?" he asked with a surprised look in his eyes.

"I was just curious. I'm getting ready to start rehearsals for a new play." She gave him a bright smile, but he winced as if he were in pain.

"You will be playing the Erlking's daughter."

"Yes," she said, studying him. There was a tortured look in his eyes she couldn't understand. "What's wrong, Mr. Berrow? Are you unwell?"

"Can I ask you a question, Miss Kauer?"

She stopped walking. The look he gave her had transfixed her with worry. She felt sympathy for him. Concern.

Until he asked her a question he shouldn't have.

Chapter Sixteen
Dark Remembrances

"Miss Kauer, was there a time you almost died?"

The question went straight to her heart, breaching all the walls she had erected over the years since that tragic, impossible night at the theater. No one knew about what had really happened. Those who had been there had seemed to forget all about it. But this sorcerer, this Mr. Berrow, looked at her as if he *knew*.

Immediately her heart began to palpitate. Her mouth went dry. An involuntary feeling of dizziness swept over her, potent enough that she must have swayed on her feet, because he was instantly there, grasping her arm to steady her. His touch sent violent shocks through her. There were only certain places she allowed people to touch her, primarily her hands.

Feeling his hand around her upper arm sent strange tingles through her—the feeling much too familiar given she'd just met him. Annalise jerked her arm away, giving him a hot look that seemed to sear his conscience as he retreated a step.

"Do not touch me!" she said fiercely. She could still feel the warmth of his hand on her arm, and her heart was beating wildly.

"I'm sorry if I offended you. I was afraid you were going to faint."

"I wasn't going to faint." A surge of indignation swept through her.

"I apologize. It seemed you were."

"I think our interview is concluded, Mr. Berrow."

"Please," he said, looking heartbroken at her words. "I hoped we could speak a little longer."

"I don't think that would be wise, Mr. Berrow. It was a pleasant enough walk until you asked me such an absurd question."

"Absurd?" he said. "Then why are you reacting this way?"

Was he accusing her of being too emotional? "I think we've spoken long enough. Good day."

She began to walk away from him, but he had the audacity to catch her hand, halting her. His hand felt positively hot through the silk glove she wore.

"Mr. Berrow!" she said in growing alarm.

"Please, Miss Kauer," he said, looking miserable with sorrow. "You have no idea how far I've come."

"Or how far you're willing to *go*, it seems," she said archly.

"It wasn't an errant question."

He had an impressive vocabulary. She had to give him credit for that. How many young men would have used the word "errant" in casual conversation? The little surge of respect she felt for his elevated language was diminished by the fact that he was still...holding...her...hand.

"If you do not unhand me, I'll be forced to cry for help." She'd actually decided to strike him with her parasol, but better not to alert him to her intentions in advance.

He did release her. "I'm sorry."

"You should be," she said. "That was very reckless, Mr. Berrow. I'm leaving. But I warn you: If you come to see me again without an invitation, you'll be met more harshly."

"But why did you react to my question that way?"

"Because it was an unseemly question to ask *anyone*. Good day."

She began to walk briskly back the way they'd come. Why was her hand still tingling from his touch? It was infuriating. Maybe he'd cast some spell on her? Perhaps there was a kind of magic that could make someone feel they knew you intimately. That you could trust them without hesitation. Those were the feelings roiling inside her, and they were completely alien to her. She hardly knew the man. How could she trust him with such a dangerous, intimate secret?

And yet...he'd known. Somehow, he'd already known.

She risked a backward glance and found him following her but at a slower pace. He was watching her intently, which made her increase her stride. The carriage was around the bend on the other side of the park. Perhaps she should run for it, but she didn't feel inclined to do so. Somehow she knew he wasn't attempting to catch up with her—rather, he was following her to ensure her safety. The thought didn't make sense, though, and it troubled her. Because she had no reason to trust this man. None at all.

Her pulse was still racing when she reached the carriage. The driver had seen her approaching quickly and had stepped off the rider's box to open the door for her.

"Was that man troubling you, miss?" the young man asked. She grasped the handle to pull herself up and risked another backward glance. Mr. Berrow was still coming up the sidewalk. He looked forlorn and serious. Surely he regretted his words to her. His impertinence.

Good. That was as it should be.

"Not at all, but the walk took longer than I thought," Annalise said blithely. "I have an appointment back at the hotel. Can we go there quickly?"

"Yes, miss."

She hurriedly seated herself, laying the parasol across her lap. The driver climbed up and gave the horses a little lash with the crop. She gazed out the window as the carriage lurched forward.

Mr. Berrow was still watching her, still walking closer. She saw a tear glisten on his cheek and couldn't account for it. But it made her heart ache for some mysterious reason.

Maud had the day off for Closure, which left Annalise alone and confused in her room at the new hotel. She wished Mr. Froman hadn't changed it. It was his right to protect his performers, but she'd gotten used to the old hotel room. The pattern of the curtains in this one was unfamiliar, as were the decorations.

She sighed and sat down on the little divan and tried to compose herself, but her agitation was only growing. Memories she had buried were surfacing again. Ugly memories of the night Mr. Froman had tried to kill her...

A decade earlier, he'd been a sort of bully to his actresses. There was always the implication that he could become violent if crossed. She'd seem him whip one of the stage boys with his cane. Had heard him bluster and rage at one spot of "foolishness" or another. But that night, that dark night, he'd turned his cruelty on her after she'd come to the defense of another girl with a minor part in the play.

When Mr. Froman was in one of his tempers, the rest of the crew tended to slip away in abject terror, abandoning whoever bore the brunt of his temper to their fate. Annalise had been sixteen years old and had keenly felt the injustice of his behavior toward the young woman who'd muddled her lines and then dared to yawn.

"Just leave her alone," Annalise had said angrily.

Annalise had been given the lead role in that play. She'd felt, wrongly, that Mr. Froman would drop the matter and skulk off. Instead, he'd acted as if she'd prodded him with a hot poker and scalded him. He had never been able to bear defiance from anyone whom he didn't esteem a peer. He'd been petty and prone to overreact to slights and imagined insults. He had blamed the caprice of the economy and poor ticket sales on the actors and actresses being worthless performers. In short, he'd been a very different man.

The other girl had escaped because he'd turned his cane on Annalise.

Bruises on the arms and the back could be hidden. You could work through the pain of sore arms. So he tended to strike there first. Because even then, he'd been all about getting the most work from each of them.

His blows hadn't cowed her. The injustice had infuriated her. After he'd delivered several hard strokes against her arms, she'd looked him in the face and said, "Is that all? I could hardly feel the blows."

A devilish rage had contorted his face. She'd heard at least one person gasp in shock at her audacious pronouncement before the sound of fleeing footsteps beating hasty retreats. Mr. Froman then began to beat her in earnest, striking her back and buttocks with his cane. Her own father had never whipped her, let alone beat her. She was so angry she didn't even feel the pain from the blows. She just glared at him as he struck her, clenching her teeth, knowing that the next day's performance would be done in agony. But she endured it until, dripping sweat, he backed away from her, holding a broken cane.

"You can't hurt me, Mr. Froman," she seethed at him. Her whole body was trembling as she lay on the stage floor behind the curtained area where props and knickknacks were stored. Her heart cooled until it was ice. All fear of him was gone. She rose shakily to her feet, squeezing her hands into fists. "You can't hurt me."

She'd defied him. She'd bested him.

He was huffing, cheeks red, sweat dripping from his chin. His abominable cane had been broken on her backside.

The maddened look in his eyes should have warned her...

Annalise rose from the hotel divan, trying to blot out the memory of what happened next as a tremulous sigh escaped her lips.

Her thoughts were interrupted by a knock on the door. She wasn't expecting anyone. For a panicked moment, she feared Mr. Berrow had somehow found her and come to ask more questions.

She crossed the room, her cheeks hot with the evil memories, and paused with her hand on the handle.

"Who is it?" she asked.

"It is I."

It was Mr. Froman. She bit her lower lip before turning the lock and opening the door.

He gazed at her black-and-white dress with a bent brow. "Are you going out?" he demanded. It was more common for her to wear a less formal gown on Closure.

Ever since that day, he had changed. He'd become another man entirely. He still had a temper, but he never beat the cast or crew ever again. Instead, he used his tongue and stern gaze to administer his displeasure.

That night had been the most terrible in her life and it still made her unsettled to think about it. She rarely did anymore. She'd accepted Mr. Froman's change in personality. She'd put the event behind her, knowing it was in her own self-interest to move on, if not forget. But the memories, at times, made it difficult to face him. She had to utilize her skill in acting, on occasion, to disguise her fear. But Mr. Berrow's question had unlocked the memories, so they were out of the box and parading about in her mind again.

"I'm not," she said, showing no emotion on her face.

"I heard from the manager that you were out this morning," he said, his eyes narrowing suspiciously.

"I took a stroll in the park."

"At sunrise?"

So that's why he was here. His spies had informed him about her deviation from her regular patterns. He was trying to get her to confess. Well, she had no intention of doing so.

"Haven't you always extolled the benefits of regular exercise and morning light?" she asked in a slightly teasing tone.

"I just wanted to be sure nothing was amiss. Have you had breakfast?"

"I'm not hungry at the moment." Then she gave him a suspicious glance. "You came all this way because you'd heard I'd taken a walk?"

"No. I learned that after I arrived."

"Then what did you come for?" she asked.

"To see if you'd heard that Mickelgate Prison was breached last night. A hundred or so sorcerers escaped."

He was studying her for a reaction.

At his words, she *did* feel a momentary surge of exultation, which she could not fully explain. Part of her was giddy with excitement.

"Oh? I didn't know all the details."

He squinted slightly at her words and supported himself with just one hand on the cane—the new one with the jeweled top—and reached out to her. He extracted the pin that held her hair up in that particular coif, and her hair tumbled down about her shoulders.

She gave him a confused look as he held out the pin for her to take.

"This looks more suitable for a stroll in the park," he said, implying that he knew she was lying. He hated dishonesty but especially when it was directed against him. That was another dramatic change in his personality since that night.

She took the pin. He tipped his hat to her, the hat that partially concealed his damaged face...

And she gently shut the door and locked it. For just a moment, she could feel his hands around her throat again. It made her shudder behind the closed door when no eyes were on her.

Kellin Carrault

Chapter Seventeen
The Cane's Jewel

The shrill whistle from the train joined the cacophony of noise and confusion in the yard at the train station in Auvinen. Kellin looked both ways, trying to catch a glimpse of the man he was searching for. The train was loaded with passengers ready to depart, but the officers of the Marshalcy had ordered a delay, believing that some of the sorcerers recently escaped from Mickelgate Prison were on board. They'd waited until the last moment to inform the chief engineer they'd be doing a search. The crowd, which had gathered to wave farewells to the passengers, was confused by the delay and had grown agitated.

Kellin was exhausted, having only filched a few hours of sleep on Closure the day before. He watched as Arbuckle strode toward him, then asked, "Any sign of them?"

Arbuckle shook his head curtly. "The informant hasn't recognized any of the passengers. Not a single one. But he *said* this was the last train they'd be using to depart."

The Marshalcy had been chasing shadows since Mickelgate Prison was compromised. They hadn't recaptured any of the sorcerers who had escaped. Thankfully, one of them had decided to turn traitor on the others and had slipped away to warn the Marshalcy about the plot, hoping for a reward for his information. At that very moment, a detective lieutenant was escorting the fellow row by row through the train to identify any of the culprits since he had told them they had all been given a change of clothes to aid in their disguise.

Kellin knew that Mr. Froman was particularly interested in this case, so he wanted to have a report for him before he went to the theater that night. He was still furious that the sorcerer he'd nabbed at the theater had escaped him, though he hadn't revealed that lapse to Mr. Froman yet. Mr. Froman was not a patient man.

It took about an hour to search the entire train, and Kellin watched in despair as the Marshalcy officers left empty-handed. The whistle shrieked again, and then the pistons began to churn. The wheels grated and screeched as the lumbering machine lurched forward on the tracks.

"No one," Arbuckle seethed, stomping his foot.

Kellin nodded toward the detective lieutenant, who was gripping a plain-clothed man by the arm. "Is that the informant?"

"That's the one. Peachley's his name."

Kellin made his way toward them, then nodded to the officer, whom he recognized. "Marks." The lieutenant looked disgruntled, and so did his companion.

With a grimace, Marks said, "I don't know what to tell you, Carrault. Maybe it was a decoy."

"It wasn't," Peachley grumbled. "This was the time. This was the train."

"Where are you taking this fellow?" Kellin asked, giving the informant a curt nod.

"Back to headquarters for now. Maybe something else will turn up."

Kellin nodded gravely, disappointment squeezing his chest. Another Marshalcy officer came running up to them, his face dripping with sweat.

The detective lieutenant scowled. "What's wrong, Statham?"

The new arrival was panting. "Bambridge Prison…"

"What about it? Speak, man!"

"Bambridge Prison is empty! Everyone is gone!"

Kellin stared in disbelief at the news. "Bambridge? How?"

"The warden let everyone out," the officer said, holding up his hands. "He was in a daze of sorts. Just roaming the courtyard, twirling his keys. They're all gone. Every single inmate."

"That's preposterous. How?" the lieutenant said, flustered.

"I don't know! It must be magic. A spell. He's acting like he's in a dream. Can't explain why he left the gate open, and he doesn't even remember everyone leaving."

"It is broad daylight," Kellin said angrily, heat surging through his chest. The Marshalcy had gathered a sizeable force for the raid at the train yard. Everyone was so focused on hunting down the escaped men that they hadn't considered another break might be in progress under their very noses.

Marks rubbed the bridge of his nose. "How am I going to explain this?"

"Something has changed," Kellin said fiercely. "The newcomer," he barked at Peachley. "What did you say his name was?"

"Hawksley."

"Surely it's not the *same* Hawksley," Marks said, glancing at Kellin.

"We can't be sure of anything. They say he was shot and killed well over twenty years ago. But was he? Was there a cover-up of sorts?" Turning back to the informant, he asked, "He was a younger man, wasn't he?"

"Looked about thirty, if I were to guess," said Mr. Peachley. "Said he was the Master of the Royal Secret. That he's the last one who had that rank."

Marks scowled. "I need to report all of this to headquarters."

"So do I," Kellin said. He glanced at Arbuckle, giving him an overt nod indicating he should learn what he could about the prison break, then hurried to the carriage that would take him directly to the theater.

✳

When he walked past the main stage, it was more than an hour before the performance was to begin, but the tension was palpable. He knew the cast would be putting on their costumes. The crew preparing for scene changes. He could hear snatches of words as he walked briskly toward Mr. Froman's office. He quickly reached the door, knocked, and entered as soon as he was invited to do so.

Mr. Froman was alone in the meticulous room. The furniture was polished and cleaned, never dusty. There were bookshelves and trinkets and the pleasant smell of pine. Mr. Froman was seated at an angle, gazing distractedly at him.

"I've some news, Mr. Froman."

"If it's about Bambridge Prison, you're already late. Someone else got here first."

Kellin's stomach coiled with dread. He didn't dare ask who had sprung the news ahead of him.

"I'm sorry," Kellin apologized.

Mr. Froman still had a faraway look in his countenance. He was brooding about something. His cane was in his hands. It had an uncommonly large jewel fastened to the top as a grip. An Aesir artifact, no doubt, although no one was likely to complain about it. Certainly he'd paid some sort of fee to someone.

"Is that all?" Mr. Froman asked in a tired voice.

"No, sir. The Bambridge news is a recent development, but I did want to share what I learned during Closure yesterday. One of the ringleaders of the Mickelgate prison break is a man who goes by Robinson Hawksley."

Mr. Froman stiffened and turned his head, giving Kellin an awestruck look. "Tell me what you've learned."

"I know it's the same name as the sorcerer who died all those years ago. One of the sorcerers who left with the others decided to change sides and warn the Marshalcy. I was just at the station. The Marshalcy attempted to apprehend some of the escapees, but none were found."

Mr. Froman chuckled deep in his throat. "How easily you are all deceived."

Kellin wondered what was meant by the statement. "I don't believe the man is truly Hawksley."

"Oh? And why not?"

"That was decades ago. The man who met with the escapees was a younger fellow."

"Describe him, please."

Kellin frowned, but Arbuckle had related the description to him, so he could pass it along well enough. "Slightly over six feet tall. Rather unkempt hair. A spare-framed fellow. Not one you'd see in the boxing ring, you know. Articulate, confident—"

"It's him," Mr. Froman said with confidence. Then he leaned back in his chair.

"You believe it is the same man, then?"

"I'm convinced of it." He gave Kellin a serious look. "Has anyone matching that description been seen around the theater, Mr. Carrault?"

Kellin swallowed. He felt the impulse to lie, but he knew Mr. Froman abhorred falsehoods. More than any other crime, dishonesty was promptly punished. "I have, sir."

"When?"

"The last performance actually. Miss Kauer noticed a man by that description in the audience."

"Where was he sitting that he was so noticeable?"

"Box six."

Mr. Froman frowned. "I'd like to find out who was sitting in that box that night. And what did Miss Kauer ask you to do? Bring the man to her?"

"She did," Mr. Froman said, perplexed by Mr. Froman's ability to deduce as much. At least no chastisement seemed to be forthcoming. "I found the man attempting to leave and persuaded him to visit with her. I took him to the private box. Chained him with nulling cuffs, but he managed to escape and locked my man Arbuckle to the seat instead."

It was humiliating to relate the truth, but Mr. Froman only chuckled again.

"So that's who met her," he mused.

"Actually no," Kellin said. "He slipped away. She was disappointed not to meet him."

"Mr. Carrault, they *did* meet that night, and she met him again yesterday at Closure at Aesir Park."

Kellin's brain was becoming muddled with all the strange news he was hearing. He still wasn't convinced the man in question was the real Professor Hawksley. How could it be? And then there was the realization that Mr. Froman was clearly getting information from sources other than Kellin. He tried to collect himself but hadn't gotten very far when Mr. Froman slowly rose to his feet, steadying himself with his cane. He came around the desk and stood before him.

"If I may ask how you came to know—?"

"You may not." Mr. Froman interrupted him coldly. "You've been a capable servant, Mr. Carrault, if a flawed one. You see what is going on around you, but you do not truly see."

"I don't see what, exactly?" Kellin asked.

"She is my daughter," Mr. Froman said. "And every time, she chooses *him*. But not this time. I'm determined it won't happen this time."

The words made no logical sense whatsoever. Miss Kauer was Mr. Froman's daughter? Surely not. They hadn't met until she was a young stage performer. Her parents were part of the public record. Or was there a scandal...?

"No scandal, Mr. Carrault. Not in the way you are thinking."

"In the way that I'm...thinking?"

It happened so fast that Kellin couldn't react. The cane whipped up and struck him in the side of the head, causing a blinding explosion of pain in his skull. He experienced the sensation of falling, but he was caught by a strong hand and lowered to the floor. Wetness tickled his ear. His vision was blurred, but looking up, he saw the jewel at the tip of Mr. Froman's cane glowing. It was a magical light, not an incandescent one.

So Mr. Froman *was* a sorcerer.

As that realization struck him, the impact as forcible as the blow from the cane, he felt part of himself get sucked out of his body. That part of him, the conscious part, joined the crystalline structure of the jewel and was seized and held fast by impervious bonds.

Mr. Froman was calm as he said, "I need your help to hunt down Isaac. He's already been in contact with Eiríka."

Another voice answered him. Kellin's voice. But how was that possible? His awareness was becoming lethargic. The magic was overpowering, succumbing to it was the only conscious thing he could comprehend as a dreamlike state was coming over him.

"I thought it was him when I plummeted to the street that night. I will find him, my lord. And I will bring him to you. Justice will be done."

"Justice has already begun."

Issac Berrow

Chapter Eighteen
The Best Disguises

Isaac walked up Brake Street with a heavy heart. All day, he had been dwelling on his interaction with Annalise at Closure, and how she'd run from him. He'd hoped that by asking about her brush with death, he would be able to start to convince her that she was a Semblance. It hadn't gone well at all, though, and he was discouraged and anxious.

Seeing the familiar house up ahead added to his pangs.

It felt like he was Robinson again, and that McKenna would be joining him there. But McKenna was gone, and Annalise wasn't warming to him...

The invisible guardians he'd established to watch over the house after the play—when he'd removed the glamour on the family as well—informed him that everyone was inside and safe. The sun was going down, which meant Annalise's next performance would be starting soon. When would be the right time to seek her out again, to try to help her remember who she truly was?

He opened the little gate and stepped around to the side of the house, entering near the kitchen. Then he removed the invisibility spell. The smell of supper was enticing. A variety of fish, by the scent of things. The family had already gathered for the meal.

"Rob!" True said when she saw him enter the dining room.

"You look exhausted," Mrs. Foster said worriedly.

"I am," he confessed. There was an empty chair next to Wickins and he took it. A serving platter was covered in strips of cod and salmon adorned with specks of pepper and thinly-sliced lemon. Mrs. Foster hurriedly fetched an extra place setting for him.

"Good to see you, old chap," Wickins said. "You didn't have anything to do with that ruckus at Bambridge, did you?"

He flashed Wickins a crooked smile. "Maybe a little."

"Is everyone safe?" True asked, reaching out across the table.

He knew exactly whom she meant and nodded. "Everyone from the prison left."

"You didn't liberate just the sorcerers?" Mr. Foster queried, angling his head.

"Most of them *were*," Isaac said. "But it added to the confusion to release all of them. I had a suspicion that someone might have betrayed us to the Marshalcy, so we spread word that the last train to Bishopsgate leaving the city would be full of escaped sorcerers. The Marshalcy was there in force instead of roaming the streets."

"Good show," Wickins said, laughing. "Now that's a clever fellow."

"But you might not always guess things right," Clara warned, giving her husband a reproving look. "There are Semblances throughout the government. We're all at risk if something goes wrong."

"I don't want anything to happen to this family," Isaac said, looking at each person in turn. He cared about them and they'd suffered enough because of him.

"If we do nothing," Mr. Foster said, "then we'll all be slaughtered. I've heard more disturbing news from the north. People are dying. Winter has already descended on the northern borders. Is there any hope of stopping the Aesir?"

Isaac reached out and served himself some of the fish and some brussels sprouts glistening with olive oil with little bits of cooked bacon mingled in. His stomach growled, but he took his time to answer the question honestly.

"There is a way," he said. "And I am working on it."

"Can we help you?" True volunteered.

"It's something I must do alone."

"Is it dangerous?" Mrs. Foster asked, her eyes narrowing with concern.

"Honestly, yes. To a degree. But there is even more danger if I attempt nothing. We're trying to rally the other sorcerers. While magical artifacts would be helpful, we know that the smoke from saltpetr will slow an Aesir down. We need alchemies to make more. We also need funds."

"People will help if they understand the need is real," Mr. Foster said gruffly. "The government is trying to quell the rumors that people are dying in the north, but news is getting out. People are asking questions."

"We've been complacent too long," True said forcefully.

"Let the poor dear eat some food," Mrs. Foster suggested, giving Isaac a look of sympathy.

He started to eat, and the excellent meal immediately improved his mood. Mrs. Foster had always had an excellent cook. After finishing his meal while listening to the family's light conversation, he wiped his mouth on a napkin and set it on the table.

He wanted to protect the family, but he couldn't always be there.

"Remember the glamour spell the *strannik* used to deceive everyone? The spell is normally guarded at the highest levels of the Invisible College because the temptation to use it is very real," he said. "But I am going to teach it to you."

"Where do you suppose he learned it?" Clara asked.

"I believe from the Erlking himself. They were in league. After he abducted McKenna, he used the spell to disguise her as a younger girl. Such illusions never worked on her, though. She could always see through them."

"I remember," Clara said. "The *strannik* was at the railyard, and he looked like an ordinary worker to me, but she saw who he really was."

Isaac nodded. "Exactly. When she escaped, she had to cross a river and got dunked in the waters. After we talked about her ordeal, I realized that being submerged in moving water multiple times can remove a glamour without magic. McKenna, serendipitously, managed to remove the spell from herself, otherwise we wouldn't have recognized her."

He remembered how overjoyed he'd felt when she'd returned to Bishopsgate with Mr. Swope. At the time, they'd all feared the worst, but she'd come to them miraculously. If only that would happen again...

"So we need to be prepared to dunk someone in water?" Wickins asked with a smirk.

"No, you're going to be the ones who cast glamours. It can be used to disguise someone's appearance but also to alter their memories. It's the spell I've been using on you to make you forget me. But now I want you to be able to cast it on your own. For example, if a member of the Marshalcy came to the house looking for me, you could cast the spell and make him believe he'd conducted an interview and nothing was untoward. That idea would be fixed in his mind until the spell was removed."

"It would be highly illegal," Mr. Foster said. That wasn't a surprising comment, coming from a past barrister.

Mrs. Foster reached out and squeezed his hand. "The law has become corrupted."

Isaac leaned forward. "We must first defeat the Aesir. Then we can go about trying to restore reason to the people. If you are uncomfortable with the deceit, I can cast a glamour and have you all forget I was ever here."

"No!" True and Clara said simultaneously. Then they grinned at each other.

Mrs. Foster gave her husband an imploring look.

"You are right, Son." Mr. Foster looked intently at Isaac. "The damage to law and order needs to be reversed. We've let weeds enter the garden, and they've choked out all the plants. It will take time and a lot of work to restore it. But I see no other way. I may be an old man, but I will do my share."

Isaac felt his heart burning with gratitude. They were all in this together.

"Thank you," he said, his voice thickening. "It means more than you know. These are the words of the spell and the way it must be sung. And you can use them to keep this house safe. *Eshi omorfi matia.*"

"There are about three hundred of us, by my count," Jack said. They were at a small pub in the theater district of Auvinen, talking over food. The performance would be ending soon, and Isaac wanted to catch a glimpse of Annalise Kauer when she left. He'd been thinking about her all day. It was difficult seeing Eiríka with yet another face, but her personality still shone through. He had to believe that if their love had endured for so many centuries, it would persist in this new incarnation.

Isaac had hardly touched his meal, but Jack was nearly done with his.

"Three hundred," Isaac said with a weary sigh. In past lifetimes, he'd had thousands of sorcerers to direct.

"I was thinking of Salisbury next," Jack said. "It's on the outskirts of town. Two closer prisons and then a farther one. No detectible pattern in that."

"Wise move," Isaac said. "Remember, they cannot react as quickly as we can act. The rings make all the difference. The Marshalcy is cumbersome. They can't communicate with each other quickly enough to keep up."

"I know," Jack said with a broad smile. "It's been nice watching them dash about."

"They'd have to break their own laws in order to defeat us," Isaac said. "How many more rings will be produced?"

"Another twenty or so by morning. I've got two men working on it, now that we have that second mold."

"How are you getting so much gold?"

"Pawn shops," Jack said. "Even though the gold is illegal, it's still valuable."

"I'm proud of you," Isaac said, reaching out and clapping Jack on the shoulder.

"I need to get going," Jack said. "True is coming down the street. I promised we'd see each other tonight." He had a wistful smile.

"Where are you meeting?"

"She picked the hotel. Said you taught them all the glamour spell tonight at supper." He arched his eyebrows.

"I want them safe," Isaac said. "And aware."

"I'm not complaining," Jack said. "I'm surprised her father went along with it. It sounds like they all did. Good work, Professor."

He started to rise, but Isaac stopped him. "Before you go. Tell me more about Mrs. Turner."

"Paige?"

"That's the one. With all we've had to discuss, it's kept slipping my mind."

"What about her?"

"She looked very wary of me. I was half-surprised that she wasn't the one who betrayed us."

"Oh, she wouldn't," Jack said, leaning against the table. "She's solid."

"I'm glad you think so."

Jack nodded. "Paige came from the slums too. Wanted so much to read books. To study magic. Saved her cuppers like a miser to afford nighttime classes. Hired a tutor to help her make up what she lacked." Jack shook his head and made a disappointed face.

"What happened?" Isaac pressed.

"The tutor tried to take advantage of her. Thought she would give in to his demands in order to keep getting lessons. She punched him in the face and walked away. Has a sore spot when it comes to academics, you could say."

"Oh," Isaac said. He'd been in the world long enough to have come across plenty of men like that, who'd take advantage of someone else because they thought they could get away with it. "I'm sorry for her."

"She'll come around, Professor. You're not like that one." His eyes shifted toward the window. "She's outside now."

"You'd better not keep her waiting on my account," Isaac said. They clasped hands, and he watched out the window as husband and wife were reunited. Jack lifted Trudie into the air and twirled her around, a sight that made his heart clench with pain and happiness. The two held each other and then furtively walked down the street.

Loneliness. There was a time it hadn't bothered him so much. He scooted away from the table, put his coat back on, and went outside. The theater was only a few blocks away, and he could tell by the swelling crowd that the performance of *The Little Barrister* was done. He saw couples holding hands and gushing with enthusiasm about the play.

If he could just get Annalise alone for a while, maybe he could repair the broken trust.

Closure was her only day off, and the thought of waiting so many days caused a surge of dissatisfaction and restlessness in his chest.

It would be unwise to accost her again when she might still be upset with him.

But when had wisdom ever overruled the longings of the heart?

Loyal, I want you to follow her back to her hotel. Find out which room she's in. Then come and get me.

Chapter Nineteen
Interdiction

Hotel Tiburg was in a fashionable shopping district in Auvinen, about a mile from the theater. Isaac walked vigorously, his fatigue drifting away as he imagined meeting with Miss Kauer again, hopefully before she went to bed. There were pitfalls to his strategy, he realized, not the least of which might be her reaction to him arriving uninvited to a hotel he shouldn't have known about. Too much was at stake, though, and his native restlessness would have made sleep impossible.

The hotel was tall, at least seven stories judging by the windows, and very narrow. Lit lamps burned in their sconces, but he'd already cloaked himself in a web of invisibility. Loyal led the way up to the door of the hotel, which had the name engraved in ironworks above the single canopied door. Isaac gripped the handle and pushed it open, a little bell jingling upon his entrance. He grimaced at the tinkling sound and hurriedly shut the door. Then he turned, finding the entryway glowing with muted light that softly illuminated the walls and paneling made of dark-stained wood. There was a little office to the left where a board with keys was mounted behind an empty desk.

A uniformed worker poked his head from an interior room of

the office and then briskly approached the door. Isaac pressed against the wall in the corridor to avoid a collision.

The man had round glasses, a thick mustache, and a receding hairline. He pulled at the door handle and looked outside into the darkened street, which rang the bell again.

"Strange," the man muttered to himself. The street outside the Tiburg was likely still empty, the way it had been when Isaac had ducked inside.

Isaac held still and watched the fellow go back into the tiny office where he opened the ledger on the desk and examined a page while running his finger down it. Isaac ventured past the office, reaching a little area for meals, with small circular tables and low chairs. Some refreshments had been organized on a little credenza with mirrored doors and a variety of wine bottles and glass chalices suspended upside down on pegs above it. There was an elevator of sorts with an iron gate behind him, near the office, and a cramped stairwell next to that.

Lead me to her room, he silently asked Loyal, who led the way to the stairs.

Isaac took the steps two at a time and passed a few floors, each containing no more than six rooms. Although the hotel was small, it was high-end and had exquisite furnishings. The carpeting on the steps muffled the sound of his shoes.

At the top floor, Loyal stopped, and Isaac felt a subacoustic whine from the doglike intelligence, warning him of a presence.

The corridor was shrouded in shadow. Isaac paused at the top of the steps, still holding the handrail. He listened for any sounds, but there were none. He wondered which of the six doors he could discern belonged to Miss Kauer. He didn't see anyone, but that didn't ease his suspicion that someone was hiding in the shadows.

He stepped forward cautiously, trying not to alert anyone to his presence with a creaky floorboard. As he exited the stairwell, a quicksilver lamp awakened at the end of the hall, revealing the man who had accosted him at the theater.

The fellow was standing by the last door in the hallway, holding the portable lamp in his hand.

"My lord thought you might come tonight, Isaac," the man said with a cunning smile. *"Kalispel!"*

An invisible blunt force slammed into Isaac's shield, which absorbed the impact and kept him upright, otherwise he would have flown backward and struck the stairwell wall.

"Apokaluptis!" sang the man, though it sounded more like a snarl, invoking an Aesir spell that revealed hidden things.

Isaac's heart, already racing, began to gallop. The man was a Semblance! Isaac was fairly certain he hadn't been one before.

Turning, Isaac fled down the twisting stairwell and immediately heard the fellow chase after him. He surrendered any attempt to mask his footfalls and used his long strides to carry him down quickly.

A warning snarl warned him of another assailant just before the man stepped out of the shadows and tackled Isaac into the railing. A fist smashed against his cheek, sending a dizzying whorl of sparks across his vision.

This had obviously been planned. A cramped stairwell was the perfect place to set up an ambush.

The man pulled his fist back to punch again, and Isaac waited for it, then jerked his head aside at the last moment so the man punched the wall instead.

The fellow bellowed loudly, and Isaac popped his fist out and struck him in the chin with an uppercut that sent the man's eyes rolling back in his head.

The pursuer from above reached them just then, tackling Isaac. The two began to tumble down the stairs, arms and legs pinwheeling and flailing. He felt an elbow in his ribs and then the man was on top of him at the landing of the next floor.

He starting punching Isaac's face over and over.

"Ex calibris duo!" Isaac sang, summoning a shield spell, which rebuffed further blows.

"Up here!" the man shouted. "I've got him! Get up here!"

There were more men down below. Isaac maintained the shield spell and rose to his feet. He was sweating and aching, but the seriousness of the situation helped steady his thoughts.

He took hold of the shield with his mind, sang an opposing note and inverted it, trapping the fellow inside of it, just as he'd done at the Great Exhibition when a Semblance had come to kill him. The man's face twisted with outrage as he tried to force his way past the confinement, but Isaac gave him a knowing look and then bounded back up the stairs.

There were sounds of confusion from down below, but Isaac clearly heard the bodyguard shout, "He went back upstairs! Get him! Don't let him escape!"

Isaac reached the top steps again and hurried down the corridor. A single curtained window waited at the end. One of the two opposing doors was likely Miss Kauer's, but it wasn't the time for a nocturnal visit. He needed to escape. He grasped the latch of the window and tugged it. Looking out, he saw it went down to an alleyway behind the hotel, boxed in by other buildings. He clambered up on the window and then jumped into the darkness.

Gravity pulled him down sharply, but he sang the command *"Apellethróno,"* which slowed his descent until he landed on the sturdy floor of the alley as if he'd stepped off a sidewalk. He walked to a locked gate, commanded it to be unlocked, and then pulled open the bars and sidled through. Moments later, he was back on the street, walking briskly, wincing at the soreness in his back and arm. His lip felt puffy.

The violent encounter brought back memories of one of his earlier existences as Isaac Berrow, when he was in charge of the imperial mint and accompanied officers to apprehend coin clippers. He wiped some moisture from his nose and saw the dab of blood on his knuckles. This settled it: He had a definite preference for casting spells over swinging fists. Physical combat was something Eiríka excelled at.

He grunted in pain, both from the injuries he'd been dealt

and from the memories of her. Soon Loyal had caught up to him and was trotting invisibly at his side with a worried whine.

"I'll be all right," Isaac whispered, more to himself than to the intelligence. Physically, it was true. The device in his pocket with the philosopher's stone would heal the injured parts of his body by morning.

He grimaced when he thought of the bulb that had revealed his invisibility.

They'd used his own invention against him. And they'd switched her to a hotel with fewer guests. With Annalise's body-guard having become a Semblance—and worse, a Semblance who was very much aware of him—it would be much more difficult to contact her.

The theater would also be more closely guarded. No doubt Mr. Froman—the Erlking—had his henchmen on high alert. Even though magic was technically illegal, the Erlking and his servants would still use it. They'd be able to find him. Track him.

All the Erlking needed to do was to keep him and Eiríka apart until the Aesir destroyed the mortal world. He gritted his teeth. He could not allow that to happen.

Annalise had given him another way to contact her—by sending a message to her maid, Maud. But was Maud a Semblance too? If she was and he sent Annalise a message, he might be walking into another trap...

But it was worth the risk. It was the only obvious way forward.

He looked backward, surprised no one was pursuing him.

After passing several streets, he realized he was walking aimlessly. He had considered going back to the Fosters' home on Brake Street, but he couldn't risk asking Annalise to meet him there. It was too dangerous for the family. And yet...it could help his cause if they met somewhere that might trigger memories of McKenna's life...

The thought struck him. They'd first met at the basement

apartment at Sarah Fuller Fiske's house. That's where he'd taught his student and begun to fall in love with her.

Sarah had fallen in with the *strannik*. She'd left with him. In the end, she'd believed that Robinson was an imposter, a deceiver. He wished he could rectify that. But there was no changing the past.

Perhaps her house was gone, overtaken by someone else, but there was a good chance it might be empty—and it was unlikely the Erlking would think to look for him there.

Feeling good about the idea, he changed course and continued to walk in that direction, using side streets. The cold of the night made him shiver, or maybe it was the soreness caused by bruises. The walk took two hours, but he arrived and found Sarah's home still intact.

The street was dark, the only sound the rustling of leaves.

Loyal, go see if anyone is living in the basement apartments.

He was grateful for his companion's quick response as it wandered down the steps and into the rooms.

He looked up the steps leading to the front door, feeling a stirring of memory himself.

A longing as deep as the sea filled his senses. He and Eiríka had found each other nearly a thousand times, but he could only remember glimpses of the past and nothing of his life before becoming Isaac Berrow. When a Semblance was near to dying, older memories began to return, and he'd had a few close shaves with death that had brought about flashes of memory. Would he ever get all the memories back?

Loyal's ephemeral form padded back up the steps, and he felt a joyful, quiet bark. There was no one presently in the apartments.

Isaac stepped down and used a spell to unlock the door.

He'd send a message to Maud and ask her to bring Annalise to the address.

Perhaps she was a Semblance and would attack him.

Perhaps she would do as he asked.

One thing he knew for certain: It was time to tell Annalise who she really was.

Annalise Kauer

CHAPTER TWENTY
MEMORIES AWAKENED

The electric streetcar lurched to a halt, forcing Annalise to grip the railing harder to keep from bumping into Maud. The conveyances were ugly and had splotches of rust, but they were the most efficient way to get from one part of the city to another. She liked to imagine a time when magical metal horses had traveled the streets.

"Brookside and Shelbourne!" shouted the conductor in a bored tone. "Brookside and Shelbourne! Next stop, Camden."

Maud hurried down the steps first and Annalise followed. Others had gathered around the streetcar to jump on board before it continued down the tracks. Annalise caught the fragrance of sugared peanuts in the air, which tickled at her memory. She'd preferred licorice candy from the time she was a child, but she'd lost the taste for it after her career had taken off. There was something deliciously familiar about the caramelized smell of the peanuts.

"This way," Maud said, guiding them down the sidewalk. When the message from Mr. Berrow had come that morning, Annalise had asked Maud to investigate the location first to make sure it wasn't in a dangerous part of town, and then—if all seemed well—convey the message that Annalise would pay a visit after lunch.

Maud had gone, spoken to him, and returned.

Ordinarily, Annalise wouldn't have responded to such a request at all. But there was nothing ordinary about Mr. Isaac Berrow. He'd made himself totally and completely vulnerable to her. She knew he was a sorcerer, and by revealing where he would be and when, he had put himself at a disadvantage. She could have sent the Marshalcy to arrest him. But his plea had piqued her interest. Maybe it was the lack of pretense in his manners she found so intriguing. His disregard for the decorum of polite society. She also felt keenly interested in him as a person, and she *did* think him rather handsome, albeit not in the popular way.

"It's a lovely neighborhood," Annalise said as they walked down the sidewalk toward the address.

"I agree. In this part of town, the homes are quite expensive. Not as expensive as Bishopsgate, of course."

Annalise's home there was also in a fashionable district. But she preferred Caddam House, her country estate in the Lake Country. It had been months since she'd last been there.

"If the trains weren't always breaking down, I'd go home more frequently," Annalise said. "Which is the house?"

"That one, with the stairs leading up to the doors. He's in the apartment at the bottom. It seemed very warm for a basement apartment."

"And he was alone?"

"As far as I could tell."

Annalise imagined one of Mr. Carrault's men was likely trailing them, although she didn't see anyone who stood out to her. But she hadn't told Mr. Carrault what she was up to. She occasionally went for walks or went shopping without telling him and just trusted that he'd have someone following her discreetly.

As they reached the steps leading down to the door, she felt an inexplicable jolt of déjà vu. She paused, blinking quickly, trying to recall if she'd ever been there before. That was impossible. Yet the basement apartment felt undeniably familiar.

"Are you all right?" Maud asked, giving her a concerned look.

"I swear I've been here before," Annalise said.

"When?" Maud asked, her brow wrinkling in confusion.

"I don't know. It feels like it was a long time ago."

They walked down together, and Maud rapped on the door.

Mr. Berrow answered it immediately. Annalise started in surprise, seeing a red scab on his lip and a fading bruise on his cheek. Maud had neglected to mention he looked like he'd been in a fight.

"Thank you for coming, Miss Kauer," he said, bowing his head formally. "Please come in. Good afternoon, Miss Jenkins." He made another slight dip of the head to her.

"What happened to you, Mr. Berrow?" Annalise asked, feeling uneasy about stepping into the apartment.

He gave her a sheepish smile. "You can ask Mr. Carrault later."

"*He* did this to you?" Annalise demanded, feeling a surge of heat in her chest. Despite what Maud had said, a cool breeze came from inside the apartment, which was lit by a magical incandescence.

"There were several of them actually. I don't think they wanted me to see you. Please come in. I know you have a performance tonight, and I appreciate you taking the time to speak with me now."

Annalise seethed with fury. It was an affront to her that Mr. Berrow had been roughed up merely because he'd wanted to see her.

She accepted the invitation and stepped inside the pleasantly cool room. It was full of rubbish for the most part—old furniture, storage boxes, and a rack with old shirts hanging from it. She did smell the fragrance of roasted, sugared peanuts, though. And another smell—a perfume that was hauntingly familiar. Though it was a drab little apartment, it caught her attention nonetheless.

"I fear I'm the one who owes you an apology," Annalise said to him after her quick appraisal of the domicile. "I had no idea you were assaulted."

He remained by the door and sang an incantation. The words were gibberish, but the sound of them was familiar.

"Mr. Berrow," she said warningly, feeling distrustful, yet confident he meant her no harm.

"A bodyguard was following you," he said. "I just didn't wish for us to be interrupted. You are free to leave anytime you wish. If you touch the handle, the door will open."

Maud rubbed her arms as if she were chilly. She looked around in confusion.

"This way," he said, gesturing to an open door. The room beyond it had some benches arranged inside. There were posters on the wall with symbols drawn on them.

Annalise looked at the door, hesitating about whether she should just leave right then. The feelings of familiarity had departed. This was a stranger's house, a stranger's room. But permitting herself to trust this sorcerer a little further, she followed him into the room with Maud at her side.

When she entered, she halted, her eyes widening with shock and surprise. Everything about the room was remarkably recognizable to her. It was a little classroom of sorts, but it hadn't been used to teach arithmetic or grammar but speech. How did she know that? How did she know what those symbols written in chalk on one of the blackboards meant?

She wandered about the classroom, overpowered by feelings that began to tremble inside her. Memories flashed through her mind. There was a brown-haired girl sitting in a seat, trying to speak a complicated sentence. A kind teacher giving encouragement. A teacher that looked exactly like Mr. Berrow.

Annalise turned her head to look at him—and found him studying her face intently.

"What is this place?" she asked.

"We used to have lessons here together," he told her.

A surge of strange conviction filled her chest—what he had just spoken was impossible, but it was true.

"I've never been here before," Annalise said, shaking her head. Maud looked disconcerted.

"This is where we met the first time," he said softly. "Well, not the first time. We have met before, Miss Kauer. In other lives."

"I think we should go," Maud said firmly.

"Do you believe in metempsychosis, Mr. Berrow?" Annalise asked. "Is that...common among sorcerers?"

"The transmigration of souls?"

"That is what it means, but there's no evidence to support its existence."

"You've been in this very room, Miss Kauer. These posters are of the Hawksley method, which I taught you in the past."

"I've never even heard of the Hawksley method."

"Do you know the Poundstone canticle?"

Annalise wrinkled her brow in confusion.

He looked at her boldly. "The seething sea ceaseth and thus the seething sea...?"

And instantly she knew the rest and finished it. "Sufficeth us."

How did she know that?

"Are you putting her under a spell?" Maud asked worriedly. "Miss Kauer, we should go at once. This is illegal!"

"I'm not putting her under a spell, Miss Jenkins." His eyes were fixed on Annalise's. "I'm trying to awaken her from one."

Another surge of emotion flooded her. His words rang true, although they made no practical sense.

"So you do believe we've met before in another life."

"You were my student. Your parents sent you to me to study the method so it could improve your defective utterances."

Those words sounded familiar to her. She didn't know why. "Did I have a speech impediment, Mr. Berrow?" she asked lightly, but there was nothing light about the weight of his gaze.

"You were deaf," he said bluntly.

Sometimes, in her dreams, she was a deaf girl. He couldn't possibly know that...

Annalise began to tremble. She had heard some men would say anything to woo a woman. But this declaration was so outlandishly surreal that no one in their right mind would swallow such a fabrication. Yet her own heart told her that what he said was true, and her secret memories confirmed it.

"Your name was McKenna Aurora Foster," he said pointedly.

Another tremor of recognition.

"And you were someone else before that, and someone else before that. And a very long time ago, you were Lydia Brewer, and you taught me about Semblances." His eyes began to tear up. "You taught me everything I know about Aesir magic."

"So I'm a sorcerer too?" she asked, giddiness welling up inside her. It had been a secret dream of hers to learn sorcery. Were her feelings more preternatural than she'd realized?

"You are the best of us," he said. "But you are a Semblance. It is a spell of the Aesir that attaches your immortal soul, your intelligence, to a mortal body. The transfer happens at death. It is a magic the Aesir never taught us. Not even you knew it. That is why I asked about your past. You've died before, Annalise. That moment was the beginning of your new life. When things changed for you."

Annalise glanced at Maud and saw a look of consternation on her face. It was clear *she* didn't believe any of it.

But Annalise felt invisible fingers around her neck. Mr. Froman had begun to choke her. Dizziness made her sway and Mr. Berrow caught her arm.

"I'm calling the Marshalcy," Maud said angrily. "We should never have come here! It's a trick!"

"Quite the opposite, Miss Jenkins. It's the truth. When you came earlier, I was testing to see if *you* were a Semblance as well. Do you remember how warm it was?"

"It was much nicer than this!" Maud said, perplexed.

"Semblances abhor the heat. That is because the Aesir can

only exist in the cold. I used an incalescent heater to warm the room up. I needed to see if you'd react as a Semblance would, Maud. You are not a Semblance. But Mr. Carrault is. He tried to harm me last night, and he will try again. Mr. Froman is also a Semblance. He is an Aesir inhabiting a mortal body."

"Are you one?" Annalise asked him, but she already knew the answer.

"I am," he said. "I'm not an Aesir, but I was born thousands of years ago. And through an agreement with the Erlking, I have been permitted to inhabit other bodies. Heat doesn't bother me the same way because I'm not an Aesir. But it bothers you, Annalise. The stage lights. You can only endure them for so long."

She was always exhausted after a play, but years and years of performing had inured her to the discomfort. Still, she favored winter above the other seasons and always swam in the early morning to avoid the heat of midday. On hot afternoons, she preferred to be indoors.

The sound of a doorknob jiggling jerked her attention back to the other room.

Mr. Berrow sighed. "We didn't have as long as I'd hoped." He reached out and took her hand. The touch went right up her arm and made her tremble. "Come back tomorrow, and I will teach you more. You need to remember who you are, Annalise. Who you *truly* are."

"Tomorrow, then, Mr. Berrow," she said, gazing into his warm eyes.

A fist began to pound on the door.

"Maybe we meet at Aesir Park at one instead," he suggested worriedly.

Chapter Twenty-One
Love's Confession

"It's the Marshalcy, thank the Mind!" Maud muttered with a tone of relief.

Annalise gave her a scolding look, but Mr. Berrow smiled smugly and shook his head. "It's one of Miss Kauer's bodyguards, I believe."

"Mr. Carrault?" Annalise asked with concern.

The pounding on the door resumed after a brief pause.

Mr. Berrow regarded her intently. "I wish I could have seen the rest of *The Little Barrister*. I wasn't able to enjoy the entire performance."

"You shall see it tonight, then. I'll leave a ticket for you at the box office under the name of Richard Mathias."

His brow wrinkled. "I thought it was sold out?"

"I'll see to it. Richard Mathias. You'll remember the name?"

He nodded. "And I'll come disguised in a spell so they won't recognize me. But you will. What are you going to tell your bodyguard outside?"

"I'm an actress, Mr. Berrow. It won't be a problem."

She dipped her head to him and then walked to the door.

Mr. Berrow had said it would unlock upon her touching it, and she wanted to test the point. Maud came up swiftly next to her, looking back at Mr. Berrow, who stood in the doorway of the schoolroom watching them. He backed out of sight when she reached for the doorknob.

A quiver of magic tingled in her hand as she gripped the knob and turned. At the door was Mr. Busseby, one of regular Trilbys Kellin assigned to her.

"Miss Kauer!" he exclaimed, furtively trying to look around her to examine the interior of the space.

Annalise walked directly toward him, which caused him to backstep quickly. As soon as Maud was out too, she shut the door behind her.

"What are you doing here, Mr. Busseby?" Annalise demanded.

"I was worried when I saw you enter this basement."

"I'm considering buying this property," Annalise said. "I like the neighborhood. What business is that of yours, pray tell?"

He opened his mouth but closed it again without a word.

"Mr. Busseby, should I have required any assistance, I would have asked for it." She fluttered her hand at him. "I expect Mr. Carrault's employees to be more discreet. If anyone learned I was interested in such an acquisition, they'd raise the price or I'd be flooded with propositions about properties I don't care to see! I can manage my own affairs, thank you. Now, be gone!"

"Apologies, Miss Kauer. Truly."

"Be gone," she said curtly.

Mr. Busseby looked around quickly before hastening back up the steps and walking away. Annalise glanced at Maud, who was barely concealing a smile.

"And you will say nothing of this to anyone, Maud Jenkins," Annalise said as they also departed.

"I'm impressed with how you handled Mr. Busseby, but I'm not comfortable with this cloak-and-dagger plan. They have some openings at Mickelgate Prison now, and I don't want to stay there."

"You didn't believe anything Mr. Berrow said, did you?"

"About him being a centuries-old sorcerer? And you a—whatever it was—a...Semblance? It's a bit far-fetched. But this I can tell. He's in love with you."

Another jolt shook Annalise, for she had the preternatural sense this was true. Her heart started fluttering madly with excitement.

"You think so?" she asked, trying to seem indifferent.

"That was strangest story I ever heard," Maud said, shaking her head. "I don't think we should linger around here."

"We're meeting elsewhere tomorrow," Annalise said.

Maud just sighed.

Annalise had lost count of how many times she'd performed this particular role in this particular play. Hundreds? She'd rehearsed it countless times. But there was something different about her performance this night. Something had altered within her. A chink in the curtains of her consciousness, perhaps? There was something beyond that curtain—and the possibilities dazzled her thoughts. Mr. Berrow had told her she was more than just an actress performing a part. Her entire life was a part—a person she'd been playing but not her true self.

As she performed her role alongside Mr. Beal, she was almost painfully aware of Isaac sitting in the seat she'd arranged for him. Richard Mathias was the name of her mother's brother, and it was a code word of sorts for her family. A message from Richard Mathias was from her parents, a way to disguise their communications and preserve her privacy. Annalise never did interviews with the press and had to regularly scold those reporters who tried to meet her through trickery.

She was eager for her next meeting with Mr. Berrow. There were questions she needed answered. She was also consumed with the need to learn magic from him. To *re*learn it, possibly. And as she pretended to fall in love with her stage partner, she imagined she was giving those marks of affection to the sorcerer instead.

Then came the moment at the end of the performance when she and the actor shared a kiss on stage. She'd never let her heart get involved in her performances. It was entirely unromantic to kiss a stage partner over and over again. Every aspect of the kiss and their posturing was schemed to arouse certain feelings in the audience.

What would it feel like to kiss someone she *wanted* to kiss? A spontaneous kiss, anticipated by both parties?

On that stage, during the kiss that had many times enraptured the audience, Annalise began to feel stirrings of memories that seemed to come from another life, a time when a young husband and wife had kissed on a steam train on their way to their honeymoon.

When she pulled back from the kiss and saw the shocked look in Mr. Beal's eyes, she realized she'd spent years blunting her emotions in order to achieve the perfection that Mr. Froman desired from her. And she was tired of pretending. What she wanted was something real. And her stage partner had felt the difference.

His eyes were moist as he delivered his lines tremulously, "Why have you left me all this time? You are not glad to see me now?"

"I was glad," Annalise answered, her voice husky. "But I prayed to the Mind not to let you see me." She tried to back away. He reached for her hand, but she snatched it from his grasp. "No, I am to tell you everything now, and then—" Her voice wilted as if she'd start sobbing. She *felt* like sobbing this time for real.

"Say that you love me first," he broke in.

"No," she said, "I must tell you first what I have done, and then you will not ask me to say that. I am not a Romani."

"It was not because you were a Romani that I fell in love with you!"

"I am to be married tomorrow. To someone else."

Even though it was just a play, she suddenly felt vulnerable—as if it were real. And she knew in her bones that it would be absolutely and totally wrong to marry anyone but Mr. Berrow.

"Throughout my whole girlhood I was taught nothing but to please him, and the only way to do that...was to be pretty." She'd spoken these lines so many times, but they felt different this time. She knew she was beautiful, that she turned heads. But there was only one head she wanted to turn. And it wasn't her stage partner's.

She turned to face the audience—and looked directly at Mr. Berrow. He was leaning slightly forward in his third-row seat. His eyes had a haunted look that caused her heart to ache as the scene continued.

"I dare say he cares more for you than you think," said her partner tenderly. She uncharacteristically sighed before resuming her lines, adding to her character's air of misery.

"He's infatuated with my face," Annalise lamented, "or he would not have endured me so long. I have twice had the wedding postponed, chiefly, I believe, to enrage his sister. I am a different woman since I knew you."

At this, her gaze lingered for another moment on the rapt sorcerer before turning back to Mr. Beal in time to see him shake his head, his gaze heartbreakingly sad.

She'd spoken these lines so many times, but they felt different this time. She looked directly at Mr. Berrow again.

"In time, perhaps, I shall have suffered sufficiently for all my wickedness." She wrung her hands and looked away from him, casting her gaze down at the stage floor. She was right on her mark.

"This is the end of it all," he said with a forlorn voice. "I loved you. Romani or no."

Annalise shook her head. "You never knew me until now, and so it was not me you loved. I know what you thought I was, and I could...I could *try* to be it now."

"If you had only told me this before," Mr. Beal said, affecting sadness by adding a choke to his voice, "it might not have been too late."

"I thought you were like all the other men I knew," she replied. "It was only my face you admired."

"No, it was never that," he said with a forcefulness that she answered with a practiced expression. It was designed to show her desire for him to recant and tell her she was pretty, eliciting bubbles of laughter from the audience. But she did not speak her complaint, and her partner delivered the line that won the audience's hearts.

"You must have known that I loved you from the first night. And you have never cared for me at all."

She drooped and shook her head no. "Oh, always, always!" she answered. "Since I knew what love was. It was you who taught me. I could not tell you who I truly was because I knew you would loathe me. I could only go away."

Annalise gave him a look of sorrow. She could evoke tears as an actress when she wanted to, but they came early this time. She began to walk to the prop door on the stage and paused, her hand quivering above the knob.

"I cannot give you up," he said with firm decision.

Annalise stood in tears. She let her hand fall from the doorknob. "Don't say that you love me still," she cried. "Oh, Gavin, *do you?*"

She turned and whirled to face him. And that's when Annalise smelled the smoke. Ribbons of green flame were licking at the ceiling of the theater.

"Fire!" someone in the audience screamed.

There was a heartbeat of stillness, and then the entire audience surged to their feet and began to trample each other to escape the flames.

Issac Berrow

Chapter Twenty-Two
With Auvinen Burning

It was the color of the flames that struck Isaac's heart with terror. This was a sorcerer's fire, a pyrophoric one, and it would consume the theater in a raw hunger, much as it had the Fosters' original house on Brake Street. Chaos had broken out as everyone tried to escape at once. Isaac was buffeted several times as he strained against the crowd to get to the stage, but it was like trying to move against an avalanche. The memories it had triggered were awful, but he wasn't going to lose Annalise. He would get her out alive. He'd get both of them out.

He could already feel the heat from the green flames as they licked ferociously at the theater's interior décor. Water could not quench such a fire—it would burn until there was nothing left to consume. Not even a spell would put it out.

Through the flailing limbs of astonished guests, he saw Mr. Carrault grab Annalise by the shoulders and lead her backstage.

Loyal, follow her!

He felt the presence of his shadowy friend race off to trail Annalise. Smoke quickly filled the theater, and the screams turned into coughs.

Isaac quickly whistled a spell into being, summoning wind to help blow the smoke back toward the ceiling. If too much smoke got into people's lungs, they'd fall unconscious and no longer be able to flee. Then, with the incantation to summon light, he created strands of light to illuminate the exit doors.

"Follow the lights!" he shouted into the cacophony. He anchored the wind and light he'd summoned into place, then continued to maneuver through the crowd toward the stage.

By the time he got there, raining embers had caused the curtains to burst aflame. Pieces of debris showered down, but he summoned a shield spell to protect himself. The wind was blowing the smoke, but it was also feeding the flames, making the timbers rage with green fire.

He turned to look back at the crowd. The chokepoints of the exit doors were thronged with people trying to escape certain death. Some had fallen and been trampled. He saw a man rubbing his eyes against the smoke, looking delirious as he stumbled the wrong way.

He was in the thick of a terrible dilemma. He'd seen more than his share of suffering in his multiple lives, and his heart panged for these people. Death would claim many this night, no matter what he did. He'd already known the Erlking didn't value mortal souls, and here was the proof. It felt like this awful moment had been orchestrated to cause Isaac as much pain and anguish and confusion as possible. To try to shift his focus from his goal. But he couldn't let that happen. If anything happened to him or Annalise, then the bargain they'd struck to save humanity would be null and void. The whole human race would be butchered by the Aesir.

As much as it pained him, he had to abandon the other theatergoers. He'd done what he could in the little time allotted to him. But he had to make sure Annalise was safe and that he did not get trapped and die himself.

Rushing across the stage floor, he hurried in the direction he'd seen Mr. Carrault take Annalise. The backstage area was empty. All had fled. A haze filled the air, making his eyes burn. He held his breath and continued to press through the corridor. A strange ringing in his ears confused him as he tried to find his way to Annalise's room.

Loyal, where are you?

He found Annalise's dressing room. The door was open, costumes still hanging on the racks. He made a brief search and, confirming it was empty, began to follow the back passageways toward the exterior of the building.

Would the Erlking leave his daughter to burn to death in the building? Or was the fire just a not-so-subtle way of getting rid of Isaac and canceling future performances of the play.

He heard a loud crashing noise, and immediately a wall of smoke surrounded him. The heat was growing more oppressive and sweat streaked down his ribs. He held his breath. He fought the mindless urge to panic and deliberately recounted the directions from memory. His eyes were burning with the smoke. The roar of the inferno was behind him.

He found the exit door, kicked it open, and escaped out into the street.

Someone grabbed him by the arm and pulled him out. He almost concussed the man with a spell until he realized it was a stagehand trying to help.

"You got out just in time!" the bearded fellow said in relief. "The whole theater is about to come down!"

The man seemed genuinely concerned, so Isaac allowed himself to be guided away. A storm of sparks and cinders were flurrying down into the street. The nearby apartments would likely catch fire too.

"Did Miss Kauer make it out?" he asked the fellow, his voice hoarse.

"She did," the man replied with a nod. "I helped her out the same door you came through. She's safe."

Thank the Mind, Isaac thought in relief. He didn't sense Loyal nearby and imagined the intelligence was trotting after her. He'd go to her small hotel and verify that she'd arrived.

"Thank you," he said. "I didn't see anyone else leave out of the back. But there are a lot of poor souls trapped inside."

"You were smart to try a different exit," the other man said in agreement. "Best to get away then, right?"

"Right. Thank you!"

Isaac followed the alley around to the front of the theater. A steady flow of people were evacuating. Officers from the Marshalcy had arrived, and some were helping carry the injured outside. The entire roof of the theater was engulfed in flames, causing shadowy images to quiver and writhe over the nearby apartment walls. Cinders were raining down. Horse-drawn water brigades were just starting to arrive but would be able to do nothing.

His stomach clenched with dread as he was assailed with horrible memories of the burning of the Brake Street house. He strode purposefully away from the chaotic scene and, several streets away, found a streetcar heading toward Annalise's hotel and boarded it.

All the passengers were talking about the fire at the theater. Some said that Mr. Froman would lose a fortune from the disaster. Isaac scoffed internally at the thought, knowing the Erlking wouldn't care about such things. His aim had always been the annihilation of mortalkind. He would not have flinched if the entire city of Auvinen were burning.

When Isaac arrived at the Tiburg, he got off the conveyance and swiftly walked to the door of the hotel. He was surprised to find Maud Jenkins in the lobby, dressed for travel, with an abundance of traveling chests stacked around her. She looked at Isaac expectantly at first and then glanced past him, apparently waiting for someone.

Isaac walked over to the little beverage area and poured himself a glass of water. The cargo and Miss Jenkins's state of dress implied she was leaving the hotel with Annalise's belongings. He decided to linger and see if he could overhear information that would help him determine his next steps.

Within thirty minutes, another person arrived.

"Mr. Arbuckle!" Maud said in relief.

"Ah, Miss Jenkins. I see you have Miss Kauer's things packed. Is that all of them?"

"Yes. Every chemise. Do you have a carriage to bring us to the station?"

"I do, but Miss Kauer is already gone. She went north in Mr. Froman's private car. I'm to escort you to Miss Kauer's car and see to it that you make it back to her estate with her belongings."

"She left without me?" Maud asked in concern.

"You can imagine the commotion this night has caused, Miss Jenkins. Can you believe it? A sorcerer's fire burning down the theater? There is no end to the evil of those people."

Isaac felt a flash of rage in his heart at the unfounded accusation. The fire might have been started by a sorcerer, but not a human one. If Isaac hadn't been there to provide a modicum of protection, even more would have died.

Mr. Arbuckle turned to the hotel manager. "Can we get some help loading the cargo, please?"

Isaac slipped the ring on his thumb and felt a jolt of pain in his temple.

I was at the theater tonight, he thought to Jack. *Unharmed, but they're blaming the Invisible College.*

I heard about it. You were there?

Yes. I need to go north. Can you meet me at the Fosters' house?

I'll be right there.

Isaac walked up the darkened street. He had lingered at the hotel long enough to ask a cat's intelligence to trail Miss Jenkins and report back to him when she was on the train and underway. Cats were more difficult to persuade to help than dogs, but he got the acquiescence and went on his way. The calm of this neighborhood was in sharp contrast to the events underway in the theater district. Disquiet was his silent companion. He still hadn't received information from Loyal about where Annalise was but assumed the intelligence was following wherever Mr. Froman was taking her.

He crept closer to the house on Brake Street and inspected the wards for intruders. They had been tripped by Jack a little while before, but he'd been permitted to enter. Isaac stepped over the fence and released his invisibility as he entered through the side of the house.

The family was gathered in the parlor with a single lamp, and Mrs. Foster hurried forward to embrace him.

"You smell like smoke," she said in concern. "It must have been awful for you to witness another fire."

He nodded and then embraced the others. Mr. Foster was scowling. "Ridiculous that they're blaming the Invisible College for the mishap," he said.

Jack and True were standing close to each other, but not so close that they raised suspicion. True's parents still didn't know about their elopement.

"I need a favor," Isaac said. "I have to leave town right away."

"You can't go so soon," True said, shaking her head with a look of worry.

"I must. I had made an arrangement to meet someone tomorrow morning at the old Aesir park. I need someone with a ring who can let me know if anyone comes."

"I'll do it myself." Jack volunteered.

"I can't guarantee anyone will come," Isaac said. "But I would like to be certain either way. The agreement was to meet tomorrow at there at one." He thought it most likely that Annalise had indeed gone north, but she might try to deliver a message to him since she'd known he was at the theater. With her separated from Maud, he had no way of contacting her, so he wanted to be prepared if she sent him a message. Still...he couldn't afford to linger in Auvinen. He would try to follow her on his own.

"Are they expecting to find *you*?" Jack asked significantly.

"Possibly. You'll need to use your judgment. As much as it pains me to leave you all so soon, trust me when I say that it is of the utmost importance. If the Aesir start another bombardment, the entire city will be set aflame. I believe I am close to stopping the war."

"Can you not tell us more about how you will do it?" Mrs. Foster asked with sympathy in her eyes.

He wasn't sure how much he should divulge. It wasn't the right time to explain to them that the woman they'd known as their daughter was, in fact, someone else for most of the time they knew her. They would need to grieve that unaccounted loss. Nor did he want them to think he could marry another. Besides, there was nothing they could do to help him accomplish the final marriage between himself and Eiríka.

"I seek the Erlking's daughter," he said to them simply. "She is the key to securing the truce with the Aesir."

The looks on their faces showed their surprise.

"And you know...where she is?" Mr. Foster asked.

"I believe so," Isaac answered. He turned to Jack. "And that's why the message tomorrow is so important to me."

Chapter Twenty-Three
A Voice of Unreason

The iron wheels of the steam train groaned to a halt at the crowded station in Bishopsgate, gusts of smelly steam issuing from the engine at the front of the connected train cars. Soot stains had blackened the walls of the station, and Isaac wrinkled his nose in distaste. He missed the way things had been.

Isaac clambered off the train with the other passengers, only to find a row of Marshalcy officers awaiting them. They were interviewing each person before letting them leave the station. He felt a tingle of unease, but he was close enough to hear some of their questions, which seemed general enough.

When he reached the front of the line, the officer before him gave him a scrutinizing look. "Welcome, sir. What's the purpose of your visit to Bishopsgate?"

"Returning from a trip," Isaac answered, giving the officer a bored look.

"Where do you live, sir?"

Isaac remembered the address of the Fosters' residence in Bishopsgate. "411 Round Street," he said without hesitation.

"Thank you," the officer said, waving him past.

As Isaac left the yard, the scene before his eyes was deeply familiar. Bishopsgate had hardly changed. There were no electric streetcars, just horse-drawn carriages and wagons. A row of two-wheeled chaises were picking up passengers along the street outside the train station. The drivers sat in pilot boxes at the back of the chaises, with long whips to coax the horses. The skyline beyond silhouetted buildings crowded together, and people were walking swiftly, as if in a constant hurried state. The clothing was more drab than what he'd seen in Auvinen, mostly in shades of dark gray or black, even the dresses and hats worn by the ladies.

He checked the time on the station clock. It was nearly one in the afternoon. He was eager to talk to Jack. In the unlikely event that Annalise had arrived at the park in person, Isaac intended to rush back at once, but he felt confident she had departed. He knew she had a residence in Bishopsgate—although he had no idea where—as well as a sizable estate in the Lake Country. It was most likely she would have gone to one of those places after the burning of the theater.

He lingered at the station, but the considerable presence of Marshalcy officers loitering persuaded him to leave to get some lunch.

He was still at a little outdoor café when the meeting time arrived. He loosened the ring from his device and twisted it onto his thumb, experiencing the familiar jolt of pain. He covered the ring with his other hand to conceal it and waited with growing trepidation.

It was possible, of course, that Annalise would send no message. That Jack would have to wait for her for hours only to wait in vain...

He had no notion of what he'd do then, but he'd find her. Somehow he'd have to find her.

The previous night, while she was performing in the play, she'd looked straight at him. There'd been a moment when he'd thought she was communicating directly with him. Telling him...

He wasn't sure what, but there had been tenderness in her gaze.

He rubbed his forehead and declined a refill of his drink when a waiter stopped by.

Professor, are you there?

He instantly responded to Jack's thought. *Did she send someone?*

A boy just arrived with a telegram.

Excitement seethed inside Isaac's chest. *What did it say?*

Caddam House. 863 Tannersville Road. Yverdon. It is signed by Maud Jenkins. Is this what you were expecting?

Isaac's excitement increased. Annalise had told him that correspondence through her maid was the way to reach her. The message had been arranged by her.

It's just what I needed. Thank you, Jack.

My pleasure. So you are really seeking the Erlking's daughter?

I am.

I wish you luck, my friend. If there is anything I can do to help you, tell me.

Isaac rose from the table, leaving some coins to pay for the food he'd eaten, and began to briskly walk back to the train station.

You've already done so much.

He experienced a distinctive throb of pain in his skull. It wasn't his own.

I've been shot.

Isaac stopped, his eyes opening wide. His heart stuttered as he was suddenly filled with a feeling of dread. *Where are you now?*

Sidewalk. Right outside of the park. A man just passed me. Pistol.

His friend's thoughts were becoming sluggish.

Jack!

No response came.

Isaac hastened his pace. He sent another message. *Nathan, this is Robinson. Jack has been shot. He's lying on the street. This is the address. Get there at once!*

Isaac's heart was pounding double-time. *Jack—can you hear me?*

He fumed silently that he'd sent Jack into a trap. Someone had tailed the messenger. Someone had been watching the apartment.

Jack?

True would need to know he'd been injured, but if Jack was dead, he didn't want her to be the first to find him...

If Isaac were in the city, he could use his device and the philosopher's stone to help stanch the bleeding, but he'd left. He'd left him alone and vulnerable. He gritted his teeth, staring at the train station just up ahead.

Jack, I'm going to send someone to help you.

But he felt helpless.

Another voice infiltrated his mind.

All is well, Professor Berrow. It felt like Jack's thought, but it wasn't. It was cold, calculating. *Now we know where you are.*

Jack had become a Semblance.

Isaac's eyes focused on his reflection in the window, depicting a calm that belied his inner turmoil. As he rested his elbow on the windowsill of the train, he directed his gaze absently at the majestic vista unfolding as the machine lumbered up a mountain pass. He would arrive in Tanhauser before midnight after going through a series of tunnels blasted into the mountainside.

He had warned the Fosters about what had happened to Jack, who had become an omnipresent voice inside his head because of the sorcerer's ring. A voice in his mind that whispered intermittent and insidious thoughts of doubt and despair since taking over Jack's body. Isaac knew that True was in anguish. She'd finally told her parents about the secret marriage once her husband—or his Semblance—knew of her. Was the Semblance tormenting her as well as him?

After Isaac had consulted with the Fosters, Wickins and Clara, and True, the family had decided to leave Auvinen for another city without revealing to him where. Concealment was their best hope. The weight of Isaac's burdens was stifling. He had sent Jack to his doom and regretted it deeply, but the Erlking would not passively await his fate. Time was of the essence.

The ochre-colored sky above the fading sun made for a beautiful scene. This particular length of tracks, bridging the distance between Tanhauser and Bishopsgate, had not been in existence during his life as Robinson Hawksley. When he and McKenna had gone to Tanhauser for their honeymoon, they'd taken the longer but flatter route past Krier. There they had seen Shopenhauer's opera—and encountered the dangerous enemies sent to abduct McKenna in the *strannik*'s name.

This time the enemy preventing their reunion was the Erlking himself. If Annalise and Isaac married, the Erlking and all the Aesir would be forced to abandon their claim on the world and find another. For the first time, he wondered where they would go. Their previous planet had been destroyed. What kind of danger would they pose to the new one? Would he be responsible for the fallout?

He opened his fingers and lowered his head into his hand. He had no way of knowing what would happen to anyone—himself, Annalise, the Fosters, or Jack. No one had ever reversed a Semblance before...

Death was the inevitable outcome, and the torment of having caused Jack's death after saving him as a child added to his guilty burden.

He lifted his head and squeezed his hand into a fist. If there *was* a way to bring Jack back, he would discover it. He knew how to capture a Semblance in a shield. He'd tried, in previous lives, to extract their intelligences, but it had always ended in the death of the host.

If only he had more time to experiment and plan!

You cannot win, Professor Berrow. Do you really believe the

Erlking can be defeated? That your cunning exceeds his wisdom? Arrogance and pride are the deformities of the mortal born. You are not immune to them, are you?

Isaac breathed in through his nose and exhaled slowly. He'd removed the ring from his thumb so as not to inadvertently reply back rashly. The smooth, condescending tone of the being's thoughts were designed to trouble him. To harass him.

Heed me, Professor. Turn yourself in to the Marshalcy. Winter will come, and only the best mortals will be chosen to serve us. You can still choose to live. Forsake her, and you will be forgiven. A new world will be given to you. A world that will intrigue your mind. Where secrets are taught in majestic abbeys and written in golden tomes. There is much you can still learn.

Isaac chuckled softly, shaking his head. They still thought they might tempt him to abandon her? A thousand lifetimes he'd loved her. He'd love her forever.

From his vantage at the window seat in the train car, he could see snow on the mountain peaks. Soon there would be more. Blizzards would make the mountain passes impassable.

When he reached Tanhauser, he would hire a carriage and driver to take him to Yverdon. A boat would be faster, since the two cities were on opposite sides of a vast lake, but surely every boat would be watched. So would her estate. But he *would* find her. If he traveled all night, he could be there by dawn.

The train's upward climb became more sluggish as it tried to crest the pass in the mountains. A shrill whistle and burst of steam issued from the front engine.

They'd reached the top.

Isaac gazed out the window again, trying to coil his anxiety and sadness into a tight, quivering mass. The voice in his head had fallen silent again, at least.

He ducked his hand into his pocket and removed the device. After opening the lid, he gazed down at the Aesir runes at the top. Three nines.

It reminded him of his purpose. It reminded him of his resolve. He would let nothing come between him and Annalise.

But he also knew the Erlking would exercise all his cleverness and cunning to try to stop him.

CHAPTER TWENTY-FOUR
CADDAM HOUSE

Isaac's feet were sore from walking on uneven ground through the raw countryside. A bird intelligence guided him through the lush and thinly wooded grounds surrounding Caddam House. A private security sentry had been posted at the entrance of the carriage way leading to the house, but Isaac had disembarked from a conveyance he'd hired before reaching the entrance, having been alerted by his invisible allies beforehand. He'd traversed the rest of the way on foot. It was on the verge of dawn, and the birds had been plentiful and colorful—yellow-breasted goldfinches, black-capped chickadees, and sky-headed bluebirds, just to name a few. He'd even spied an eagle's nest on the way through the country, just off the road.

He'd sent a mental summons to Loyal, hoping to find his friendly companion already at the estate. But the summons had gone unanswered, which meant either Annalise wasn't at the estate yet herself or that Loyal had departed to find him, and they'd taken separate paths along the way. When McKenna had been abducted by the *strannik*, Loyal had gone missing for weeks.

The sun rises on your failure, Professor. Another town has been destroyed by the Aesir. Our coming is inexorable.

Isaac climbed a little knoll, hoping to get a view of the estate.

He'd walked for several miles at least, following the bird intelligence's guidance. The insidious voice in his head mentioned sunrise, which had not happened yet. But he was in a valley in a mountainous region, so Auvinen would see the sunrise earlier than he would. Hopefully that meant the Semblance believed he had not left town.

When he reached the sparsely wooded top of the knoll, he saw the shimmering waters of the lake first and then, to his delight, the estate half-hidden at the edge of a clearing. It was not a fanciful house—it was plenty spacious but had a rustic quality. From his vantage point, he saw a rock-and-mortar chimney in the middle of a gambrel roof structure with other segments fixed to it. A triangular roofed area jutted out to the left of the chimney and a longer, slanted roof to the right. There was a patio deck supported on stilts because the grassy ground sloped sharply away from the house at its rear. Rock walls helped grade the land down to the lakeshore. The trees were majestic and some still gorged with leaves in a splendid variety of autumnal colors with patches of fallen yellow ones littering the ground.

There were an abundance of windows on every level, which must have provided a breathtaking view of the surrounding countryside. At the shore of the lake was a dock with posts and a single rowboat tethered there.

Caddam House was a costly, secluded property. Only the very wealthy could afford to live in the area. Both the mildness of the climate and the beauty of the scene entranced him. It reminded him slightly of Mowbray House in Siaconset, only this estate was much larger.

The eastern sky was brightening, suggesting sunrise was imminent. He sang the invisibility spell and then began to walk down the slope of the knoll and onto the spacious lawn on that side of the house. He observed the little road coming along the way.

Are there any people about? he asked the intelligence that had been guiding him. He sensed the creature flit away to investigate.

His shoes squished in the damp lawn. Not having slept well

since the fire at the theater, he felt the full weight of his exhaustion. Rest could wait. He feared he'd come all this way only to be wrong. There was a good chance Annalise wasn't even there. No telltale plumes of smoke came from either chimney—for he spied another smokestack on the farther end of the house. Most of the trees on his side had been de-limbed except near the top, which would provide a more unobstructed view from the house.

The bird intelligence returned excitedly, so he followed it back to the lakeshore.

Isaac's heart began to pound with excitement, and he immediately changed course, following the slope down. He jumped the short distance off the first retaining wall and then quickly strode down to another one and hopped off that one too. The retaining walls stretched along the shoreline, nested next to and in between some of the tall maple trees.

He spied a little shack near the water's edge and had to shield his eyes when the sunlight began to glare off the water.

Isaac strode to the edge of the shack and collided with Annalise, who was dripping wet and clutching a thin blanket to her shoulders.

Her hair was drenched, and she wore swimwear that was undoubtedly popular but dissimilar from the fashions of twenty-three years earlier.

She'd rebounded off his invisible form and stood looking confused, as water dripped down her arms and legs.

"Show yourself!" she demanded.

He felt chagrined for having been found out, although he hadn't set out to deceive her. He released the invisibility spell and appeared at the edge of the shack in front of her.

"I got your message and came at once," he said, embarrassed to have greeted her in such a way. She immediately covered herself with the blanket.

"Your arrival was unexpected, Isaac."

She'd called him by his first name. It made his heart jolt with delight. "I had to see you."

"I like to swim in the mornings," she said. "I normally don't entertain guests in such a state. You'll have to excuse me while I dress."

"I wasn't sure anyone was home," he said, feeling his cheeks heat.

"You could have knocked, I suppose," she answered, but she then started to laugh. "This is quite a scene."

"I could wait—"

He started to speak, but her own words interrupted him. "Maybe you could wait—"

They both chuckled. She bit her lower lip. "Maybe you could wait here in the shed? I'll come back when I'm ready. And then we can contrive a way for you to arrive more...properly?"

"I apologize most profusely—"

She held up her hand. "There's no need to apologize. I invited you. I just didn't think you'd arrive so soon." Clutching the blanket with one hand, she gestured to the shack's door with the other.

Isaac found it open. Inside there was a little changing area, a set of oars leaning against the wall, and a bench. The windows were lined with curtains.

"I'll wait for you here," he said.

"I won't be long," she replied, and it felt like a promise with the inviting look on her face.

Isaac started awake when he felt her fingers brush the hair at his brow. He'd fallen asleep on the bench, arms folded, his legs stretched out.

"You look exhausted," Annalise said in sympathy, just the hint of a smile on her mouth.

He was struck by her presence, which reminded him forcefully of McKenna. She'd liked stroking his hair too. Annalise wore a white muslin dress hanging loosely from her shoulders, exposing her throat and a jeweled necklace with a diadem on the front. Her hair, still damp, was coiled back rather untidily, indicating she'd hastily dressed herself in order to return and see him.

Isaac felt a surge of homesickness—that blend of loss and longing that he'd become all too familiar with over the years. Even the expression on her mouth reminded him of McKenna. He rose to his feet. She looked as if she might touch him again but withdrew her hand.

"I haven't slept since the fire at the theater," he said. "I'm glad you're safe."

"I was worried about you," she said. "I saw you in the audience of course. I arranged for the telegram so you'd know where I was. Mr. Froman thought it best for me to come here and recuperate."

"Is he here?" Isaac asked worriedly.

She shook her head. "He's in Tanhauser. I'm expecting a visit from him by Closure in two days. Would you like to come to the house?"

"I would," he said.

"My cook, Jynnifer, is preparing breakfast," she said. "I normally don't have visitors, so she was surprised to hear someone was coming."

"What did you tell her?"

"I don't have to tell her anything," she said with a confident look. "It's my house."

He offered his elbow to her, as he would have in the past. She wrinkled her brow as if slightly confused but took his arm, and they walked toward the house together.

"Why did you look at me that way?" he asked, peering at her.

"It reminded me of something," she said offhandedly.

"Would you tell me what?"

"When we spoke last, Isaac, you told me about Semblances. About where my strange memories come from, and why heat bothers me but cold does not. I'm never cold after swimming in the lake. I crave it. I have two chimneys but rarely build fires in them. But I asked Jynnifer to start one so you'd be comfortable."

"Do you believe all that I told you?" he asked, his heart wanting to burst.

"I do," she answered, gazing up at him. "And I want you to tell me more. In my past life, one of them, you said I was deaf." She looked at his face for confirmation, but he could tell she already knew it was true.

"You were," he said.

"And my name was McKenna Aurora Foster."

"Yes."

She paused, looking down at the little earthen path as they walked up to the house. "Your name was Robinson."

His throat grew thick. "Yes. Robinson Dickemore Hawksley."

"I know that name. The famous inventor who betrayed us to the Aesir. But that was always a lie, wasn't it," she said, as if to herself, her gaze still fixed on the path. "When I saw you asleep, you looked so familiar. Like I'd seen you dozing before." She glanced at him, almost shyly. "Were we...?"

"We've known each other before, Annalise. You are just beginning to remember it. You were my wife."

"That explains certain...memories," she said, smiling involuntarily. "I went to Covesea once, on holiday. And I had to leave because the feeling of déjà vu was so powerful. Like I was a bride." She gave him a significant look.

"You were," he said, feeling his own memories stir.

They crossed the lawn to the back door. Smoke had begun to puff lazily from the flue. Annalise released his arm and pulled the door handle, leading him into a spacious open living area with plush seating, fine-built furniture, and tasteful decoration. The thing that caught his eye immediately, though, was the splendid harp in the corner of the room. There wasn't a servant about.

"Do you play the harp?" he asked her in surprise, and she nodded brightly.

"I've played since I became an actress and Mr. Froman paid for the permit," she said. "It's my favorite instrument."

"Play for me," he asked, his heart churning with emotion. "I would love to hear you play."

Annalise gave him a dimpled smile and walked around the harp to the padded stool that sat beside it. Her arms were long and lithe, and she positioned her hands just as a true musician would. Everything about her fascinated him, made him hope that the terrible waiting was over. She knew. She had to know!

Isaac felt tears sting his eyes when the first chords she chose were the beginning of the aria of the Erlking's Daughter.

And as she played, it was as if she cast a spell on him.

No communications from Iskandir, Daylen, or Halt after the first snowstorm. Barometric readings show a strong cold front has struck the northern portions of the empire. Imperial city of Andover preparing for blizzarding conditions. Advise the royal family be relocated farther south. Early reports indicate this may be the coldest winter on record. Winterthur has already accumulated thirty inches of snow in the mountain passes. Advise evacuating the Lake Country, as weather in that region is unpredictable.

—Signals Intelligences, Gresham College, Bishopsgate

Annalise Kauer

Chapter Twenty-Five
The Power of Music

Annalise was impressed with the set decorations in the renovated Volksoper theater. Work crews had been on site for months in secret, creating the elaborate design, which was so reminiscent of an ancient age. As she walked down the aisle toward the stage, running her hand along the tops of the cushioned seats as she passed them, she saw Mr. Froman standing near the conductor's box with his cane. All the windows of the theater had been covered up with paper to prevent the eager and inquisitive from peeking inside and seeing what was being done to the interior.

It was the most fabulous set Annalise had ever seen. Surely Mr. Froman had outdone himself with this production. The investment had been massive, judging by the faux-stone columns and pillars that helped create the illusion of an Aesir palace.

Tanhauser was famous for its concerts and performances. People would come from all over the empire to see this play. To see *her* in its titular role.

But despite the grandeur of the set, she was filled with an uneasy desire to return to Caddam House, her estate on the other side of the lake where Maud Jenkins should have already arrived to prepare for having a guest. Annalise had missed her friend's companionship since the fire in the theater had upended her plans.

The prevailing story was that rogue sorcerers had started the fire, but she didn't believe it for an instant. She had no idea how many might have been injured, but surely Isaac would have made it out safely. Maud had sent her a telegram that the plans had been made, so Mr. Berrow should be arriving at her estate in a day or so, she imagined, and she wished to be there when he did, to see for herself that he was all right. Still, her sense of unease persisted, and she was trying to think of a reason she could depart earlier for her estate.

As she drew nearer to the stage, she could overhear Mr. Froman talking to the conductor.

"That third violist's instrument was out of tune. Did you have it corrected, Maestro?"

"Of course, Mr. Froman. The orchestra will be gathering this afternoon to rehearse. The permit has been secured and paid for. Will you be there?"

"Not today, Maestro. Miss Kauer and I are having a late lunch together."

The conductor, a tall man with wavy auburn hair and a professorial demeanor, nodded and rocked back on his heels. "We will do our best to achieve perfection. It is the music, after all, which will transform this, *ahem*, humble theater and carry everyone away on the wings of their imaginations!" He sounded a little proud of himself as he said it.

"I should like to hear the overture myself," Annalise said when both men turned to acknowledge her arrival.

"In time," Mr. Froman said with amused eyes.

"Who is our lunch with?" Annalise asked, for she'd been completely unaware of the plans.

"Banker Harwell."

She detested the corpulent man. He was in his mid-sixties and was another one of the wealthiest men in the empire. She had the feeling that if he didn't know he'd be rejected out of hand, he'd try to persuade her to marry him.

An image flashed in her mind of a wedding scene in a greenhouse. Mr. Berrow was there, looking at her admiringly. A judge stood in front of them. The image made her dizzy.

"Are you all right, Miss Kauer?" the conductor asked.

"Quite all right," she answered, flashing him a smile. "I'd like to speak to Mr. Froman."

"Of course." The conductor gave an accentuated bow and walked away, weaving through the array of chairs and music stands, pausing once to adjust one he'd nudged in passing.

Mr. Froman's eyes were inquisitive as he waited for her to speak.

"Banker Harwell? You know I detest that odious man."

"You should be grateful that you rarely have to endure his presence. I have reservations at the Pallisades."

It was an excellent restaurant, but she still felt uneasy.

When she'd left Auvinen in her private car, she'd fancied a brief rest at Caddam House. She missed the Lake Country and its privacy. After working for months in Auvinen, she was ready for some peace and quiet, and since the rest of the shows needed to be canceled, she would get some. She was also desperate to learn more about the Invisible College and Mr. Berrow, and Caddam House would provide the private sanctuary she needed. But with their arrival in Tanhauser, Mr. Froman had insisted she stay.

"I'd like to go *home*," she said plaintively.

"We're going there in two days," he said, looking confused. "On Closure, as we agreed. It's only two more days."

Her anxiety spiked, but she kept it from her expression. She hadn't told him she had ulterior motives, nor about the man she anticipated meeting. If he knew about Mr. Berrow, he would forbid her from going. But did he have the right to control whom she associated with? He was her employer, her business partner, and her mentor, but she was her own person and could make her own choices. Though, even after ten years without further harm, she could not deny a slight frisson of alarm at the recollection of his potential for violence when crossed.

"I should like to hear the score soon at least?" she cajoled. "I've heard you sing part of it, but it will be quite amazing with the orchestra, I imagine."

"I hope so," Mr. Froman said. "I want the audience to be swept away by it. To imagine, if you will, a different culture, a different way of life. A contrast to their own dreary existences."

What an odd thing to say.

"What makes this play so different from the ones you've done before," he said, "is that it highlights the virtue of duty over emotion."

"Because she chooses her father over her lover," Annalise said. She'd started reading the script on the ride north and had already begun to embody the role she'd be playing as the Erlking's daughter.

"Not duty over *love*," he countered. "She chooses duty and learns that her lover is and has been unfaithful to her. It is a play about emotional blindness. Duty and honor prevail."

"Does she ever find love? If not, I fear it will unsettle the audience."

"There are many emotions, Annalise. Vindication is a particularly satisfying one. Believe me, the audience will be thrilled by it. Especially when the lover receives his comeuppance in the end."

Froman's version of the once popular story presented her with an intriguing role, to be sure. Her stage partner, the mortal who had fallen in love with the Erlking's daughter, would appear to the audience to be forthright and display all the virtues of respectful manhood. Yet it was all a charade. He intended to hold her for ransom and deceive her, but his plan would be foiled in the end. The plot did have some emotional heft to it.

"We'll be rehearsing during the winter, then?" she asked. "For a spring performance?"

He gave her a slight bow. "That is the intention, my dear. And

Banker Harwell wants to be assured that all will be ready in time. I'll have a carriage arrive at your hotel at one o'clock."

A late lunch indeed.

Annalise deliberately dropped the spoon, and it rattled on the edge of the porcelain soup bowl. Mr. Harwell, who was deep in discussion with Mr. Froman, abruptly stopped and turned his attentive eyes to her.

"Miss Kauer, you look unwell."

Annalise pushed away from the table, bringing her hand to her mouth as if stifling a burp. "I'm feeling...rather nauseous," she said hurriedly. "Please excuse me."

"Annalise?" Mr. Froman said worriedly.

"I think I should go back to the hotel and lie down," she said. "I don't wish to make a scene."

As the first course had progressed, she'd been offering little hints that she was in distress. Being an actress had its advantages. She knew how to pretend anything. In this case, she hoped she'd convinced them she was on the verge of vomiting.

"Let me escort you back," Mr. Harwell urged. He tried to scoot back in his seat, but his girth prevented any easy action.

Annalise hurried to her feet. "You have business to discuss and I'm unwell. I'll take the carriage back if that's all right?"

She gave Mr. Froman an imploring look. His gaze was fixed on her face. Was he trying to discern any duplicity in her?

She feigned a stomach spasm and quickly covered her mouth.

"Go," he said, his wariness shifting to disgust. He was always appalled by displays of drunkenness or any lack of sobriety or illness.

Annalise took her purse and parasol and fled the table. Because it was a late lunch, there were fewer patrons. As soon as she was out of their sight, she hurried to the maître d' and asked for Mr. Froman's carriage to be brought to the front. She continued to feign agitation.

Well, she *did* feel agitation, but the stomach ailment was a pretext. Something inside her was causing irrepressible worry. Like a dog whining to be let out.

In short order, the carriage came to the front, and she told the driver to take her back to her hotel and then return to pick up Mr. Froman.

"Yes, Miss Kauer," he said deferentially.

She quickly climbed into the carriage and shut the door. A man in a suit approached and exchanged a few words with the driver. She looked out the window surreptitiously and saw the concern on the man's brow. Probably one of Mr. Froman's bodyguards stationed at the restaurant. The man nodded and then the carriage lurched forward, the motion nearly knocking Annalise over. She maintained a queasy expression until they were out of sight, when she allowed the pretense to lapse.

She was *going* to Caddam House.

The hotel was not far, and when the carriage arrived, the driver hopped down quickly and she feigned illness again.

"Can I take your arm?" she asked, gripping his arm with one hand and holding her stomach with the other.

"I'm so sorry, Miss Kauer. Let's get you inside."

With his solicitous assistance—she'd always fancied the word "solicitous" for some reason—they were inside. One of the hotel managers came to them immediately with a look of alarm.

"Miss Kauer, how may we help you?"

"I'm feeling unwell," she said. "I'd like to lie down, but can I have one of your maids attend me? Mine is gone."

"For certain. I will have Miss Corrigan wait on you."

"The girl who came this morning, Miss...?"

"Miss Balzen, I believe."

"Yes! Could you have her come instead? I would be so grateful."

"Absolutely. I'll send for her right away."

"I'll gladly pay her wages," Annalise said. "If she could stay with me as long as I'm indisposed."

"I'm sure she would be honored, Miss Kauer. Mr. Briggs, please find Miss Balzen and send her to Miss Kauer's room at once!"

Annalise almost smiled. She'd made arrangements with Miss Balzen before leaving. There were many charter boats that ferried people across the lake on a daily basis, and she knew one would be leaving before the luncheon with Banker Harwell wrapped up. By eventide, Annalise would be back at Caddam House. And Miss Balzen would be deflecting queries for her.

With the manager supporting her on one arm and the driver the other, they took her to her room, where she continued to rub her stomach and look ill.

Miss Balzen arrived shortly thereafter.

"You do as she tells you," the manager said strictly. "Anything she needs, anything at all, you get it for her."

"Yes, sir," Miss Balzen said with a curtsy. The two men left the room, and Annalise looked at the maid and smiled.

"I brought the outfit you asked for earlier," Miss Balzen said. "It's under your bed."

Annalise had played many parts in her career. One thing she'd learned was that people always overlooked the staff.

"Thank you, Miss Balzen," Annalise said, already feeling affection for this girl who was her accomplice in the deception.

"What if someone insists on seeing you?" the other girl asked nervously.

"You don't know when I left or where I went," Annalise said. "Just be truthful."

Chapter Twenty-Six
The Sanctuary of Home

A good costume was all that was needed. Annalise had donned the hotel's servant garb and used Miss Balzen's instructions to get out of the hotel without being noticed. At a local shop, she'd procured a dress, a frumpy hat, and glasses, and then adopted the manners of a nervous middle-aged woman as she walked down the busy street. She rather enjoyed herself and the role she'd invented and was confident she'd eluded the vigilant bodyguards Mr. Froman had assigned to watch over her at all times.

She arrived at the wharves with thirty minutes to spare and hastily procured a ticket for the ferry heading along the coast. It had a single smokestack and could hold cargo as well as passengers for its daily jaunt along the shore of the vast lake. There were fewer passengers than Annalise had expected to see, but that was not so unusual this late in the season. She sat in the closed dining portion and took a seat by herself, positioned to watch the gang-plank for signs of trouble. At the proper hour, the crew detached from the bridge, the engine room rumbled, and the ferry lurched into action. As she watched the wharves shrink into the distance, she felt a giddy feeling of triumph and relief.

"Any tea for you, ma'am?" asked a serving girl from the kitchen.

"Yes, and a little scone if you please," Annalise replied.

From her seat, she watched the wake of the ferry as they passed the small estates and homes along the shoreline, many of which had private docks with moored boats. The closest town to Caddam House was Montreux, where she could hire a cab, but if she spoke to the captain, she might be able to persuade him to drop her off directly at her estate. Doing so would mean revealing herself, but it would save time. There were two other stops along the way.

After a small wait, the serving girl returned with the tea and scone.

"Not many passengers today," Annalise mentioned in a friendly way.

"You're right, ma'am. The captain said a storm is coming."

"A storm? I hadn't heard."

"A winter storm, ma'am. Coming from the north."

An oppressive feeling settled in Annalise's heart. It was still early in the year for a winter storm to strike. She hadn't even begun to prepare the household for it. This was good information. Perhaps the captain knew more about it.

"Can I speak with the captain?" Annalise asked.

"He's very busy, ma'am. Doesn't like to be disturbed."

"I don't want you to get in trouble. I'll ask for him myself."

The girl smiled and nodded and moved along to attend to other guests.

Annalise thought the scone a little dry, but the tea was warm and soothing. The unsettled feeling continued to grow within her. She'd stayed at her estate during the winter before. Snow might be an inconvenience, but the thought of an approaching Aesir army from the north caused deep concern in her bosom.

A memory stirred in her mind. Of a snowy mountain pass in the heart of winter. Flying creatures made of desiccated hide flew across the pass, with glistening warriors mounted on their backs. Bog beasts.

A chill of recognition went down her spine. It was a pleasurable feeling but also a warning. It wasn't just the storm she feared. It was what might be coming *in* the storm.

"Thank you so much, Captain Belvor," Annalise said, reaching out to shake his hand. The ferry was slowing as it approached Caddam House. It was eventide, just as she'd predicted. The captain offered one of his crew to row her to her dock, an offer she'd gladly accepted. Once he'd learned her true identity, he was only too willing to assist her in returning home, and he respected her need to travel incognito. He'd laughed at how well her disguise had worked, but he'd seen her in plays in Tanhauser and had recognized her as soon as she'd doffed the hat and glasses.

She'd learned from him that the winter storm had cut off communication from northern outposts in the empire. The captain's brother, who was in the Signals division of the military, had alerted him about the coming blizzard.

"It's my pleasure, Miss Kauer. How long will you be staying at Caddam House? Would you like me to return on the journey tomorrow? The estates on this side of the lake are pretty isolated."

"I don't want to be an imposition, but I would appreciate it if you'd come back," Annalise said. She needed to get back to Tanhauser before she was truly missed.

"I should return to these parts around ten in the morning," he said. "Light a beacon if you'd like me to stop."

"That is very grand of you, Captain Belvor. Would my companion be able to join me?"

"We have enough room," the captain said.

A crewman approached.

"This young man will see you safely to your dock," Captain Belvor stated. "Thank you for revealing yourself."

"If you could keep it secret, I would appreciate it," Annalise said, giving him a pointed look.

"I would never betray your trust," he replied and tipped his captain's hat to her.

The crewman escorted Annalise to the rowboat, which had been lowered into the water behind the drifting ferry. He climbed inside first, and another crew member helped her down. She could see the dock and her own rowboat tethered to it.

The crewman was young and handsome but too shy to speak to her as he rowed her to the dock. The sun had set over the mountains, although it still cast sufficient light. The crewman stopped rowing and guided the boat to the dock before gently easing up and butting against it.

"There we are, miss," he said.

"Thank you." She reached into her purse to pay him for his help, but he quickly shook his head.

"My pleasure, miss."

She gave him an appreciative smile, and once she had made her way onto the dock, she took in the sight of her glorious house.

Water lapped against the wooden beams. She breathed in the smells of the trees and lawn, and memories of her first time at the estate came bubbling into her mind. The switch from being a penniless actress to a famous one able to afford such accommodations truly baffled her. Mr. Froman's guidance had produced her accomplished life. If he had been a different kind of man—warmer and less controlling—she may have felt a little guilty for having deceived him, but it wasn't his right to dictate how she spent her free time. And she had never again been foolish enough to directly antagonize him after that horrific night.

She walked across the dock and turned to wave goodbye to the crewman as he pulled on the oars to return the rowboat to the ferry. Smoke belched from the smokestack as it waited.

As she crossed the dock, she glanced again at the house. She doubted Isaac Berrow had arrived quite yet, but she dearly hoped he'd come before she had to leave. He would teach her things that were forbidden, and she knew there was more to herself than she understood. She was eager to learn it. To understand herself in a way she never had.

She walked up the side trail leading to the house and saw that the interior was well lit. Maud had clearly arrived. It would surprise her that Annalise had come home without sending word first.

She followed the path to the stairs of the deck, deciding to enter through the back of the house. The grounds were wreathed in dusky light, and the temperature was falling rapidly without the sun. But it was a comfortable feeling.

She finished climbing the steps at a languid pace only to stop in her tracks on the deck. Through the window, the ample light inside clearly illuminated two people on the couch in the center of the room. They were holding hands and facing each other.

Annalise recognized them both—it was Mr. Berrow and Maud, and she watched in disbelief as they started kissing each other in a way that denoted more than just friendship. Annalise watched the act with a surging feeling of jealousy and betrayal.

The tumultuous feelings inside of her echoed with feelings of past pain. Somehow she knew she had witnessed a moment like this before. She couldn't deny that her immediate instinct was to plunge a dagger into Maud's ribs. Such violence was not part of her actual temperament, and she recoiled from it, but watching Isaac Berrow kiss someone else was deeply painful.

How had things between these two developed so quickly? Maud had been genuinely worried and distrustful of Mr. Berrow just two days earlier. Had even suggested calling the Marshalcy to apprehend him. Such a drastic turn in feelings was inexplicable. Or was it? Was Mr. Berrow a cad, a rogue sorcerer who used his magic to dupe and seduce?

Turning her gaze, Annalise saw the lights from the ferry had moved along the shore, so she was effectively stranded at Caddam House. When she looked back, the kiss was becoming more amorous, the scene on display before her eyes incensing in every possible way.

She'd been duped. Taken advantage of. Not just by Mr. Berrow but possibly her confidante as well. Unless a spell had overcome Miss Jenkins, her behavior was inexcusable.

Part of her wanted to flee. To pretend she wasn't seeing this. She could go to the front door and pretend to have just arrived home. Give them time to compose themselves so she could see how they acted in front of her. Would they betray themselves with stolen glances and touches?

No, she couldn't—wouldn't—subject herself to that. This was *her* home. Those were *her* couches. And she'd just as soon cast them out and banish them from her life immediately.

There was no understanding her heart and the confusing emotions at war within it.

Annalise strode to the back patio door and wrestled the handle.

The lovers must have heard her approach because Mr. Berrow had pulled away from the kiss and was rising to his feet. He saw her at the door, hand on the handle, and his eyes widened with shock.

Annalise jerked the door open. She gave him a fierce look, one that threatened him with the coldest of perditions.

"Have you made yourself quite comfortable in my home, Mr. Berrow?" she demanded.

He looked from her to Maud and then back again, dumbfounded. There was a look of blazing guilt in his eyes that said enough. That he'd been *caught*.

Issac Berrow

CHAPTER TWENTY-SEVEN
FORGOTTEN GLAMOUR

The two women looked identical in physical features and differed only in their manner of dress and the styling of their hair. Isaac stared at the Annalise standing at the patio door, eyes blazing with outrage. Then he slowly turned and looked at the other Annalise, who rose from the couch with an equivalent look.

"Who are you?" demanded the Annalise he'd just been kissing. "This is my home. What sort of trickery is this?"

"Your home?" said the other, matching her twin's incensed tone. "Maud, how dare you!"

"Maud? That's the name of my maid. I'm Annalise Kauer."

Isaac's insides churned with confusion, and mortification stained his cheeks. He instantly realized that a glamour spell was in effect. And that he was being deceived by it. But which woman was the fraud? Or were both? Had he spent the day confessing his undying love to an imposter? In his excitement, he hadn't given the idea much thought because he persuaded himself into believing the early-morning swim would have removed any glamours.

"You are Maud Jenkins," the newcomer said. "And you will leave my employ. I dismiss you."

Isaac felt familiar hands grasping his arm. "She may look like me, but I tell you, this is a trick. This is sorcery."

Indeed, it was, but he was growing more certain that the Annalise he'd spent the day with was the deceiver. He felt so ashamed of himself, even though none of it had been deliberate. He'd underestimated the Erlking yet again and blundered into another trap.

But was this newcomer the real Annalise or another decoy? He had to settle this. He had to be sure.

"There is magic involved in this situation," Isaac said, pulling away from the Annalise he'd just been passionate with. His conscience was in flames, but he had to think clearly!

Glamour spells did not work on Eiríka. She was immune to them. So that meant, logically, that the woman he'd spent the day with was likely Maud Jenkins and that she'd been glamoured to believe she was Annalise Kauer. Her intimacy with and knowledge of the real woman would only have added to the effectiveness of the spell, but much of the conjuring happened in the minds of those who *believed* what they saw.

Had Maud played the harp so proficiently earlier that day, or had Isaac only imagined the notes being played correctly? The potency of a powerful glamour spell was astonishing, but thankfully, there was an easy way to reverse it.

The counterspell. A single word. Lydia Brewer had taught it to him.

Isaac could not remember it.

His heart began to accelerate its rhythm. Confusion twisted his mind. He knew the counterspell. He absolutely knew it. He'd used it recently, in fact.

But the glamour was shielding it from his memory.

The newcomer, the Annalise in the drab-colored dress, entered the room as if she were ready to strike the other woman across the face.

Isaac interposed himself between them. "Hold on a moment."

"This is my home," said the newcomer furiously. "I purchased it. That woman is Maud Jenkins. You've met her before in my presence! I don't know what sort of fantasy you're playing at, Mr. Berrow—"

"This is no fantasy," Isaac protested. He pointed to the other Annalise. "She looks *exactly* like you."

Confusion and anger mottled the newcomer's face. "We look nothing alike."

"You're mistaken, imposter," said the other version. "We *do* look alike, although I'd never wear such a dreary dress."

"Stop, both of you!" Isaac said, holding his hand out to each of them. "There is a powerful incantation called a glamour spell. It can deceive the senses. Make someone appear to be someone different than who they really are."

"That's what I'm saying, *she's* the imposter!" said the well-dressed Annalise.

"But I don't see her as me at all," replied the other.

It made sense, and Isaac wanted to believe that the newcomer was the real Annalise. As much as Isaac wanted to believe that meant she was the real Annalise, he cautioned her, "That could be another layer of glamour that makes you see her that way, to sow uncertainty in all of us."

And he still couldn't remember the counterspell. There had to be another way.

"Jynnifer will verify who I am," said the well-dressed Annalise. "I can't believe this is happening. Wait until the Marshalcy finds out."

"She would be equally deceived," Isaac said to the woman he'd spent the day with. "We had dinner with her earlier, and she was under the same impression, but we must undo the glamour to get to the truth."

"Then do it, Mr. Berrow!" demanded the new Annalise archly.

A memory stirred. When McKenna had been abducted by the *strannik*, he'd put a glamour spell on her to disguise her as a child so as not to draw attention to her during their travels. People tended to overlook children.

The spell hadn't altered her perception of herself, but it had affected others.

After she'd escaped, McKenna had crossed a river. The water was very deep, and she'd had the impression, so she'd told him, to immerse herself thoroughly in the river.

What would be considered thorough? There was significance to the number three, especially within the Invisible College. Isaac had long believed, and taught, that the number three was a perfect number. Mortal perception involved beginnings, middles, and endings. Birth-Life-Death. Triangles were the shapes capable of bearing the strongest loads in construction.

"I can remove the glamour," he said, looking at one Annalise and then the other. "We must go down to the lake."

Bathing in a tub would not remove the effect of the glamour. It had to be moving water, like a river, lake, or a waterfall. It had grown dark outside, so Isaac summoned a will-o'-the-wisp of light to guide the way to the water's edge. The night was full of sounds of nature: night birds calling in the darkness, crickets, a bullfrog croaking in the distance. Both of the Annalises came willingly. Both insisted they were the same person.

When they reached the water, the one he believed was the true Annalise spoke first. "So what do we do next?"

"I will immerse each of you in the water three times. Three is a powerful number."

"I'll go first," she said instantly.

"I will," the other chimed in. "I'll prove to you that I'm the one."

Isaac pointed to the one he thought was the imposter. "It is unlikely but possible you are *both* imposters. So both of you will be immersed. Let's start with you, though. You'll each get a turn."

He was answered with two nods of acceptance.

Isaac removed his coat and vest and laid both down on the bank with the towels they'd brought for drying off. Then he loosened his necktie and set it atop the pile. Neither woman looked inclined to disrobe in front of him, but that was no matter, for there were changes of clothes back at the house.

Isaac offered his hand to the elegantly dressed version of Annalise, feeling again the pain of embarrassment. If there had been a magistrate close to the house, it was possible he might have already been married. They'd discussed the most convenient way of getting married legally, which was to send for a magistrate from Tanhauser.

The Erlking had been cunning in his deception. If the false Annalise had swept him away, he might not have even discovered the ruse for some time.

He wondered how the other Annalise had come upon them, but he'd ask later—after assuring himself of who she really was.

Hand in hand, they walked into the water together. It was frigid and he felt his legs begin to tremble. The Annalise by his side didn't seem troubled by the cold at all, just as she hadn't been that morning. Swimming in the lake wouldn't have broken the glamour unless she'd been completely submerged for a suitable amount of time. It was also possible that it might take longer in a lake because the water wasn't moving as quickly as a river.

They walked in until they were about waist-deep. He felt the wet cold on his legs as his pants soaked up the water. Annalise looked at him imperiously. "What next?"

"Put your hands like this," he said, demonstrating by bringing his to his chest and crossing his wrists. She copied him, and he put one hand at her wrists and the other at her back. "Perfect. That will give me better support to lean you backward, and you can just bend your knees if you would."

Isaac glanced at the Annalise who stood on the shore, watching them intently. The sorcerer's light hovered near her, giving her an ethereal presence.

Isaac gripped the wrists of one possible pretender, gently pressing against her back, and carefully eased her down into the water. After she was completely immersed, he pulled her back up to a standing position. Isaac was surprised when it was still Annalise's face that came up out of the water. The drenching of her gown had turned it diaphanous, but he kept his eyes focused elsewhere and released her wrists so she could brush the water droplets from her face.

"Are you ready for the second time?" he asked. McKenna had only submerged herself once, but Isaac had the idea that if the Erlking himself had been the one to cast this glamour, maybe it would require that power of three to break it.

She nodded, her soaked hair hanging down her back. He clasped her wrists again, pressed her back, and lowered her the second time. When she came up, she quickly brushed her face once more.

"I don't feel any different," she said to him. "No change at all."

Isaac hoped the third time would work. He would feel a little ridiculous if it didn't. Not to mention bewildered.

"Once more," he advised. She crossed her arms again, and he pressed her back and lowered her into the water.

Isaac pulled Maud Jenkins up the third time.

The woman blinked in startled surprised and immediately began to tremble with cold.

"Oh dear," she whispered in shock. She looked at Isaac with self-conscious horror. "Oh no!"

"The spell is broken," he said. "You remember now?"

Maud nodded vigorously. "It's like w-waking from a d-dream," she stammered, her teeth chattering. Then she whirled and looked at the woman on the shore. She brought her hand to her mouth in utter mortification.

"It's not your fault," Isaac told her. "Let's go grab a towel, shall we?"

He gripped her by the arm and led her back to the shore. Their clothes were dripping wet. Isaac was soaked up to his shoulders, but he felt fine. The magic was being dispelled and he felt the truth enter his thoughts again. The waiting Annalise held out a towel.

"Do you remember when it happened?" Isaac asked Maud while she clutched the towel to her bosom and shivered. "Do you remember who cast the spell on you?"

She nodded. "I didn't understand the words, but it was Mr. Froman. He did it at the train station. 'Eshi…morfi'? Something like that?"

Isaac nodded in recognition.

"And he tapped me with his cane," Maud said. "Lightly. On my temple." She wrinkled her brow. "I've never played the harp before, but today I could. I've always been a little jealous of Miss Kauer's…abilities." She turned to Annalise with a miserable look. "I'm so sorry! I wasn't trying to deceive you. I really felt I *was* you."

Annalise flinched when she'd said the word "harp," but her expression quickly relaxed. She nodded and patted the woman's shoulder. "There are things I still don't understand. But what's done is done. Let's get this over with." She grabbed Isaac's arm and pulled him to the water's edge.

He went willingly, and the trembling Maud waited for them at the shore and watched while clutching the towel.

When they were waist-deep, Annalise crossed her arms but didn't meet his eyes. She still looked troubled. Was it anger? Hurt? He couldn't judge her expression.

"Proceed," she said. Her dark dress had absorbed water, but she was clearly unaffected by the cold.

He immersed her three times in quick succession. She didn't even wipe her face clear. After the final one, there was no change. His heart, which had been afraid, began to unclench. It was her. It was truly Eiríka.

"It's you," he said softly, wanting to kiss her, yet knowing it would be highly imprudent to do so at that moment. "I'm sorry, Annalise," he whispered to her.

"Now it's your turn," she said, tilting her head. "We had to endure the test and so must you."

"Me?"

"Don't be proud. You're soaked already. Three times. On with it."

He felt a smile tug at his mouth at her directness, and he succumbed to her request without resentment. She immersed him in the water three times, and when he came up the third, the glamour that had been put on *him* was broken.

He knew this because he remembered the counterspell. *Alítheia.*

The veil over his memories parted, and he recalled emerging from the burning theater and finding a man there. The veil over his memories parted, and he recalled seeing Mr. Carrault at the stables outside the Tanhauser train station. Isaac knew he was a Semblance and remembered the man invoking the glamour to trick him. His memory of the event had been snatched away as they'd allowed him to continue on his path to encounter the false Annalise, without the ability or thought to question her identity. To marry the wrong woman.

"Do you feel any different?" Annalise asked him, reaching out and wiping some water from his nose and cheek.

He couldn't believe how close he'd come to making a horrible mistake. Anger at the Erlking flared in his chest.

"I do," he said, looking at the damp tresses framing her face.

"I suppose I should be grateful I took the ferry this afternoon instead of waiting for Closure. Who knows what else you might have done?" Her tone was partially teasing, but it was full of genuine relief.

"Are you cold?" he asked, taking her hand.

"No. But we should go get some dry clothes, don't you think? Unless you intend to stand in the lake all night?"

Smiling, he took her hand as they walked back to the shore. It was an unconscious gesture on his part because the ground underwater was unsteady. But she didn't pull away.

Chapter Twenty-Eight
A Coming Storm

"Are the clothes dry yet?" Annalise asked as Isaac bent over the chair with the incalescent heater he'd set up on the ledge in front of the fireplace. He was currently wearing a borrowed pair of work pants and a wool knit sweater, which belonged to the old groundskeeper. He squeezed the fabric of the clothes draped there and felt dampness still.

"Not quite, but they should be dry by morning," he answered. A lit candle on the low center table by the couches provided the only light. It was probably after midnight, but he didn't feel sleepy.

Annalise sat on the couch in a nightdress with a crocheted blanket on her lap. Maud had gone to bed an hour earlier. She'd mostly resolved her embarrassment from having briefly swapped identities with her employer. None of it was her fault at any rate.

Isaac straightened and brushed his hands together. "Are you tired? I could sleep on the couch."

"I have plenty of guest rooms," she said with a little laugh. "But I was hoping we could talk a little longer."

"I'd like that."

"There's something familiar about this situation. I...I think perhaps I stayed up all night talking with you in a past life."

Isaac felt the pull of fond memories. He and Lydia Brewer had stayed up late talking the night she'd used magic to break in to his small university apartment.

"We've done that many times," he confessed, dropping down on the couch opposite her.

"I take it, by implication, that we've been married before?"

Isaac rubbed his legs, looking down. "Oh? What makes you think that?"

"Is it true?"

Isaac nodded, swallowing. He was still embarrassed for having kissed the wrong woman earlier that day, but sorcery was responsible for the mishap.

"Look at me," she said.

In the soft candlelight, she looked so radiant his heart shuddered. Eiríka's personality was still intact, although in a different form. Her legs were tucked up under her, hidden beneath the blanket. Her hair was loose around her shoulders, which gave him the urge to sweep it aside and kiss her neck. That thought caused a spasm of desire, which he quickly tried to quench. They were *not* married yet in this iteration of their lives. And he would not take liberties, especially after what had happened earlier.

She propped her head with one hand, the other hand resting on her lap.

"Would you...come closer?" She invited him by patting the cushion next to her.

"It might be safer if we remained farther apart," he said.

"I'm not inviting you to ravish me, Mr. Berrow," she said with a smirk. "I just wanted you to lay your head on my lap."

He quirked his eyebrows at her and she patted the couch again. Cautiously, he moved to the portion of the couch next to her and sat down. He eased his head down onto the crocheted quilt, which was very soft, and looked up at her face with open curiosity.

"I had this memory, you see," she said, reaching down and

tousling his hair with her fingers. "Of a moment like this. Your head on my lap. Me stroking your hair. It is quite untamable."

"I am rather neglectful of it," he said, feeling a shiver go through him as she touched his hair.

"A spasm, Mr. Berrow?"

"A shiver. Call me Isaac."

"I intend to. It just felt more...appropriate to keep the formality between us a little longer. This is an unusual experience for me. Very unusual." She continued her gentle ministrations, then stroked the edge of his cheek.

"How so?" he asked.

"There is no script, you see. In every play I've ever been in, there are scenes of dialogue, set instructions, feelings to feign in order to trick the audience into believing the characters on stage are really falling in love. It would be so much easier if I knew what lines I was supposed to say next. But I like it this way. It's unpredictable."

"In times like these, we can only speak what is in our hearts."

"And what is in *your* heart?" she asked him.

He gazed up at her face, seeing tenderness in her expression. Familiarity. She was every woman he had ever loved. "That I've loved you for ten thousand years. I'm not sure it has actually been that long. But it feels like that at the moment. And I will love you for ten thousand more."

He watched her tongue dab her lower lip as she contemplated his words. "How many times have we married?" she asked him. Her finger slid down his nose.

Isaac reached into his pocket, pulled out the device, and opened it. He held it up for her to see.

"You showed me this earlier. You imply we've been married over nine hundred times?"

"Yes." His voice was getting huskier.

"What happens when it has been a thousand, then? Does that thing break?"

"No," he said with a chuckle. "When we've married a thousand times, the Aesir curse will end."

"What curse is that?"

"Their war on mortalkind. The Erlking has promised to leave this world. To allow us mortals to be its caretakers. They will abandon it and go to another. If we find each other one thousand times, marry one thousand times, proving humans can be consistent. That our love can be consistent."

"The Aesir will leave? Willingly?"

"They will. That is why I didn't tell you before what the numbers meant. I didn't want to frighten you."

"You are a master at keeping secrets, Mr. Berrow."

"I've had some practice," he said, feeling emboldened.

"Well, if *we* are going to get married, Mr. Berrow, we'd better do it before Closure when all the magistrate judges have the day off."

"That would mean...tomorrow." He tried to sit up, but she held him down. "Do you really mean it?"

"We need to work on your lines." She lifted her hand to her bosom in a theatrical pose. "You should say, 'I cannot live another day without you.' Something like that."

He twisted in her lap to see her face better. "But you are not joking?"

"I'm not, Isaac. I've constrained my feelings for so long. But now they've come loose, and I'm remembering things, like the time we spent at Covesea. I feel so recklessly attracted to you I'm not sure what to do about it. I'm just upset that Maud ruined it with the harp." She tossed her head and looked away.

Isaac stared at her in confusion. "What do you mean 'the harp'?"

"It's beneath me. I shouldn't have mentioned it."

"Tell me. I noticed you were upset when Maud mentioned it."

"I'd rather not speak of it."

"Please, Annalise. Tell me. I won't judge you."

"Ah, but I judge myself. Very well, since you are so endearing to me right now." She began to stroke his hair again. "Being an actress, I have a preference for the dramatic. I've always had a fancy of a man declaring his love to me while I played the harp. It's such an elegant instrument."

"It is," Isaac murmured.

"I almost made a suggestion to Mr. Froman once that I wanted to be in a play about a woman who falls in love with a man while playing the harp. But I was too self-conscious."

Isaac started and quickly sat up.

"It's a silly thing. And very personal."

He looked at her face, her cheeks a little pink with embarrassment.

"But you never told him?"

"I never told anyone," she answered. "Until now. That's why it was particularly irksome to hear that she'd played the harp for you today."

"He can read your mind," Isaac said. His thoughts were whirling quickly. There'd been evidence of this in past encounters. The Erlking's mind was not hampered by the constraints of mortal intelligence. He could perform vast calculations with effortless ease, and if Isaac's theory were true, he had. Wearing a ring cast from Aesir gold could allow a person to communicate thought to thought over great distances. But this was different. The Erlking was capturing thoughts that had not even been expressed. Skimming the cream from the milk as it were.

"Who can?" Annalise asked. "Mr. Froman?"

"I'm convinced of it. He's been guarding you in your present incarnation." He paused, then put his hands on her shoulders. "As I told you, he's really the Erlking. And you're his daughter."

He felt her stiffen when he said it. Her eyes widened with surprise. "Are you saying I'm one of the Aesir?"

"Not just anyone. You are his daughter. He has tried to stop us this entire time."

Her eyes widened with astonishment, and she stared off in the distance. He could tell she was thinking, her brilliant mind hard at work.

"He will do everything in his power to stop us from coming together," Isaac said.

"Even burn down his own theater?" she asked.

"Yes. That fire was tinged green. It was a pyrophoric conflagration."

"A what?"

"The only humans who know how to make that kind of fire are in the Invisible College. But the Erlking also has that knowledge. And so do you. You were the one who taught *me* about pyrophoric gases."

"While I was on stage? For what reason?"

"Because he knew we'd already met," Isaac said. "I'd been trying to keep it a secret from him, but he already knew. Because he also has the ability to read your mind. It's the only thing that makes sense."

"Didn't Maud say that he touched her with his cane?" Annalise said, meeting his gaze again.

"She said he tapped her with it on her temple," Isaac said, nodding in agreement. "Maybe it's a magical relic. Has he always had that cane?"

"No," Annalise said, shaking her head. "Not that one, the other one broke after..."

She stopped, her brow knitting.

"After what?"

She shook her head, her hair grazing his hands. He squeezed her shoulders. "When did he start using that cane? How long ago was it? I cannot tell you how important this is."

"I don't want to remember it anymore," she whispered, her expression showing him how badly the memories haunted her.

"Tell me, Annalise. Tell me what he did to you." His eyes were fixed on her, giving her a look of deep sympathy. He was in turmoil to see her so scared.

When she lifted her hand to her neck, he felt his stomach drop. Tears began to gather in her lashes.

"I was sixteen," she said faintly, lowering her hand into her lap. Her fingers twined together, convulsing with her inner torment. A tear trickled down her cheek.

Anger and resentment raged inside Isaac's chest. He wanted to soothe her. To make the hurt leave. "What did he do?"

She lifted her head and met his gaze. He could see Eiríka in her eyes. "That was the night he killed me."

Annalise Kauer

CHAPTER TWENTY-NINE
THE UNDOING

Annalise had built internal walls to protect herself from the memories. It was easier to pretend that night had never happened, especially since her life had changed so drastically afterward. She had never told another soul about it. But the concern in Isaac's eyes and the burgeoning, familiar tenderness she felt toward him lowered her defenses. In her heart, she knew she could trust him. And she recognized that she had trusted him before. Every impossible thing he'd told her was true. There was no other explanation for how deeply her feelings had evolved in so short a time.

"You died that night?" he asked softly, taking her hand in his and giving it a gentle squeeze.

"Yes."

"How do you know you were dead?" he asked, tilting his head slightly. It wasn't disbelief in his tone but curiosity.

"Because I saw my body lying on the floor. My awareness, my consciousness, was outside of it. I could see I wasn't breathing. I saw Mr. Froman put his ear to my chest, listening for a heartbeat. Or breath. Finding none, he began to panic, and I was grateful. More than anything else in that moment, I wanted revenge on him. I wanted the Marshalcy to find my body and send him to the gallows."

"You mentioned the broken cane."

Annalise pursed her lips and looked away from his compassionate gaze. Images of violence flooded her mind, and an acidic taste formed in her mouth.

"He used his cane on the cast at times, especially the vulnerable. If someone forgot their lines, he might rap them on the head. Or deliver a blow to their back. I'd been in plays since I was an infant, and I was always diligent about memorizing my part. That was long before I'd met Froman."

"You were in plays as an infant?"

Annalise nodded, feeling the hint of smile tug at her mouth. "There was a baby required for a certain scene, and my mother, who was an actress, offered me for the part. I'd always been a good student, but my passion was for the theater. The principal of my school tried to persuade Mother to send me to the academy so that I could become a teacher, but I pleaded and persuaded her, at fourteen, to let me try the theater first. I followed my dream, even though practically everyone said it was impossible to succeed. It was impossible for my mother at any rate."

"You proved them wrong," Isaac said, offering her a thoughtful smile.

She liked the feeling of him holding her hand and caressed the back of his palm with her thumb. "Froman found me a year or so later and offered me the chance to be in one of his plays. Mother and I had been scraping by. Father died when I was eleven, you see. She felt guilty that we were so poor and destitute, but I told her"—Annalise straightened her shoulders and recited the line from memory—"'I am merely accustoming myself to the vicissitudes of an actor's life.'"

Isaac grinned at her.

"Why are you smiling?" she asked.

"I'm imagining you startling your mother with the use of that word. 'Vicissitudes.'"

"I love words, Isaac. It's why the principal thought I'd be such a good teacher."

"You've always loved words," he said to her. "For as long as I've known you."

"You can understand why I enjoy acting, then. All we have to go on are the words on a page. But they come with so many possibilities. Each script delivers us a new life, and we get to know our characters by the words they say. Those words fascinated me from the youngest age. I would think about them, dream about them, and act them out before the mirror, my only assistant being my imagination."

"Persistence and diligence author success."

"I believe that," she agreed, squeezing his hand. "Mother asked me why I practiced so hard, and I'd tell her 'Sufficient preparation is more than half the battle. The rest is steadiness of purpose mingled with the power to wait.'"

"With that attitude, you would have been recruited to the Invisible College at a young age," he said.

"I want to know more of the words like the ones you taught me," she said, her heart full of wonder. "I want to do more than just summon wrinkles of light."

"That's an interesting way to describe them," he said with a laugh. "Wrinkles indeed."

"I want you to teach me everything, Isaac. I think you'll find me an insatiable learner."

"I can teach you what you previously taught me in one of our all-night sessions. But first, you haven't told me about what happened. Why did Mr. Froman kill you? I don't understand his motives. You were diligent, ambitious, talented. Why throw all that away?"

"Because I lacked the quality he prized the most in his slaves. I wasn't very submissive."

Isaac's lips pressed firmly together. "Did he...did he try to take advantage of you?"

"Not in the way you're suggesting. He dominated everyone. And sometimes he'd give in to his temper, and his punishments were more extreme than the matter deserved. It caused great resentment within me to watch him punish the understudies. There was a girl, Joanna, who was younger than me. A meek little soul, but she loved to act. She was desperate to please him, but she forgot some lines during rehearsal one night, and then she yawned during a scolding. What an offense! He started to beat her with the cane."

Isaac shook his head, brow furrowing with consternation. But he listened, giving her his full attention. She rarely had that kind of intimacy with anyone. It wasn't the same as people admiring her on stage for a character she played or her position as a famous actress. This time the attention was for *her*.

"The other members of the cast watched in horror as he lost control, and many began to slink off, looks of disgust on their faces. No one intervened, and it felt so unjust. To strike a girl like that on the back and arms for being tired! It was probably nine o'clock. We were all weary, and he'd kept the pressure going. She took the blows, whimpering and crying, and the sounds she made just pierced my heart. I knew she'd have bruises the next day and would have to act despite her pain. I just...I couldn't watch it happen."

Isaac shook his head in disbelief. "What did you do? What could you do?"

"I grabbed his hand that brandished the cane and shouted for him to leave her alone, told him he was making a fool of himself for punishing Joanna like that. That we were all tired and would do better with some rest."

"Oh, dear," Isaac gasped. "You defied him. In front of others."

She met his gaze. "I couldn't bear to watch it a moment longer."

"He beat you with the cane next?" Isaac asked.

She nodded her head. "When he switched his focus to me, Joanna crawled out of reach and then I don't know what happened to her because he grabbed me by the arm and started hammering at me. I was shocked, startled, and so upset that it didn't actually hurt very much. I pulled my arm away from his grasp and scolded him. Said he was a coward and a knave and that I wouldn't work for anyone who treated me like that. I was determined to quit."

"Was your mother there?"

"No. She wasn't part of that production. It was my earnings that were supporting us both. But I wouldn't stand for such treatment a moment longer. Performances were to begin in a few weeks, so replacing me would be painful to him. The look in his eyes. The rage. I tried to leave, but he threw me to the floor and then went back to striking me with his cane."

"What did the others do?"

Annalise snorted. "They left me alone with him. He beat my back and arms, but the strange thing was I was so furious that it didn't even hurt. He saw that it wasn't having the same effect on me as it had the others he'd punished. I was lying prostrate on the floor, and he beat me on my backside over and over until the cane broke!"

Isaac gaped in surprise.

She reached out with her other hand and smoothed some hair from his brow. "I shouldn't tell you the rest. I can see this is disturbing you."

"No, do go on. I was a very stubborn child and was punished corporeally as well."

Annalise felt her heart hurt for the little boy he'd been. "Poor thing," she said, cupping his cheek. "Neither of my parents struck me. Not once."

"He broke his cane on your backside?"

Annalise nodded, feeling her emotions swirling as she relived that awful night yet again. "I heard the crack, and when I turned, I saw him kneeling over me, his face dripping with sweat, his mouth agog at his broken cane. I could feel the swelling in my arms, my back. My legs. But it still didn't hurt. And I looked at him, propped up a little on the floor, and I said, 'You can't hurt me. You...can't...hurt me. I'm not afraid of you. I'll never be afraid of you. And you are going to jail for this.'"

Annalise sighed, trembling. "The look in his eyes at that moment... I should have kept my mouth shut, but I wanted to hurt him with my words. *I* wanted to frighten *him*. But he didn't look frightened. He looked enraged. And without another word, he grabbed me by the throat"—Her words had been picking up speed and vehemence, but here, she paused and breathed deeply to collect herself—"and began choking me," she said in almost a whisper.

She looked down again, not wanting to endure the pain she saw in his eyes. With a hand, she reached up and touched her own neck. "I couldn't breathe. And I died. And whatever part of me that lives beyond death came out of my body and stared at the scene. There was no pain, just...pity for myself and a desire for revenge on him, our tormentor."

She could feel tears burning behind her eyes, but she held them back. "When he came to his senses, he realized I wasn't moving or breathing. Then he started to shake me, to try and revive me. Listened to my mouth and chest. From that place above it all, I simply stared at the scene as the panic began to overtake him. It was no longer prison he faced but the noose. He pushed my chest, trying to get me to breathe. He smacked my face. And I just watched him, feeling tired and a little resentful that my brief role on the stage of life was ending so soon and so tragically." She paused again to sigh. "He hurried away, and I felt something tugging at me to depart. I fought it. I wanted to see the end, to see him pay for the injustice."

When she grew quiet, Isaac prodded her to get the rest out. "And what was the end?"

Annalise looked up, saw Isaac's grief and pity, but it was the compassion, shining from his eyes, that opened her mind to the memories, and she related the final act, which she had blocked completely for so many years. "He returned with a pistol. I feared he was going to put it in my dead hand and make it seem like I'd been the one trying to kill *him*. But he used it to kill himself. He still bears the scar."

"Do you remember when you awoke?" Isaac asked softly.

Annalise nodded slowly, with wonder on her face. "I saw a mist creep into the area. A little wisp of fog. I watched it enter my body, and my back arched up off the floor. I gasped and came awake, and I was back in my body again."

"What happened then?"

She responded hesitantly, as the memories coalesced in her mind. "Mr. Froman revived too. He was surprisingly strong for a dead man, and he carried me to one of the changing rooms and laid me on the bed. He had a stone, a brown stone. I'm only just remembering it, but it's like the one in your device. He told me to hold it and it would heal me. He told me it was Aesir magic."

After so many years of having a blank space in her memory of that night's events, the details surprised her. "He was utterly different the next day. Exacting, perfectionist, but he never lost control of his temper the way he used to. And no one remembered what had happened that night. Not Joanna, not the stagehands, not any of the cast. They acted as if *nothing* had happened and that Mr. Froman had always been demanding but never severe." At long last, it made sense. She finally understood why she was the only one who remembered that awful night. "It was a glamour spell. But it didn't work on me."

Isaac shook his head. He reached out and brushed the hair away from her neck to press his fingers against her skin. "That is when you became a Semblance. And when he did. Annalise and Mr. Froman both died that night."

"So I'm not who I thought I was, even though I have all the memories of my childhood?"

"Those memories are still intact. They must be because all the Semblances I've met have had access to them somehow. I believe all your past lives may have been preserved. If that's true, then all the memories might be restored."

"My memories?"

"Mine too," Isaac said. "From all our lives. But if I'm right about his ability to read minds, which, based on his efforts to always keep you close to him, I believe can only happen if he is in the immediate vicinity, it means that he will know what happened here tonight if you think about it around him.. What I've told you. What we've learned. You can't go back to the theater."

"He's expecting me." She lifted a hand to her lips, recalling what he'd told her about the new play. "This play he's written. It is *about* the Erlking and how his daughter chooses to stay with him."

Isaac smirked. "Not very subtle, my lord king. Not subtle at all." Then he winced and lifted his hand to rub his temple.

"What's wrong?" she asked.

"I'm getting messages from a foe. I think he's been asleep because I haven't heard from him in a while. He's a Semblance who took over my friend's body. He's telling me he's arrived in Tanhauser. That he's going to find me and kill me."

"And he's speaking to you right now, mind to mind?" she asked, still trying to wrap her head around this new information and the many ways her world had changed.

"In my mind, yes. I can't stop his voice. I choose not to respond to it."

She put her hand on his leg. "Does he know where you are? Will he come here?"

"I don't think so. We can't stay here, though. We need to get to a magistrate. Do you have a carriage and horses? Maybe we could leave tonight."

"The ferry is going to stop by tomorrow on its way back to Tanhauser. The captain promised he would stop and see if we need a ride back."

Isaac smiled. "Tomorrow would be perfect. Maybe we should both get some rest."

Annalise shook her head. She leaned forward and boldly kissed the corner of his mouth. "I want you to teach me, Isaac. Teach me everything I taught you."

CHAPTER THIRTY
TILL DEATH US DEPART

Annalise and Isaac were standing hand in hand at the shoreline when the first rays of sun peeked out from behind the hills on the horizon. Annalise was tired but so, so happy. As an actress, she'd conjured the effects of falling in love fluidly enough to deceive audiences in theaters throughout the empire. But her feelings of bliss, safety, and connection felt so natural and instinctive it was like she and Isaac had been married for a long time already instead of being on the cusp of matrimony. Well, they *had* been married before. Almost a thousand times. But not in this body, not in this awakening. She leaned against his shoulder, clasping her other hand to their joined pair. She wanted this feeling to last forever.

"How many mornings have we enjoyed like this?" she asked him.

"I've lost count," he said, and he inclined his head to kiss her hair. She was still in her nightdress, he in his caretaker garb. "There is something powerful about a sunrise. They are never the same. Each one is unique."

"Each one whispers possibilities," she said. "And today the whispers are louder. We'll be married by sunset. And the world will change for good."

He squeezed her hand and turned to face her with such a look of tenderness and devotion that it made her breath catch.

"I think I'd like you to kiss me, Mr. Berrow," she confessed.

"Gladly, Miss Kauer," he said saucily.

He pulled her into a gentle embrace and pressed his lips against hers. His short whiskers tickled slightly, although the sensation made her interested in what they'd feel like on her neck. She returned his fervor with her own, pulling him closer and enjoying the lack of artifice in their ardor. Her heart sped up, and the swell of giddiness was very real.

"That was its own kind of magic," she said, giving him a mischievous smile.

They'd been up all night discussing and practicing and singing spells. Each of the incantations had come effortlessly to her. She had always been impeccable at memorizing lines and could easily modulate her voice with accents and singing. They'd gone through probably a hundred spell variations, and she'd mentally rehearsed at least thirty throughout the night so she could recall the phrasing and tones of each. Before they'd walked to the lakeshore together, he'd told her that she'd be a tenth-level sorcerer in the Invisible College already. All she lacked were the initiation rites.

"It was," Isaac declared in agreement, resting his chin on her head. "I'm not prone to jealousy, Annalise, but watching you perform on stage definitely provoked feelings. I wanted to be man you were wooing."

"Even though you knew it wasn't real?"

"It seemed real enough at the time. A tribute to your talent."

She felt a sense of giddiness. Isaac was quick with compliments, and she rather enjoyed them. She was used to shallow praises from strangers. His felt more intimate.

"Well, we should put on some real clothes, I imagine," she said. "The ferry will be here in a few hours. What should we do about Maud?"

"I've wondered about that. If she goes to Tanhauser with us, she will be in danger. I propose casting the glamour on her again before we leave, making her look and seem like you. Let's perpetuate the illusion until we're married and can end this farce permanently."

"I'm not sure I like the idea of her pretending to be me," Annalise said. "But it's just for one day. And I don't want her to come to any harm."

"I don't like it either, but the whole world is at risk. If we don't succeed today, then Closure is tomorrow and the storm you mentioned last night strikes. The change in the weather could be coincidence, but we cannot take that for granted. The Aesir can affect the weather."

Annalise leaned up and kissed his cheek. "We should hurry, then. We'll have to glamour the staff so that they don't remember we were here or what we've done."

"I don't know if the Erlking's staff can pilfer smothered memories," Isaac said. "We shouldn't make assumptions one way or the other."

She patted his chest. "We'll figure it out, Isaac. I have confidence in you."

They walked hand in hand up to the house, and Annalise imagined living there with him, enjoying the views of the lake, visiting the cities of the empire together. When the Aesir finally left, would all their previous memories be restored? She hoped so. The glimpses she'd had of McKenna's life had made her hunger for more, though she knew not all her memories would be so pleasant. He'd told her the story of how she'd been put into the dying body of the unfortunate Lydia Brewer. She was eager to hear about more of their lives together, all of them, but there were important things to accomplish. *One thing in particular,* she thought giddily.

When they reached the house, they found Maud sitting on the couch drinking a steaming mug of tea. She looked startled to see them.

"Were you awake all night?"

"We've had a lot to talk about," Annalise said. "We're going to catch the ferry back this morning."

"I'll help you get ready. Would you like me to come with you?"

Isaac shook his head. "It would be safer if you stayed. If any of Mr. Froman's people come, they'll be expecting to find you as Annalise."

"But the spell has been broken," Maud said, looking confused.

"I'll disguise you once again," Isaac said.

Maud directed a worried look at Annalise.

"This time you have my permission," she said. "Have Jynnifer make some breakfast for us, and we'll be on our way shortly."

Isaac went to the device he'd set up to dry his clothes and checked them before nodding. "They're dry."

"I'll change as well. Maud, can you help me with my hair?"

"Gladly," Maud replied.

It was a smooth ride on the ferry. Captain Belvor had greeted them personally and she'd paid the fare for two. The ship was more crowded than it had been the previous day because many were seeking to get ahead of the coming winter storm by going to Tanhauser. She and Isaac nestled together on a bench in the covered area. Isaac had started dozing, so she'd suggested he lay his head on her lap. She'd begun stroking his hair again, which had promptly put him to sleep.

She was tired but too keyed up to want to sleep herself. Ever since she was sixteen she'd eschewed the idea of marriage. Other than that particular fantasy of being wooed while playing a harp, she'd felt no inclination to marry anyone. She'd feared that all the acting and pretending to be someone else had damaged her capacity to truly love someone. But she'd come to the conclusion that it was *because* she'd been waiting for Isaac to find her. Here she was, Annalise Kauer—the Erlking's daughter—hurrying to Tanhauser to find a magistrate to marry her and her betrothed that very afternoon. And she was so eager for it!

It was possible, of course, that this was all an elaborate ruse. An unscrupulous sorcerer's ploy to win her affection. How could an intelligent woman not consider such things carefully? But Isaac had never come across as duplicitous. The question he'd asked her in the park, about when she'd died, had struck a nerve because of the story only she had known. His explanation of Semblances, about the sudden change in Mr. Froman's behavior following his suicide, and even the collective amnesia everyone else seemed to suffer about that night fit the events perfectly. She was no fool. She knew truth when she saw it.

She noticed one of the uniformed crew talking quietly to passengers, group by group, which caused worried looks to bloom on their faces. As he made his way closer to them, she shook Isaac's shoulder to wake him. He yawned and sat up.

"Something's happening," she said quietly to him. "That member of the crew is sharing news."

Isaac immediately went on his guard, and she heard him humming gently to invoke a shield spell. Why hadn't she thought of that? She added her voice to his, humming in harmony with him to amplify the spell.

The crew member reached them shortly thereafter. "We'll be arriving in Tanhauser within the hour, but Captain Belvor wanted me to announce that a storm from the northern mountains is catching up with us. The seas will be choppy before we make it to port. Some passengers experience extreme nausea, so we wanted to forewarn you."

Isaac glanced at her and then back at the crew member. "Can the captain increase the speed?"

"He's already ordered that, sir," said the crew member. "But the clouds are going to overtake us. Our engines won't go faster than the wind. We weren't expecting the storm until this evening, but the weather can be fickle on this lake, I'm afraid."

"Thanks for the warning," Annalise said, feeling her chest constrict with worry.

The crewman nodded and moved on to the next set of passengers. Isaac rose from the cold bench and took her hand. After helping her rise, he led her toward the stern of the boat, which faced the way they'd come. The sky had been slightly overcast earlier, but she could see a disturbing slash of clouds growing on the northern horizon, closing fast. It looked like a rift in the sky with some dense black thunderheads and a wall of fog connecting it to the sea. The dark gray, seething, foamlike clouds bore tints of green and azure, giving it the look of a scab that stretched the entire distance of the lake.

"Those are ominous clouds," Annalise said, feeling her concern growing.

The first lurch of the boat caused them both to reach for the handrail.

"That's no ordinary storm," Isaac said in a low voice, his eyes tightening with fear.

She knew he was right, even though she didn't know why. Something preternatural warned her that it was a sign of imminent danger.

The ferry lurched more frequently as the rippling waters became more violent. Annalise gripped the handrail hard when the swaying became stronger. She began to regret the hearty breakfast they'd enjoyed earlier.

"What do we do?" she asked him, but his gaze was fixed on the approaching storm and fogbank.

"A stormbreaker is coming," Isaac whispered.

She watched in alarm as a sky ship emerged from the overhead rift. The hull was mottled as if it were made out of stone. Tall pillars, like masts, protruded up from the middle, but there were no sails. She felt the vibrations of musical magic deep in her bones as the leviathan floated into sight.

"Look at that!" a nearby passenger shrieked. "In the sky!"

It took only moments for pandemonium to break free.

"Is that an Aesir ship?" cried another. "I thought they were all dead!"

"Coming right at us!" wailed another. Panicked noises filled the stern-side compartment. Some passengers rushed toward the front, fleeing the sight at the back of the ferry. A few intrepid ones joined Annalise and Isaac at the railing and gazed in horror and awe at the colossal sky ship that had cleaved the sky.

"We're going to die!" screamed one woman, adding to the atmosphere of terror.

Isaac put his hand on top of Annalise's. "We need to sing the protection hymn."

She looked at him in surprise. "They'll all know we're sorcerers, then."

"If we don't, we won't make it to shore," he said firmly.

Annalise breathed a sigh. "You're right, of course. We can do no less, Husband-to-Be."

He gave her an intense look and squeezed her hand harder. "Till death us depart."

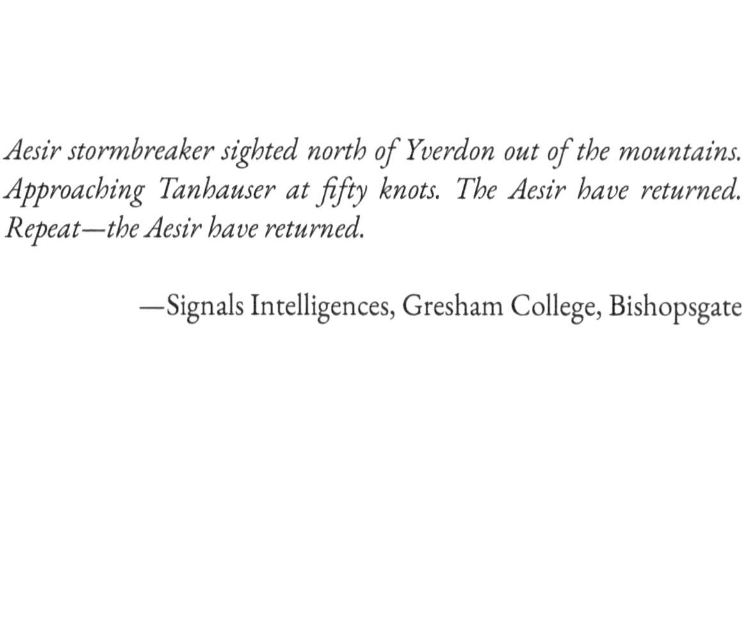

Aesir stormbreaker sighted north of Yverdon out of the mountains. Approaching Tanhauser at fifty knots. The Aesir have returned. Repeat—the Aesir have returned.

—Signals Intelligences, Gresham College, Bishopsgate

Issac Berrow

CHAPTER THIRTY-ONE
TRIUMPH OF DESPAIR

The air had become so cold that Isaac saw the breath leaving his mouth as he exhaled. Every moment, the chill became more pronounced. Fog completely shrouded the ferry, and rime ice had formed on all the metal structures on the exterior of the ship. It was preternaturally cold, but the ferry was unharmed. The Aesir sky ship hadn't bombarded them yet, but he could hear booms in the distance.

The other passengers on the ferry had retreated to the interior passages for warmth and protection. Only Isaac and Annalise remained outside on the aft deck.

The engines of the ferry lowered in throttle, and the great ship began to still, save for its rocking motion in the water. The winds had ended when the fog overtook them. Isaac felt his ears tingling with the cold, along with the tip of his nose. At such freezing temperatures, bodies lost heat rapidly and could succumb to hypothermia. His device prevented him from getting frostbite or losing body temperature to that degree, but it was still uncomfortable.

Annalise didn't look chilled at all.

"The captain slowed the engines," she said, giving him a worried look.

Isaac squeezed her hand, and they walked to the crew stairs leading up to the bridge. The crunch of the ice particles under his shoes prompted him to grip the frozen wooden railing to avoid slipping. They hurried up the steps, and he thrust open the door to the bridge.

Captain Belvor was at the helm. He gave them a quick surreptitious look before turning stiffly to gaze back at the fog-laden view through the windows. Puffs of steam came from his lips.

Isaac cast the incalescence spell on the steering column. The metal would begin to warm on its own and defy the cold.

"Why did you cut the engines, Captain?" Isaac asked.

"We're close to shore, but I can't see a thing out there," Belvor responded. "This is as close as I dare go in this fog."

"The lake will freeze, Captain," Isaac said. "We need to reach the docks."

"I can't see them!" he growled in a perturbed voice.

"I can guide you."

The captain frowned. When Isaac and Annalise had sung the shield spell, the passengers and crew had been grateful for the protection they'd offered. Especially when the ship had passed overhead without harming them. No one had seemed frightened or worried...except for the captain. Isaac could sense the prejudice in the man's demeanor, and he had a strong suspicion that Belvor would notify the Marshalcy after arriving at the docks if left to his own resources.

"How?" Belvor asked. "Do you have an uncanny sense of direction? I've sailed this lake for ten years, and I would never try to reach the shore without the lower lights burning."

"I have an uncanny sense of hearing," Isaac said. "But you're right. Without being able to see far, our sense of reckoning is immediately impaired. I can guide us to the pier with sorcery."

The captain grimaced on hearing the last word. "All the passengers' lives are my duty, my responsibility. I cannot do anything to endanger them."

"If we remain still and the waters freeze around us, we'll be in a worse predicament."

"He's right, Captain," Annalise said, coming forward and putting her hand on Belvor's arm. "If you listen to him, he will guide you true."

"Miss Kauer," the captain said doubtfully.

"Sir," said one of the crew, probably the first mate, judging by the decorations on his uniform jacket, "I think we should heed them. They're both risking prison by helping us."

Isaac gave him a smile of gratitude. He could glamour the captain and the crew if need be, but he hoped persuasion would be enough.

"Very well," Belvor said with a sigh. "I'd rather be on dry ground if we're facing an invasion. I thought the Invisible College was in league with the Aesir?"

"It's not true," Isaac said. "It was founded to protect against them."

Belvor looked doubtful but did not argue.

"Can we open one of these windows so I can hear better?" Isaac asked, pointing to one of the forward-facing windows. The first mate hurried and opened it, and a blast of frigid air came in.

"Strange, the wheel is warming up," the captain said, pursing his lips.

"That's sorcery as well, Captain," Isaac said while crossing to the window. Annalise came and stood beside him, placing a hand on his arm.

She leaned closer. "You're going to summon an intelligence to guide us?" she whispered.

He gave her a quick nod, still looking ahead.

"Can I try it?" she asked. "I'd like to practice."

"By all means," he said, giving her a grin.

She closed her eyes, lowering her head, and he could see the act of concentration wrinkling her forehead. She lifted her head after a moment. "I tried finding a waterfowl, but there are none."

"Too cold," he said. "They would have started to flee with the cold front. Try the native fish. There are some that must linger near the docks for the food and crumbs that spill.”

“Good idea,” she said and bowed her head again.

While she did that, Isaac reached out mentally for Loyal. Given their rapid movements over the last few days, he wasn’t surprised the faithful doglike intelligence hadn’t caught up with them yet.

“Oh my,” Annalise said in surprise, widening her eyes.

“What did you find?” he asked, curious at her changed expression.

“This lake has many sturgeon,” she said. “They are rather enormous fish. I found one that just died and was more than willing to help lead the way. I can sense it just over there,” she said, pointing into the fog.

“Have it guide us into the harbor,” Isaac said. “I’ll listen for the change of sound, like the water slapping against the dock posts.”

He saw the triumphant look on her face as she nodded. Then she turned. “That way, Captain.” She angled her arm to the left and pointed.

“Increase engine speed to five knots,” the captain said.

“Increasing speed, five knots,” said the first mate.

After the orders were relayed, the thrum of the engines started up again, and the vessel lurched forward.

“Make sure we have enough warning to slow down,” the captain said. “It takes time to send the word down.”

“If you send your first mate to the engine room, I can communicate with him directly,” Isaac suggested.

“How?” the captain asked.

Isaac reached into his pocket and pulled out the device, twisted the dials to unlock the center ring, and then put it on his thumb. The stab of pain was immediate. He turned and faced the captain.

Like this, Captain Belvor.

The captain gazed at him in surprise.

After a slow and tedious approach, the ship reached the dock for them to find it completely empty. Some of the able-bodied crew managed to jump onto the dock on the approach and helped secure the vessel to the pier. Isaac and Annalise were the first passengers to disembark, and they walked swiftly down the fog-shrouded street.

"I need to summon something to guide us to the magistrate's court," Isaac said.

"I know where it is," Annalise told him, clasping his hand with both of hers. She chafed some of the coldness away with her touch as she rubbed his hand vigorously.

An explosion sounded in the distance, but Isaac thought he heard music. A flute was playing somewhere far away, its light notes dancing in the air. But he couldn't tell what area it was coming from, though he'd been to Tanhauser many times, because the fog had completely disoriented him.

"I hear a flute," he said. "Do you?"

They didn't pause as they listened. "I think it's coming from over there," she said, pointing. "But the magistrate's offices are closer to the center of town."

Snow had started coming down fast and heavy, and already, it was caking his shoulders and shoes and hair. He wanted to help the sorcerers defend the city, but he knew that the best thing he could do to stop the attack was to get married to Annalise. So he continued onward, his heart heavy with the knowledge that the people of Tanhauser were afraid and in danger.

They encountered no one along the way. The gas lamps were all off, but that wasn't a surprise given it was around noon. He saw the time displayed on a clock as they passed a shop.

The sound of the flute abruptly stopped. Isaac felt his stomach clench with dread. He wondered what had happened to the sorcerer who'd been playing the instrument.

Annalise squeezed his hand, and then they stopped as well. They were able to make out a field of rubble ahead.

"Isaac," Annalise whispered, halting in shock.

Rubble was strewn over the street. Entire buildings had collapsed in the center of town, and he could see frozen bodies half-buried in shattered bricks and snow. The Aesir had wreaked havoc on Tanhauser, and it was no accident that they'd struck the center of town. The government buildings, the magistrate offices, all lay in ruin before them.

A feeling of hopelessness and desolation racked his soul. He'd witnessed such scenes of devastation countless times. A simple harmonic shield spell would have prevented the horrible destruction. The sorcerers of the Invisible College, just ordinary people in society, had banded together over the centuries during the Awakenings in order to protect the people. This was the result of the misinformation that had abounded since his last conflict with the Erlking.

"We have to keep trying," Annalise said, stirring him to action.

They pressed forward through the detritus, seeing a few blank faces of the deceased lying crushed in the streets. Several mangled street signs protruded from the ground at odd angles, street names obscured by dust or snow. He was tortured by the thought that if they'd managed to leave earlier, instead of spending the night talking, that he might have been able to prevent such carnage.

Once again he had failed to anticipate the Erlking's cunning and determination—his absolute ruthlessness.

"It's gone," Annalise said, coming up short again. She pointed. "That was the magistrate building. There's nothing left of it."

"They're all dead?" Isaac wondered aloud, a sickening feeling roiling inside.

"Maybe some evacuated in time," Annalise said. "We have to keep trying, Isaac! Even if we need to go to another city."

"And leave this one to its doom?" he asked her in anguish.

She cupped his cheek in a tender way. "I'm grieved as well. But we cannot abandon hope. We cannot let him win. We'll find another magistrate."

"They are all...gone...away."

Isaac recognized the voice instantly. Stepping out of the fog was Jack Farmer, wearing a long coat dusted with snow and a hat on his head. He held out his hands expressively, a cunning smile on his lips. "Look what you've done, Professor Berrow. Look what you've done. Where were you when they needed you?"

Isaac knew the Semblance was taunting him deliberately. Trying to provoke a rash action. He began to hum a shield spell, although he knew the device would protect him and Annalise from elfshot or bullets.

"It is good that you've arrived at last," Jack said. He shifted his gaze to Annalise. "Your father is expecting you."

There could be no doubt as to his meaning.

"We're not planning to stay," Annalise said with defiance in her tone.

"But the safest place to be in the world is in the Erlking's presence. He didn't fall for your little ruse of sickness at the restaurant. You forced him to hasten his work. But you *will* see him."

"No, Jack," Isaac said. "We're ending this now."

Isaac thought it implausible that one man, one Semblance, would have been sent to retrieve them. No, Jack must be a decoy. Someone to draw their attention forward.

He looked up as a bog beast came lunging through the fog from above, dilapidated wings unfurled, two clawed limbs reaching for Isaac and Annalise.

He had only an instant to react, one spell he could utter. *"Kalispel!"*

With the blunt-force spell, he knocked Annalise away from him just as the claws ripped into his middle and hoisted him off his feet.

CHAPTER THIRTY-TWO
THE EYE OF THE BASILISK

One of the bog creature's claws was embedded in Isaac's side, causing excruciating pain with every movement, but the stinging shards of ice against his face made it impossible to gauge the seriousness of the injury. They were flying over the rubble, which he could barely make out. After shielding his face from the whipping snow with his hand, he was able to discern the warrior atop the beast, clinging low over the saddle and harness of the flying monster.

His mind raced as he tried to determine what spell he could sing to save himself from being carried up into the sky to a stormbreaker. If he did something to force the bog beast's grip to loosen, he would plummet to the ground unless he could summon help to slow his fall as he'd done near the hotel in Auvinen. A fall from such a height might not kill him—people had survived falls from great heights before—but it would take days for the shattered bones to heal, even with the philosopher's stone inside his pocket. Over the lake, he might have risked it, knowing the water would help break his fall if it wasn't already frozen.

Before he could finish conjuring a plan, the bog beast slowed, its wings flapping more fiercely as it lowered itself to alight on the roof of a building. He'd hardly registered his change in circumstances when the creature's claws opened, and he fell onto the snowy rooftop. Despite the snow, it jarred his elbows and knees as he struck the surface.

The bog beast continued to flap its desiccated wings as it landed nearby, before letting out an ear-piercing shriek.

Isaac scurried to his feet, backing away from the beast and the armored warrior mounted on its back. She was a Disir, one of the female warriors famous among the Aesir for being fearless in battle. She had silvery hair and a face the color of snow, with purple smudges around her eyes and cheeks. Her eyes were opaque, no pupils or irises, which was unusual and made him wonder if she were under some sort of spell that was shielding her vision. He recalled the legends of the basilisk, those fearsome serpentine creatures that could purportedly slay a man with their gaze alone.

"What is your name?" he called to her, grunting in pain from his injury. She was probably six and half feet tall, encased in Aesir armor, with a spear in one hand and a curved blade sheathed at her hip. Her silver hair streamed in the wind, and she looked perfectly at ease in the storm.

"You may call me *Angorbyda,* mortal," she said haughtily.

He knew the Aesir tongue. Her name meant "sorrow bringer." He gazed around the rooftop. They were on a square-shaped flat roof with a railing. From his vantage point, he knew he was several stories above street level. Ahead of him was a curving, sloped roofline that looked familiar and distinctive. He was at the Volksoper opera house in Tanhauser, where McKenna had taken him on their honeymoon.

The bog beast lifted its sinewy neck and let out a barking call. These creatures, he knew, were prehistoric in nature. They'd perished in the tundra and were covered by glaciers. Powerful Aesir magic had animated the corpses and imbued them with the gift of life, and the Disir flew on them when attacking.

"Why have we come here, Sorrow Bringer?" he asked. He

glanced at his side and saw a sizeable bloodstain on his coat. He gingerly pressed his palm against the wound.

"I obey the commands of the Erlking, mortal," she said. "We will reclaim our stolen lands at last."

"Is the Erlking here?" Isaac asked. He edged backward toward the border of the roof. Jumping might be his best way to escape her.

"Be still, mortal," she said. "Before I accost thee."

Aóratos. He thought the mental spell for invisibility, then spun and rushed to the edge of the rooftop. He intended to vault over it to the lower roof of the building he remembered next door —presuming it was still there. There were glass windows along the front, and he imagined he could shatter one of them with a spell and get inside the building.

She snatched him as he leaped and held him with one arm, dangling him over the edge of the roof.

"I see thee, worm," she sneered. He could hear the hum of power coming from the gemstone embedded in her arm bracer, giving her supernatural strength. The Aesir were also faster than mortals, so attempting to run from her was pointless.

The door at the corner of the roof opened, scraping against the snow, and four men wearing Marshalcy uniforms emerged onto the roof. Snow pelted them as they trudged through the snow toward the Disir warrior.

Angorbyda brought Isaac back from the precipice and whistled a spell that removed his invisibility. There were spells he could use to damage her, but fighting wasn't the solution to the problem. Even with elfshot, he probably didn't have a hope of physically besting her. No, he needed to rely on his intelligence to outsmart the Erlking and his minions. And that meant discerning what the Erlking intended to do with him.

If they'd wanted him dead, he'd have been dead already. The Disir could have easily dispatched him. That meant he was wanted alive—for the moment.

Why?

The four officers approached them, and the Disir flung Isaac onto the snowy roof. In that position, Isaac hurriedly twisted the sorcerer's ring off his thumb and squeezed his hand into a fist.

"Bring him below," Angorbyda said. "The Erlking awaits him."

"Did you serve Eiríka?" Isaac asked in a challenging tone, rising to his feet as the officers arrived.

"Thou art unworthy to speak her name, dissembler," said the Disir angrily.

Isaac took a quick look at the men. He could hear the faint thrum of magic coming from them. One had a harrosheth blade strapped to his waist. The others had pistols, but not elfshot ones.

"Does it displease you so much that she chose one of us?" Isaac said to the Disir, using the opportunity to stall for time so he could think. He suspected all four of the Marshalcy men were Semblances.

Two of the men grabbed him by the arms. He pretended to resist, but quickly surrendered. He began to shiver, even though he wasn't that cold.

One of them produced a set of iron cuffs, and the two men holding his arms wrenched his wrists behind his back.

"Wait," he said to the man with the cuffs. "Can I have a coat? I'm freezing to death."

"Foolish mortal," said the Disir. "Winter has scarcely begun."

He kept his eyes fixed on the officer in front of him, who looked at him with disdain. "These coats aren't the warming ones," he said. "They keep us cool."

Isaac had noticed the bespelled buttons on the jackets and had assumed they were the same as those the military used to summon incalescence to heat the wearer. But the symbol on them was different. It was the Aesir rune for a winter wind. It made sense that the Semblances had found ways to adapt to the warmer climates in the empire. An idea was forming in his mind. A subtle one.

"I'll take it anyway," Isaac said. "It looks w-warmer than what

I'm wearing." He was letting his legs tremble, his voice become slurred. Annalise was a far better actress, but he knew the sensation well enough to give in to it.

The officer shrugged off his coat and helped Isaac put it on. It had hardly any body warmth. After they'd put it on him, they secured his wrists behind his back with the cuffs. They were nulling cuffs. He knew the word that would deactivate them, but did they? He had to assume that any knowledge he'd taught Jack Farmer was in his enemies' hands.

"Search his pockets," said the higher-ranked officer, the one who'd given up his coat. "It looks like a pocket watch."

Yes, they knew about the device. No surprise there. But did they also know that if they took it away from him, it would reappear in his pocket later? He'd bespelled it to ensure it couldn't be taken from him by anyone.

Quickly enough, they found it. The head officer examined it, his brow furrowing as he opened it and read the numbered runes. He clicked it shut and tucked it into his own pocket.

Ideas whirled in Isaac's mind. Could he escape from the cuffs? Maybe. He had the ring clenched in his hand. He could get it back on his thumb, but whom could he summon for help? Would Wickins come? Could he arrive in time? Probably not. People were likely fleeing Tanhauser in droves, not traveling there.

The officers began to haul him over to the doorway at the edge of the roofline. Isaac glanced back and saw the Disir warrior had mounted the bog beast again and was gazing at him with those basilisk eyes. Her expression was full of confidence. She believed they'd won. They had prevented him and Eiríka from marrying the last needed time.

He needed to know if he could still use magic.

Usually, incalescent buckles and other Aesir magical artifacts were activated by thought. He gave the thought impulse and heard the buckles hum. He could feel a coolness begin to soothe his shoulders and armpits. A magical jacket that made things cooler...

Yes, perhaps he could make this work.

They marched him down a set of stairs. From this perspective, he could see the interior workings of the rooftop, with its scaffolding, beam struts, and pulley wheels. Theaters had a lot of rigging to allow scene changes to happen quickly.

Finally, they reached the lowest floor and then passed through several doors before they reached the stage. It was illuminated by glowing quicksilver lamps. The decorations and setting all gave the impression of an Aesir fortress. It was the most elaborate set he'd ever seen, showing in meticulous detail the graceful architecture of the Aesir. This was a replica of the Erlking's palace. There were two thrones, one for the Erlking and the other the Erlqueen, who had died being merciful to mortals.

The officers brought him to the center of the stage where a rope dangled from the rafters. The officers brought him to the rope and one of them quicky tied the end into a noose.

Isaac took a moment to calm his mind. The noose wasn't just a prop. It was part of the play. The Erlking had staged this last encounter down to the minutest detail. All the pieces came together...

The Erlking was going to offer Eiríka a final choice. The choice between her father and her love.

Once the noose was made ready, the officer put it around Isaac's neck and cinched the back of it, though not tightly.

The theater in Auvinen had been burned to the ground to shift the scene to Tanhauser. A scene that had been set for Eiríka's final decision. This was it: choose the Erlking and an Aesir life and live forever. Or watch your mortal husband strangle to death and become mortal forever without him.

It was cruel. It was terrible. And the Erlking believed he knew what Eiríka would do. He believed she would choose to return to her people, that she would forsake the mortal world once and for all. She'd lived almost a thousand lives among them.

But if Isaac died, his soul would be swept away to another body and there would be no time for them to find each other again. Not if the Aesir destroyed all humanity as quickly as he believed they could...

Isaac heard footfalls coming, along with the thunk of a cane on the polished theater floor. The officers who'd been handling Isaac stepped aside.

Mr. Froman stepped forward, gripping his cane, his eyes narrowed and cunning.

"Give me his device," Mr. Froman said when he arrived. He clenched the cane in one hand and held out his other.

The officer passed it along. Mr. Froman didn't open it—he just put it into his own pocket.

"I'm bleeding," Isaac said. "You don't want me to die too soon, do you?"

Annalise Kauer

Chapter Thirty-Three
A Fateful Decision

After being shoved into the snowy debris, Annalise craned her neck and watched in horror as the monster flapped its wings and carried Isaac off in one of its claws. It would have snatched them both if he hadn't acted so quickly. The rider of the flying beast looked vaguely familiar. She'd never seen a real Aesir before, yet she knew this elegant warrior was one of them. Her gaze fell to the woman's weapon as they disappeared. That's what Annalise suddenly hungered for as a shielded memory broke loose inside her after seeing it. A memory that she knew how to use it. Her wrist ached from catching herself, but that was insignificant next to the worry blazing in her chest. She had to get to him. This was her last chance...

She heard the crunch of boots on the snow and turned to see the man who had addressed her earlier as the Erlking's daughter. She rose to her feet, massaging her wrist, and studied him warily.

"Where is she taking my husband?" Annalise asked, hoping a little deception would further her cause.

He smirked at her, continuing to approach, and she began to backstep. "Whatever vows you may have exchanged privately would not fulfill the covenant. And you know this."

"How do *you* know we're not married?"

"Your father knows. Now it's time to go to him." He lunged for her, but she pivoted to one side and kept out of reach.

"I prefer my freedom," she said. *"Percutis malleo!"*

The sung spell smashed into him and sent him tumbling backward. She broke into a run, going in the direction she'd seen the Aesir woman heading, and almost immediately collided with a shield spell that jolted her and nearly knocked her down.

"Two can play at that game," her attacker said, rising from the snow and brushing it off.

She and Isaac had stayed up all night, and she'd learned dozens of spells, but in the panic of the moment, her mind struggled to recall one that would be useful in the situation.

"Aparato!" she sang, sending a chunk of stone flying at him.

He ducked the stone and charged her, seizing her by the arms. He was larger than her, physically stronger, and she couldn't wrench either arm from his iron grip.

"You are coming with me," he snarled.

She stomped hard on one of his feet, and his hold loosened just enough that she got one arm free. She struck him hard across the face, a stinging blow that barely had any impact on him. He pulled her around, her back hitting his chest, and wrapped his forearm around her neck. A distant recollection came: an echo from another life. This was a kind of choke hold—one that would render her unconscious in seconds. She jabbed him in the stomach with her elbow. He grunted but then closed her airway, stopping her from breathing.

"Gently now," he said in a singsong voice by her ear.

Another memory stirred. Without even thinking, she gripped his forearm with both hands, lowering her chest by leaning at the waist, and then twisted her hips and stepped around his leg. The position opened her throat again for air, and she torqued on his wrist and flung him to the ground while twisting it, putting him in an arm bar that controlled him at the shoulders.

She almost smiled when she saw his startled expression at the sudden reversal. This was no natural instinct of hers but a memory from a lifetime before. From the Erlking's daughter.

Then she remembered the inverted shield spell Isaac had taught her, the one that could trap a Semblance and block it from communicating telepathically. She jumped back from the man, singing the complicated notes quickly, and stared in surprise and vindication when it worked. The man struggled against invisible bonds while lying on the ground. He pushed against the barrier, and a look of horrified recognition came to his face.

She backed away from him. "Happen to you before?" she asked, breathing heavily, feeling thrilled that she'd defeated him. He'd be trapped in the shield until she canceled it or the spell wore off. That would give her time.

"You can't keep me here," he said.

"Oh, I can keep you there long enough," she answered, laughing softly.

He reached into his belt and pulled out a pistol. The shield spell would protect her from a bullet, but then another remembrance struck her...

A Semblance who had been hunting Isaac had shot himself to avoid being apprehended. She had been there, as McKenna Foster.

He would kill himself in order to escape the mortal body. She recoiled from the idea, her only thought to protect the host body.

Dropping the shield, she said, *"Aparato!"*

As he lifted the pistol to his temple, a stone struck him on the head, knocking him unconscious.

Annalise approached the still body. The man looked slightly familiar, and Isaac had called him by the name Jack, which was also familiar to her. She'd seen him before but was confused as to the circumstances. Bending low, she wrenched the pistol from his hand and stuffed it into the pocket of her dress. She rose, and noticed that snow had started falling heavily around them.

It was time to disappear.

Aóratos.

There was no way to find Isaac in the snowstorm. What if the Aesir woman had taken him up to the sky ship? She needed help, so as she walked through the empty street cloaked in invisibility, she tried to summon Loyal. Isaac had explained the doglike intelligence to her and how he'd used it to find Eiríka over the centuries. As she walked aimlessly, she continued to send thoughts to the intelligence.

At last, she felt an excited feeling of urgency, like the giddy sensation of soaring on a swing set. She experienced the spectral dog's presence through her feelings.

Take me to Isaac, she pleaded to the intelligence.

A warning feeling came over her. A feeling of concern and danger.

Please, Loyal. Take me to him.

Although there was no audible whine, she felt the intelligence's obvious reluctance. It was difficult to comprehend what her feelings were saying, but it was more that Loyal didn't want to, not that it couldn't.

Please. I must find him. Take me there.

Acquiescence. That was the feeling that came next. She felt the pull to follow a different way. While she was familiar with Tanhauser, it looked very different in a snowstorm, which compromised her sense of direction and made the familiar sights strange to her.

Loyal led her down a street, past another, and then everything became familiar. No more ruins. She was in the theater district. As she passed another building, she saw the theater house where Mr. Froman was preparing to release the new play.

Another whine reached her consciousness. Not exactly a whine, but a worried feeling that niggled in her breast. Part of her mind thought she should be cold, but the winter storm felt pleasant, comforting even. She blinked some of the snow from her eyelashes, then started down the alley leading to the building. Another warning feeling assailed her.

But she was invisible. No one could see her approach.

Before she reached the end of the alley, she paused and listened. A memory of another snowy night struck her. Light flakes. A racking cough. Searching for Isaac in a cramped street. Lydia Brewer. Even the memory made her throat tickle.

She firmed her resolve and walked away from the alley. The clouds were so low they obscured the top of the theater's roof. Stanchions of light were glowing on the walls, lit by orbs of sorcery.

She knew she was walking into a trap. The lights were an obvious invitation to come closer. To spring it. She paused midway there, trying to reason it through. She needed to find Isaac and free him from her father. Then, they had to find a judge to marry them, even if they had to walk all day and night in a blizzard to find one.

Is he in there, Loyal? Is Isaac here?

A throb of warning came, but also acknowledgment. Yes, he was in there—in the theater with all the decorations for the play. Going forward felt hazardous. Loyal was warning her away, and she knew he was right about the risks. Her father would, if he could, try once again to persuade her to choose the Aesir over the mortal world. Each time she had rejected it. She was determined to reject it again.

Glimpses of previous lives fluttered before her eyes. They would give her the strength to proceed. This was the only way to end the war forever. She had to make the right decision, no matter the cost to her personally. No matter how the Erlking threatened her.

Annalise strode forward and reached the doors of the theater. They were locked.

Of course. Why would anything be easy?

"Annixe," she sang and heard the lock click.

To calm her nerves, she began to recite lines from her last play in her mind. She patted the bulk of the pistol in her pocket and then pulled the theater door open. All was dark inside. She could smell the carpet, the varnish. She stepped inside quickly and shut the door, searching the darkness for signs of life. Loyal was at her side. She knew the intelligence would accompany her no matter what.

The carpet muffled her steps. The doors ahead would lead to the audience seating and the stage. *No crowds to see this performance,* she thought with a feeling of dark humor. There was no script either.

Submit to the Erlking's will. Or lose the one you love.

She took a few more steps. Just darkness and silence.

She was halfway across the carpeted front hall when the door leading to the general seating opened and a man appeared with a glowing orb hovering over his shoulder. She recognized him instantly as her bodyguard from Auvinen. Kellin Carrault.

"Welcome, Miss Kauer," he said, holding the doors open. "So glad you could come."

Chapter Thirty-Four
Marriage of True Minds

Annalise was still invisible. She paused. Did Kellin see her, or was he assuming she was there? A knot of worry twisted her stomach. There was still time to run. No, she had a purpose, and she would achieve that purpose.

"Miss Kauer, remove the spell," Kellin said in a kindly way. "There is a Disir perched on the rooftop of the theater, and she saw through your invisibility as you approached. The way forward is the best way. Mr. Froman is waiting for you on the stage."

"You mean my father?" Annalise said, watching as Kellin's head turned slightly to face the direction her voice had come from. He couldn't see her.

"Yes. The Erlking. Your father."

Annalise felt the coil in her stomach tightening even more. She was blasted with the memory of facing him in the snowy courtyard at Nirshoye. McKenna's deafness had saved her from the excruciating storm of magical sound emitted by the bulbs. The memory came and then it went, as capricious as the wind.

"Where is Isaac?" she asked, knowing any information could be helpful.

"He is also on the stage," Kellin said. "What happens next is up to you."

She dropped the invisibility spell, as it no longer served her purposes. His gaze fixed on her with a look of familiarity. Not just as a bodyguard. This was a different look. An intimate one.

"Who are you, Semblance?" she asked him.

"I am the one who has guarded your barrow these many centuries," he said. "To protect it from mortals who wandered too near."

"My barrow? Was I buried, then?"

"In water, my lady. With a philosopher's stone that keeps your Aesir body alive. If you decide to return to us, that is where you will awaken."

She could tell from the tone of his voice that he was hoping she would choose to return. Perhaps in his lonely vigil, he had grown to care for the woman he guarded. She did not know him. There was nothing in her scant memories to suggest it. But there was no mistaking the pleading tone.

Annalise walked toward him, and as soon as she reached him, she gave him a smile and then encased him in the same shield spell she'd used on the Semblance in the street.

Worry creased his brow when he tried to leave the space and could not. "My lady, please..."

"You stay here while I speak with my father," she said. She wanted a way to escape if things did not end well. She sang another shield spell into existence to block off the foyer after she passed the Semblance and entered the theater at the back of the floor seating. Options. She needed to have options.

The theater had been a place of solace for her in this mortal life, but it was no longer comforting to her. There were will-o'-the-wisps of light throughout, providing sufficient illumination for her to see the stage. Mr. Froman stood with his cane near Isaac, who was wearing a Marshalcy jacket and had his hands behind his back.

Glamour spells did not work on her, so she was certain of the identity of the men down below. The stage was set with the props depicting the scene of the Erlking's palace, including a majestic throne and several pale faux-marble pillars that disappeared above the curtain rim. Her heart hammered with trepidation as she started down the aisle steps to the front.

Mr. Froman stepped away from Isaac and approached the edge of the stage, his cane thumping as he walked. With the house lights off and no audience, the massive theater was chilly. Of course the Erlking would prefer it that way.

As she drew nearer, she saw Isaac looking at her with a worried smile. That's when she noticed the noose around his neck. The rope stretched up past the curtains. She immediately halted.

"Excorsia," she sang, uttering a command to sever the rope.

Nothing happened, but a proud little smile stretched across Isaac's face as if he was impressed she'd thought to use that particular spell.

"Welcome, Daughter," Mr. Froman said, giving her a cunning look. He gripped the cane with both hands and stood poised at the edge of the stage. "The rope is invulnerable to magic. I'll just save you further wasted effort."

"Let him go," Annalise said forcefully.

"That is easily arranged, my dear. Just swear an oath that you will come back to the Aesir court and abandon and forsake mortality. He will be set free at once. You have my vow."

Anger began to sizzle inside of her. She wanted to wrest the cane from his hands and beat him with it. But the Erlking had always been a prodigious warrior. Even in mortal form, it would not be easy to best him. And she didn't have all her memories back, which gave him another advantage.

"If I refuse, then what?"

Mr. Froman frowned. "It's rather obvious, isn't it?"

"There must be a clear understanding between us. If I refuse, what will you do?"

"You will watch him die. There are several men waiting to hoist the rope. I have his philosopher's stone, so he will strangle to death. The choice is yours."

It was what she'd expected. He wished to torment her with an impossible choice.

"And if he dies, I can find him again?" Annalise asked.

"Yes, but the next Awakening is in eighty-nine years. There will be no mortals left. You will be stranded as disembodied intelligences. I will be thorough in my extermination of humanity, Daughter. You may count on that."

"Release him and we will discuss this," Eiríka said, wanting to stall for time.

"I decline your request. When I give the command, he will be hoisted into the air. He'll lose consciousness in approximately ten seconds. I've witnessed this form of execution many times, Daughter. Most mortals cannot survive asphyxiation beyond five minutes. That is how much time you have to make your decision."

Five minutes? And that was if Isaac even survived that long. She felt a horrible combination of pain and helpless rage mixed with a determination to save Isaac at all costs. This was the last time. Their last chance.

Mr. Froman began to lift his hand to execute the command.

"Can I speak to him first?" Annalise said.

"By all means. But you may not approach him. My men are at the ready, and they will dangle him beyond your reach if you try. These are my terms. If you desire him to live, then you must make your vow and swear it on the Mind of the Sovereignty. If he perishes because you waited too long, that is not my fault but yours."

Annalise studied the calm expression on Isaac's face. Surely the situation had been explained to him before she'd arrived. If he could have escaped, he would have already. Anguish flooded her. She had to do something to change the terms. Both choices were horrible, but only one of them would lead to Isaac's death. If he lived, the Aesir would still attack humanity, but he could help protect people from the onslaught.

There was a staircase leading up to the stage and she ascended it, but Mr. Froman stood at the top step, clenching his cane in both hands like a weapon.

She gazed at Isaac imploringly. "What should I do?"

"You ask him? He'll beg you to spare his life," Mr. Froman said disdainfully.

"No," Isaac said. "Let them kill me. It is better this way. Your freedom is more important to me."

Annalise was surprised by his answer, and by the startled look on Mr. Froman's face, he was even more so.

"How can I let them kill you?" she said, her heart tearing to pieces. She glared at Mr. Froman. "And if I choose to save him, how do I know you won't kill him anyway?"

"He was always going to die, Daughter. You taught him to create the stone, to become master of a royal secret he never should have learned. I will destroy the stone and allow him to fulfill his natural lifespan. Even if he is the last mortal, I will spare him until he expires of natural causes. You have my vow. Now, do I have yours?"

Annalise looked back at Isaac. He shook his head. "I do this willingly."

"I don't want to lose you," she said, her emotions in upheaval.

"You can't lose me," he said with a tender smile.

"But we were so close!" she said in misery, tears gathering in her eyes.

"Now," Mr. Froman said starkly. She heard the grinding of gears, the stretching of the rope. Isaac was yanked off his feet. He took one last huge gasp before the rope cut off his air and circulation. His ankles were bound. His hands behind his back. She saw his eyes bulge as the constriction started. His body bucked and thrashed.

Annalise grabbed the cane with her right hand, but Mr. Froman was expecting that—what he wasn't expecting was for her to pull the pistol out of her pocket and plant the muzzle against his skull. His eyes popped wide with surprise.

"Let him down, or I'll pull the trigger," she threatened.

Mr. Froman leered at her. "Do it!" he snarled. "You cannot know how I detest this frail form! Do it!"

"*N-nuh!*" A feeble groan came torturously from Isaac's lips. Still holding the pistol to Mr. Froman's temple, Annalise glanced at Isaac and saw a look of true horror on his face. Not from pain, but from what she was about to do.

"Let him go!" Annalise shrieked, jutting her face into Froman's. She wanted to pull the trigger, to end his life as a consequence for ruining hers. Memories of the ruthless way this man's body had choked her to death flooded her. She knew how Isaac felt. But the Erlking was probably counting on that—on her to be impulsive rather than coolly collected.

She could see Isaac's body swaying in her peripheral vision. His head slumped forward as the unconsciousness set in. How many seconds had passed, just a dozen?

"Choose," Froman said. "Spare him. Or not. You've chosen him every time. Why not now? Why hesitate? Pull the trigger!"

"*Eshi omorfi matia!*" she sang, invoking a glamour to deceive the men in the upper scaffolds into believing they needed to rescue the man by letting him down.

"Your spells will not work when I can counteract them!" Mr. Froman boasted. "Without blood flow, his brain is perishing. I restored all his lost memories, which I've been saving. If he dies, they'll be lost! Every one of those lives! Save him, Daughter! If you love him, save him!"

"I *do* love him!" she yelled and sobbed. Should she use the bullet in the pistol to end Isaac's suffering? Or end her own?

She knew she couldn't go back to the Aesir. Not after this. Not after the deliberate torment her father had chosen for this last incarnation.

Annalise lowered the pistol and tossed it aside. She turned and looked at Froman's face as her empty hand joined the other on his cane. "Save his memories," she pleaded. "Don't let them vanish forever."

"Only if you vow to come with me. I will give you this scepter, and you will have those memories to comfort you. Make your choice quickly, child. He's almost dead."

She saw Isaac's body was growing still. He wasn't fighting it. The twitches became less pronounced.

If he died, she'd lose all of him. But would the memories sustain her? She had so few of her own.

Tears ran down her cheeks as she watched the final twitches end. Isaac's face looked peaceful. Serene.

"A minute more," Mr. Froman said dispassionately. "Just to be sure."

She knew the awful grief she felt would linger with her forever. Isaac had willingly sacrificed himself for her. And she would have done the same for him had their roles been reversed. The ache was unbearable. She looked at the pistol lying on the stage floor. Would oblivion end her torment?

What if the Erlking was right, and there were no bodies for them to take over as Semblances next time?

She had to hope humanity would survive. They'd found each other so many times. Maybe they could do it one last time...

"Lower him," Mr. Froman said curtly. The rope creaked and the body was let down until it lay supine on the floor.

"Give me my memories back," Annalise whispered, looking up at Mr. Froman with loathing. "All of them." She released the cane and bowed her head.

If Isaac's memories were to be scattered to the winds, so would hers. She felt the gem of the cane tap her skull. A flood of memories unleashed within her. A thousand lifetimes, surging through her like a river. Some long, some short. The fragments were becoming whole. Her breath caught. It hurt too much to breathe. How many times had their love been tested? How many times had they seen each other die?

Annalise sank to her knees, with hardly any strength left, and crawled to the still body of her beloved. She covered her mouth as she gazed at the peaceful look on his face. He was so handsome to her. This last form had survived so many incarnations, and she remembered them all, including the first.

It had happened so many generations earlier, in a world lit by fire and struggled over with sword and shield. She'd been a Disir, searching the dead for him in a snowstorm.

She opened her eyes and pressed a kiss to his brow, and then she loosened the strangling rope on his neck. Hurriedly, she tugged the loosened rope from his neck and pulled it off and threw it aside.

A puff of cold mist exhaled from his lifeless lips.

Chapter Thirty-Five
A Ship's Captain

Annalise knelt by the body, enduring the familiar grief anew.

This was what it meant to be mortal. An unending series of sorrows. Yet she would not have given up the joy and bliss she'd also known from living in their world.

"We go to Auvinen next," her father said, impervious to her distress. "Justice claimeth its own. I bequeath what remains of this town to you, Daughter. It will be your final refuge before the end. I hope you may endure it well."

She did not look up at him. If she'd learned one thing from living among the mortals it was that they clung tenaciously to life. Her father might think the mortals would be easily extinguished, but she couldn't believe it. There might be one last chance to start again. New bodies. New memories. She reached out and stroked Isaac's cold brow.

The sound of her father's steps and the thump of his cane announced his departure. Noises from the rigging above punctuated the retreat. The Semblances were all leaving, and soon all the will-o'-the-wisps of light vanished with their departure.

"*Hoxta-namorem,*" she sang, heartbroken.

A will-o'-the-wisp appeared just as another tendril of mist crept from Isaac's lips. And then another. Then his chest expanded and a large bloom of mist came from his mouth. His eyes opened and he turned his head to look at her.

"They're gone," he whispered. "Help me with the bonds."

She couldn't believe her eyes, and for a moment she wondered if a cruel glamour had been used to deceive her. But no, he was alive. He was alive!

Isaac squirmed against his bonds, trying to free his arms and ankles. She hurriedly untied the rope around his ankles, then rolled him onto his stomach, surprised by how frigid the coat he wore was to the touch. She'd scarcely noticed it earlier, her attention fixed on his face and his suffering.

The nulling cuffs on his wrists clicked open and fell away, and he instantly rose to his knees and pulled her to him in a fierce embrace.

"I'm sorry you had to endure that, darling," he said, breathing into her neck. "But I couldn't let you know. Not until they were gone."

"How are you even alive?" she gasped in surprise, pulling back a moment, taking his face in her hands.

With a grin, he pushed aside the officer's coat, ducked his hand into the jacket pocket, and retrieved the device. "He didn't know about the enchantment I put on it. The one that recalls this back to me. I mostly relied on pretending I was doomed. I can't suffocate. But I had to pretend it was happening."

"But I saw your breath come out," she said. "The mist—the sign of a Semblance dying."

"It's the jacket," he explained. "Instead of summoning heat through incalescence, it summons cold, similar to the properties locomotivuses used to chill their internal parts. I focused on the buckles at the collar and made them as cold as possible. That way, when I exhaled, it came out as a fog."

She leaned in and kissed his mouth, so proud of him for the trickery that she was willing to forgive the torment she'd endured. Not that it was his fault. She'd needed to believe he was dead so that the Erlking would believe it too.

"You deliciously clever man!" she said, shaking her head after the kiss. "And your memories are restored too?"

"All of them," he said. "And yours?"

"Yes. I feel the thousand lives brimming inside of me."

"We can't delay," Isaac said. "We need to find a magistrate before the stormbreakers make it to Auvinen or it will suffer the same fate as Tanhauser."

He opened his fist and displayed the sorcerer's ring in his palm. He'd squeezed it so hard she could see the imprint of it in his skin. She lifted his hand to her mouth and kissed it again.

"That was a dazzling performance, my love. I'm so impressed."

"Maybe being in a theater helped me," he said, twisting the ring onto his thumb. "The only person I can think of is Mr. Foster. I don't know as many magistrates as he does and who might be the closest."

"Where are they?" Eiríka asked, feeling a twinge of worry about her past family. With all McKenna's memories restored to her, she loved them dearly. Mother, Father, Clara, and Trudie. If they were still in Auvinen, they were in grave danger.

"They are hiding from the Marshalcy," he explained. He bowed his head, and she could see the concentration on his brow. Reaching out, she stroked his hair again.

Eiríka waited, barely able to contain her joy. Isaac had come up with a brilliant scheme to outsmart her father. How had he known that she would choose to watch him die? It seemed like his whole plot revolved around his knowledge of her character. But he knew her better than any living person. He certainly knew her better than her father did.

Isaac's head jerked up, his eyes suddenly wide. She bit her lip and grasped his hand, fearing awful tidings.

Then the startled look on his face relaxed and he began to grin. He quickly rose to his feet and pulled her up with him, clinging to both of her hands. He nodded, as if having a silent conversation with another party, his expression brightening.

A smile of elation spread across his mouth.

"What is it?" she demanded with intense curiosity.

"Captain Belvor," he said in wonder.

"What about him?"

"Captain Belvor can marry us. Mr. Foster said that in this region, because the distance between townships is greater, ship captains like Belvor are authorized to act as magistrate judges to settle disputes in their jurisdictions. I asked him specifically if that also included the right to marry people, and he said they can perform any duty a magistrate judge can fulfill, including performing a marriage."

"Does every ship captain have that right?"

"No," Isaac said. "I'd never even heard of this before, or I would have thought to ask Belvor when we were crossing the lake. But leave it to Mr. Foster to know more about the law than I do!"

"We have to find Belvor," Eiríka said excitedly.

"I've already sent Loyal to see if he's still at the ship."

The snow was deepening in the streets, coming down in endless torrents that reminded Eiríka of countless storms she'd weathered before. She clung to Isaac's hand as he led the way. Loyal had found Captain Belvor in his home near the docks. He lived far enough from the city center for his home to have survived the bombardments from the stormbreakers.

Snow was thick in their hair and on their clothes, but they walked swiftly through the drifts and finally arrived at a quaint hilled area near the shore of the lake just at the edge of town. The distant mountains surrounding the lake were veiled by the storm, the wind whistled over the flat plain of the frozen lake.

Captain Belvor's home was a beautiful three-level structure with steeply sloped roofs, a half-dozen chimneys, and an assortment of snow-laden trees. The lawns were completely hidden by the results of the weather.

Isaac and Eiríka hurried up to the doorstep, and he pounded on the door.

"Easy, Loyal," Isaac said.

Eiríka could sense the invisible dog's eagerness. Every moment that passed felt like a huge delay, and she squeezed Isaac's hand with her own in anticipation and pressed the other to his arm.

She heard the sound of footsteps and then the door opened and Captain Belvor appeared holding a pistol in one hand.

"What are you doing here?" he demanded, his brow wrinkling in confusion. "Are you fleeing the Marshalcy?"

"May we come in?" Isaac pleaded.

"Of course," he said, lowering the pistol and putting it in his belt. "When we landed, I saw the destruction and hurried home to protect my wife. They say the Awakening has happened and the Aesir are attacking again."

"It's true," Isaac said. They entered the house, and Captain Belvor shut the door. He was still wearing his clothes from earlier, except his captain's jacket was gone, replaced by a long plush robe.

"The world is coming to an end," Belvor said with a sigh. He looked at Eiríka. "I can't take you back to your estate. The lake is frozen."

"We need you to marry us, Captain Belvor," she blurted. "Right now."

He gave her an astonished look and then lifted his brow questioningly at Isaac.

"If the world is ending," Isaac said, "we'd like to end it together. As man and wife."

"Now, that's the oddest request I've had in a while," the captain said, rubbing his chin.

His wife, a friendly-looking woman, appeared in the doorway. "Did I hear that right?" she asked, approaching them. "I'm Janae Belvor. Is that you, Miss Kauer?"

"Hello, Mrs. Belvor," Eiríka said, nodding to her.

"My husband told me that you'd been his passenger these last two days," she said eagerly. "And you want to get married? That's so sweet."

"Please, sir," Isaac said. "It is urgent we do this."

"I'll get the book," Mrs. Belvor said.

"How many witnesses do we need?" Isaac asked.

"Two are typically required," Captain Belvor said.

"I'll fetch Alice from the kitchen," Mrs. Belvor exclaimed.

Eiríka squeezed Isaac's hand again.

"Let me get my captain's jacket and hat," Belvor said. Eiríka felt a burst of warning from Loyal.

"Someone's coming," Isaac said. He pulled his hand free and hurried to the door to gaze outside.

Captain Belvor returned with his jacket and hat, and soon afterward, Mrs. Belvor appeared with the ledger and a woman in an apron who appeared to be their cook.

Isaac put the curtain back and began to sing a shield spell.

"Please perform the ceremony," Eiríka said urgently.

"I need your names."

"Isaac Berrow and Annalise Kauer," she said.

"You should both be holding hands, standing here before me," the captain said, brow wrinkling with worry.

"Quickly, Captain," Eiríka said, then began adding a harmony to Isaac's song to bolster his shield.

Mrs. Belvor glanced at the couple worriedly. This was probably different from any wedding her husband had done before in all likelihood.

"We are gathered today to witness the union of this man and this woman. Do you, Isaac Berrow— *hmpfh*"—upon saying the notorious name, the captain rolled his eyes disdainfully before continuing—"take Annalise Kauer as your lawful wedded wife?"

"I do," Isaac said, glancing back at the door.

Eiríka kept singing, squeezing Isaac's hand. The door's handle rattled.

"Someone else is here," the captain said, looking over their shoulders.

"Eshi omorfi matia," Eiríka sang, conjuring a glamour to prevent the captain and his household from being distracted by the noise.

The captain smiled broadly as if nothing were amiss. "Do you, Annalise Kauer, take this man, Isaac Berrow, to be your lawful wedded husband?"

"I do," she declared with all her heart.

"By my duty as a magistrate judge in this region and under the authority of the emperor—"

A fist began to pound against the door. Then a boot struck it. The shield held.

The captain continued as if nothing were wrong, "I pronounce you, Isaac Berrow, and you, Annalise Kauer, husband and wife, legally married till death you depart."

"Till death us depart," Eiríka breathed.

"Till death us depart," Isaac said, his shoulders slumping. He fished his hand into his pocket, pulled out the device, and opened it. His brow wrinkled with concern. From her perspective, she could see the number hadn't changed.

A body slammed against the door.

"It needs to be recorded!" Isaac said, looking at Eiríka.

"How could we forget!" Mrs. Belvor said with an easy smile. She opened the ledger and took it to the table. Cracks appeared in the glass in the upper part of the door, spreading like spiderwebs. But the shield held firm.

Captain Belvor asked for the spellings of their names, and Eiríka provided them while her husband maintained the shield spell and kept glancing at the door.

The captain wrote the information in, then handed the pen to his wife, who signed in the witness column. Alice, the cook, signed it next, although she did so very slowly.

Isaac looked down at the device again, and they both watched as the three numbers vanished, leaving the crystal void of runes.

Two witnesses. One magistrate. And words scribbled on paper. That was all it had taken.

Eiríka gazed at the door. The pounding had stopped.

Issac Berrow

Chapter Thirty-Six
The Royal Secret

The weight of a thousand lifetimes sloshed inside Isaac. The memories. The emotions. But they were murky, hidden for so long that it would take time to re-assemble them all. He was relieved too, of course—deeply relieved that he'd accomplished what had seemed impossible. The inaudible sense of Loyal barking frantically cut through his surging relief. He could sense the Semblance who had been Jack Farmer was still outside.

Isaac glanced at Eiríka, comforted by the warmth of her hand in his own, walked to the door, and lowered the shield. Up until the wedding ceremony, he had experienced the screaming of Jack's thoughts in his mind, trying to threaten or cajole him into not marrying her. It was all he could do to block those thoughts, but they'd suddenly ended after the vows had been recorded.

It seemed likely that the Erlking had discovered the ruse and Jack had been the only Semblance close enough to try to intercede. Had the rest abandoned their mortal bodies and returned to their Aesir ones? He didn't know the answer for certain, but it felt like a reasonable guess.

Isaac twisted the handle and opened the door, and a gust of snow came across the threshold. Jack stood there, shoulders slumped in defeat. Many spots on the window had fractured and the glass showered down now.

"The Erlking is coming back," Jack said listlessly.

"Has he conceded?" Isaac demanded. He gripped Eiríka's hand tightly.

"Yes. All the bombardments have ceased. The stormbreakers will return here to Tanhauser. We will gather as the Erlking prepares to open a rift in the sky to another world. We need all the ships to gather in one place to make the transit."

Isaac's internal relief was palpable, but he worried about what would become of the other world the Aesir journeyed to.

"And by the covenant, the Aesir can never return here," Isaac said.

"The Erlking cannot violate his oath. Unlike mortals." There wasn't any disdain in his voice. In fact, he sighed.

"You don't want to go?" Eiríka asked, her voice showing confusion.

Jack looked at her. "In a former life, I was Joseph Crossthwait. I served General Colsterworth and hunted down Semblances unwittingly. Some of us...some *preferred* living in the mortal world. And now we must go."

Isaac stared at him. "You would choose to stay if you could?"

He nodded glumly before meeting Eiríka's gaze. "You were not wholly alone in your beliefs, my lady. Justice demanded we serve the Erlking. But there were some who were rooting for you. Others will be only too grateful to abandon this heated rock."

"But can you choose to stay?" Isaac asked.

Jack shook his head. "We have no choice but to abandon the world, per the covenant. The only way to change that fate would be if you, Eiríka, permitted it. If you had mercy on those of us who would wish to stay."

Isaac looked at Eiríka's face and saw she was listening keenly. "You desire...mercy?"

"It was mercy that started this war," Jack said. "And it is

justice that has ended it. You were shown no mercy, my lady. Not once during your many lifetimes. We cannot expect you to—"

Eiríka held up her hand to forestall him. "But is it even possible for you to stay? What happens to our Aesir bodies?"

Jack looked at both of them before answering her. "For Semblances, the intelligences are exchanged. Without an intelligence, even an Aesir body will die. The Erlking's scepter enables this transfusion. The intelligence of Jack Farmer is in my Aesir body at the moment, keeping it alive. Trapped, if you will. That is why the transfer must happen at the brink of death. When the untethering of the body from the intelligence happens."

"If you stay," Isaac asked, "will that sever the connection permanently?"

"It will," Jack answered. "It means we inherit a body that ages and can die. Unless we have a philosopher's stone like yours."

"Can you access Jack's intelligence? You have access to his memories right now?"

"I do, because of the connective magic that makes all of this possible. Most Semblances want to remain connected to our Aesir forms. Some of us want the transfer to be permanent, even if we lose immortality as a result."

"Can you both inhabit the same body?" Isaac pressed. He didn't want to lose Jack. To have him severed from his body forever. To make True a widow.

"It would be a sharing of lives, yes."

"But you couldn't have your own?"

"Not without the magic of transition, which only the Erlking knows."

Isaac wanted to be sure he understood this correctly. "So the Erlking can put Jack's intelligence back into that body and put yours into another one? He has that authority?"

"He does. But I dare not even hope..." He gave Eiríka a beseeching look.

Eiríka reached out and touched his shoulder. "You may dare."

Jack's expression filled with wonder, and then he dropped

hastily to his knee. He clasped his hands together tightly. "If you would allow me, and others, to stay, I cannot express my gratitude. I cannot say what it would mean to us."

Eiríka looked at Isaac and quirked her brow. Some emotions, when experienced for the first time, were overpowering. He was proud of her for being willing to allow some Aesir to remain behind. There was much they could learn from each other.

The Erlking arrived at the still intact theater in the middle of Tanhauser. The storm had ended, although the cold had sheathed everything in hoar frost. Isaac and Eiríka stood hand in hand by the entrance to the theater. Jack stood off to one side, as did several other Semblances who had come to petition Eiríka to remain with the mortals.

The Erlking had shed the Semblance of Mr. Froman, and he appeared in his regal glory, much as he had when they'd encountered each other at the University of Nirshoye. He still had scars on his face from that elfshot blast. The Erlking stood erect, holding the ancient jeweled scepter he'd transformed into a cane to use in his mortal disguise. With the imperiousness of the look on his face, the disdain he had toward them could be viscerally felt. His armor gleamed in the sunlight. While Isaac could see his own breath, he could see no puffs of mist coming from the Erlking as he advanced and stopped in front of them. Bog beasts were flying in the sky over the ruined city, like vultures over carrion.

YOU HAVE SUCCEEDED, MORTAL. BEYOND EXPECTATIONS.

The force of his thoughts banged around in Isaac's mind like a bell ringing in a tower.

"Can we speak out loud so that your daughter may hear?" Isaac said.

The Erlking's lip twisted into a snarl. "So be it." He probably preferred the shout-like mental commands.

"Thank you for honoring the terms of the covenant," Isaac said, showing meekness. He still felt vulnerable. The Erlking could easily draw his two-handed Aesir blade and cut them both in half with it.

"I can do no less," said the Erlking dispassionately. "You have made your choice, Daughter. I will honor mine. But there is a matter we should discuss."

"Those who wish to remain here," Eiríka said.

"I demand that you refuse all of their requests," the Erlking said. "They are bound to me by oath. Their loyalty has ever been precious to me." He said it in a condescending way that showed he was furious at those who'd declared their wish to remain behind.

Eiríka looked more confident with all her memories returned. "And they must abide the terms of the covenant...unless I permit them to stay. I can grant them mercy."

"And why would you wish to redeem those who sought your harm? Who obeyed my commands even if it meant killing those you loved?"

"What is it to you if I agree?" Eiríka asked.

"Defiant child," the Erlking snarled.

"Impatient father," Eiríka said simply.

Isaac felt the tension rising between them and decided to intercede. "In your brief sojourn as one of us, Your Majesty, I am sure you have come to appreciate the vicissitudes of mortal emotions."

He felt Eiríka squeeze his hand. Maybe she was approving of his choice of words?

"They are tedious and bothersome," the Erlking said. "Mortals seek to dupe and trick one another. They preen and posture for eminence. They participate in folly."

"This is true," Isaac said. "But they can also be compassionate. Fiercely loyal. And demonstrate remarkable creativity."

"Most do not," the Erlking said with savage contempt.

"I agree," Isaac said. "Most are victims to their circumstances."

"They pollute the air, the waters, the ground. They maliciously deceive and annoy one another. And a few will even kill if they believe they'll not suffer for the misdeed."

"All true." Isaac agreed. "But there is freedom to act, to make decisions, to build or destroy. To create or to burn. We accept that good comes with the bad."

"Insufferable," the Erlking said, puffing out his chest. He looked at Eiríka. "So you are serious about allowing them to *choose* to wither and die? To forsake their inheritance of immortality and beggar themselves for base emotions?"

"For those who choose to, yes," Eiríka said, refraining from lashing back. Isaac pressed her hand gently.

"Their attachments to their Aesir bodies must be forfeit," the Erlking said. "They must accept mortality. Full of sickness. Bile. Subject to illness, fatigue, emotional malaise."

"They have already experienced these things," Eiríka said. "And if they choose to embrace this world, I will permit it on one condition."

"You have no right to demand anything of me!" he growled.

"I do not," she said. "But it would be the honorable thing to return to the bodies those intelligences that were taken away without consent."

"A worm does not consent to be stepped on," said the Erlking flippantly. "Yet it is still a worm."

"I seek justice and mercy," Eiríka said. "Those who are willing to coexist may be granted that opportunity. Those who wish to have their bodies back—"

"But they were already dead," the Erlking protested. "Their lives were forfeit. They can keep the bodies they have now."

"But how many of those mortals were killed by our people?" Eiríka said patiently. "They did not die of natural causes."

"Yet they could have died minutes later, run over by one of those abominable machines. What difference does it make?"

"It makes a difference to me," Eiríka said. "Teach me the magic that creates the bond. Or transfers it. You have always jealously guarded that final secret."

"You accuse me of jealousy?" the Erlking said with anger flashing in his eyes.

Eiríka sighed. "I meant it in another manner, Father. It also means 'to fiercely protect or be vigilant in one's rights and possessions.' There are many nuances in language."

Isaac almost grinned when she said it, especially since her alternative definition mollified her father.

The Erlking weighed the comment and nodded in agreement. "As I should be. It is my right to be so guarded."

"It will take time to sort out those who choose to stay. And you should not linger, for that would not be just." She arched her eyebrows at him.

"The word you seek is a powerful one," the Erlking said. "I forbid that it be taught to anyone, especially within the infernal order of the Invisible College," he added bitingly, giving Isaac a glare. "Which has been lax in sharing our secret knowledge. The word is vital to life itself. Only one of royal lineage may be taught it."

"Am I sufficiently royal?" she asked, tilting her head.

"I will teach you, Daughter. Guard it *jealously*."

Thirty-three Aesir stormbreakers had gathered in the sky over Tanhauser, and they made for an imposing sight. Over the centuries, no one had known how many Aesir ships there were. Thirty-three was an auspicious number, a master number in some traditions. The knowledge that these ships bore the remnants of the Aesir race made Isaac nervous and wary.

Isaac and Eiríka waited just outside the theater building. All the Semblances who had chosen to remain behind and accept a mortal life had gathered to the theater and remained inside to avoid the ire of the Erlking for their lack of loyalty. As soon as the Erlking left, their attachments to their Aesir bodies would be severed, and there would be no way to rejoin their people. What surprised Isaac was how many had chosen to adopt a mortal life. There were eighteen, an equal mix of male and female.

Through the spell the Erlking had taught Eiríka, all the mortal intelligences had been restored to their original bodies, so they were adapting to the strange sensation of having an Aesir alter ego within them. After the Aesir were gone, it would be up to Isaac and Eiríka to find new bodies for those who wanted to separate.

WE ARE READY TO DEPART.

The thought echoed loudly and forcibly in Isaac's mind. He quickly screwed the sorcerer's ring onto his thumb.

"Is it time?" Eiríka asked, seeing what he'd done.

"They're leaving now," Isaac said. For him, it would be a vast relief once they were gone. The war between their peoples was finally ending.

She squeezed his arm, craning her neck to look up into the sky and watch.

Safe journeys, my lord, Isaac thought to the Erlking.

YOU ARE WEARISOME TO ME.

Isaac knew the Erlking would never give a traditional farewell.

Your wisdom and understanding have benefited us. I thank you for your generosity.

ENOUGH FLATTERY, MORTAL. I GIVE YOU ONE LAST SECRET OF LEARNING. HOW TO SHIELD AND UNSHIELD A MIND FROM PENETRATION. IT IS THE SPELL THAT PREVENTED MY DAUGHTER FROM BEING SUBJECT TO GLAMOUR AND THE WHIMS OF MORTAL THOUGHTS.

Isaac had wondered whether Eiríka would be susceptible to glamour after the Aesir were gone. He'd assumed her father was behind her immunity, and also her inability to hear thoughts sent by one of the Aesir rings. It would make sense if the Erlking were behind that since it had made it more difficult for her and Isaac to find each other over the centuries.

You are beneficent.

YOU ARE TEDIOUS. BUT NOT UNWISE.

Not too short of a compliment, so Isaac accepted it.

THE PHRASE IS 'SKOTIA PHAINEI,' SUNG IN THIS TRIAD. Isaac heard the music in his mind, sung in perfect pitch.

TO REVERSE IT: 'SKOTIA KATELABEN,' IN THIS TRIAD. It was a different sequence, the triad in reverse, which made sense, the one triad undoing the other one. He thought it interesting that the Aesir word for darkness—*"skotia"*—was part of the spell. In the extreme regions where the Aesir lived, up at the axis of the planet, half the year was spent in perpetual darkness.

YOU MUST PRESS YOUR FINGER ON HER FORE-HEAD TO DO OR UNDO IT. OR TO ANY MORTAL WHO NEEDS TO BLOCK THEIR THOUGHTS. THIS IS MY LAST GIFT OF KNOWLEDGE BEFORE I GO.

Will you teach me the spell to open the rift between worlds? Isaac implored eagerly.

THAT KNOWLEDGE IS FORBIDDEN YOU. ONLY THE UNWEARYING ONES MAY LEARN IT.

Isaac had no idea what that meant. *Who are the unwearying ones?*

YOU GROW TIRESOME, MORTAL. THEY ARE THE EMISSARIES OF THE MIND OF THE SOVEREIGNTY. MESSENGERS OF WRATH AND DOOM. BEWARE OF THEM. THEIR COMING IS BUT A HARBINGER OF MISERY.

How will I recognize one?

THEY COME IN MANY GUISES NOT MADE OF GLAMOUR. BE WATCHFUL. BE WARY. BE WARNED. THEIR MAGIC MANIPULATES FEELINGS. YOU WILL WANT TO TRUST THEM.

What else can you teach us of these beings? he thought frantically.

FAREWELL, MORTAL. WE HAVE SHIELDED YOU FROM THEM THUS FAR.

Isaac wanted to ask more, but then he heard a beautiful sound, an anthem of power coming from the ships in the sky. It was a chorus sung by the Aesir that made the air throb. His emotions were stirred by the uncanny sound, which grew louder and louder. A whorl of color formed in the sky, like the gathering of rose petals with each a different hue. A vortex bloomed in the middle and opened until he could see a gathering blackness brimming with stars at its center. The pavement trembled at the music.

These were sounds from instruments he hadn't even known existed.

"Shades," Eiríka whispered in awe, gripping his arm more tightly.

A rift had opened to another part of the universe.

Isaac stared as the stormbreakers, led by the Erlking's vessel undoubtedly, began to aim toward the rift and then disappeared within it. One by one, all thirty-three ships ventured into the blackness of space. And then the shimmering, multicolored wreath of lights wrapped in on itself and disappeared, and the majestic anthem that had summoned it was silenced.

"It's gone," Eiríka said, stiffening.

"They are gone," Isaac said.

"No, I mean the connection." She let go of his arm and pressed her hand to her bosom. "I felt something snap inside of me. Like a taut strand was cut. I know where my Aesir body was. I've always felt connected to it, but that connection is gone now." He detected in her voice a twinge of sadness, or was it regret?

The door of the theater opened and Jack Farmer came out, along with the other Semblances who had chosen to stay behind.

"The Erlking said that would happen after they left," Isaac told her. "All of the connections were severed."

He wanted to tell her about the warning he'd received from her father, but it wasn't the right moment. As Jack and the others approached, he and Eiríka turned to face them.

"I felt it the moment they were gone," Jack said, patting his chest.

"How does it feel having another soul inside you?" Isaac asked.

"I'd be lying if I said it wasn't an odd feeling," Jack replied. "When I was in the Aesir body, it felt like I was asleep. And the only way I could feel like myself again was through dreams. But now we're both sharing this one, and he's taken some steps back. He wants his own body again. Interesting fellow."

"He was a military officer who hunted Semblances," Isaac said.

"I know," Jack said, tapping his forehead with his finger. "I have his memories still. I'm going to head south to Bishopsgate. I need to let True know I'm still alive. I miss her very much."

"I'm sure you do," Eiríka said with a lovely smile. She grabbed Isaac by the arm. "Do you think it's safe if they go back to Auvinen? To the house on Brake Street?"

"I don't know," Isaac said. "The laws still forbid the use of magic."

"The laws can be changed," said one of the others who had gathered near. A woman. "We were in the upper echelons of government. All of the Semblances in positions of power had to abandon their mortal bodies to return to their Aesir forms. There will be some confusion, but they will need an explanation of what happened."

"They'll need the Invisible College again," Jack said, looking at Isaac seriously.

"It could be helpful," Isaac said. "But to be honest, someone else needs to lead it. I could use some rest." He patted Eiríka's arm.

Jack smiled knowingly. "You need to tell the Fosters the truth."

Isaac looked at Eiríka, an idea forming in his mind. "Gather the family to Brake Street if it's safe. But give us a few days here first. We haven't had our honeymoon yet."

Most of the boats that had been made to be propelled by intelligences had been decommissioned or retrofitted with steam engines. But with Captain Belvor's help, they discovered one in storage at one of the lakeside properties. Belvor knew the owner and persuaded him to let Isaac and Eiríka borrow it so they could quickly return to Caddam House on the other side of the lake.

When they returned, before dusk, they removed the glamour from Maud Jenkins, restoring her own memories, and told her the story of what had happened in Tanhauser and that the Aesir had left for good. Jynnifer arranged a lovely dinner for them all to share before twilight settled in. Snow still covered the grounds and fir trees, but the storm had passed and patches of snow were already starting to melt. The view outside the windows was mesmerizing, and Isaac felt a calmness that he hadn't known he could feel again. He stared out at the landscape, but his mind was still a little wary of possible dangers. There was a nagging worry about where the Aesir had gone off to, but he hoped it was another ice-filled planet where they could build new palaces and create a world that would endure for millennia to come.

He hadn't even known Eiríka had slipped away—nor how long he'd stood at the bank of windows—until she returned wearing a nightdress and walked over to the harp.

He realized he didn't hear any sounds in the house except for the soft footfalls of her bare feet on the floor.

"Where is everyone?" he asked, giving her a look of admiration. His emotions and longings stirred. With all they'd been through since they'd left Caddam House, to return two days later, they'd hardly had any time alone, except for an interlude at the same hotel where they'd spent the first night of their honeymoon as McKenna and Robinson.

"I told them we'd appreciate some privacy since we're so newly married," Eiríka said, giving him an inviting look. He swallowed, feeling himself react to her words.

"I would love to hear you play," he said, joining her at the harp as she sat down on the little seat and positioned herself with the harp between her legs. He stood behind her, hand on her shoulder.

She lifted her arms and began to pluck at the strings. A web of music filled the room as her body swayed to the rhythm of the song. It was a piece he didn't recognize, but the melody was gentle and lovely.

Isaac bent down and kissed the slope of her neck.

"You're making it difficult to concentrate," she murmured.

Dropping to one knee behind her, he pulled the collar of the nightdress down, exposing her shoulder, and kissed it.

"Isaac," she breathed, the notes muddling a little. Then she stopped and twisted her neck to face him, and they kissed slowly, tenderly, sharing the warmth of their exchanged breaths. The kiss became passionate, and then he broke it off and leaned back a little.

"Why are you stopping?" she said, reaching for a fistful of his shirt.

He lifted his forehead to hers and sang the triad. *"Skotia phainei."*

Her nose wrinkled slightly. She looked around and lifted an eyebrow. "I don't think your spell worked, Isaac. The darkness isn't shining. Were you trying to summon the dawn?"

"I knew *'skotia'* meant *darkness*, but I wasn't sure about *'phainei.'*"

"What was the spell supposed to do?" she asked.

He reached into his pocket and produced the device. Then he slid the sorcerer's ring onto his thumb.

We've had many lives together, he thought to her. Her eyes widened with surprise and delight. *Some were cut very short. Cruelly short. But I thought tonight, we might go back to the one that inspired me to create the Invisible College. It started in a shabby little dormitory on a snowy night.*

"You want me to be Lydia again?" she asked, touching his hand tenderly. "How sweet. But you can't be that awkward young man anymore. The glamours don't work on me."

"Well, they do now," he said, leaning down and kissing her throat. *"Eshi omorfi matia."*

He transformed both of them. He became that studious young man without any social graces. He placed her in the dress he'd bought for her on their hastened wedding day rather than the threadbare rags she'd worn upon their first meeting.

And it wasn't just the looks, but they both remembered everything about how it had felt that first time, when she'd revealed who she was to him. And he had fallen in love with her without understanding what love meant.

A delighted smile lifted her lips. "This could be *very* fun, my clever husband," she said, leaning in and kissing him until they were both breathless.

Mckenna Aurora Foster

Epilogue
Reunion on Brake Street

Rob and McKenna turned the final corner and she could see the house at last. Since arriving at the station that morning, every sight and smell was achingly familiar. And in this life she could finally *hear* Auvinen, the bustling town of her childhood, which had once been the epicenter of the industry of magic. Gripping Rob's hand, she walked through the teeming streets, seeing it with new eyes because she remembered everything that had happened both before her time here and after. But visiting the family home at Brake Street was something she'd been anticipating all day.

They paused there, taking in the nostalgic sight, hand in hand. The last time she'd been there, only the incinerated remains of the home had been left behind. But it had been rebuilt not long after the convocation. The walk was lined with plum trees void of leaves. In her mind, she remembered spring blossoms.

"Is it how you remembered?" Rob asked her. They had assumed the personas of Rob and McKenna, along with the clothing, and for Eiríka, the appearance of the Fosters' daughter. A glamour spell was in full effect, though they still remembered their true selves. There was no magical amnesia this time.

"One of my favorite memories," she said, leaning her head on his shoulder, "was when you escorted me home that night during the blizzard."

"I didn't think you were going to come for a lesson that afternoon," he said with a laugh.

"And miss getting tutored by my handsome and caring teacher?" she teased, giving him a smile.

She saw his cheeks flush a little at the compliment. "I fell in love with you very quickly that time," he said. "And I made you furious by assigning you to work with Miss...oh, what was her name?"

"Miss Hurst," McKenna said, with a pang of sympathy. She'd always had a good memory. Ella Florence Hurst. And she'd died from the Aesir plague that had been unleashed on Auvinen. She felt the loss still, although it comforted her to know that no further magical diseases would be unleashed on the populace.

"That's right. Miss Hurst. I'd become so fond of you by then that I didn't feel it was proper to teach you privately when I was more inclined to woo you."

"I thought you were much older than me at first," McKenna said. "Little did we know that *I* was the older one! By far!"

Rob laughed. They lingered at the street corner for a few moments more, until she was ready to continue. Jack was already at the house, as were Clara and Wickins.

"I think I'm ready," McKenna said with a sigh. "I wish the street was thick with snow the way it was that night."

"I'm even missing Aunt Margaret standing sentinel on the porch, awaiting our return," Rob said.

"If only she'd known the truth," McKenna said. "If I hadn't gone with her to Mowbray House, I wouldn't have almost drowned and it might have taken a little longer for us to come together. I think Father would have preferred if we'd waited a few more years."

"He came around, though," Rob said with a twinkle in his eye.

"I miss them so much," McKenna said, her heart swelling. "You've had chances to see them since the Skrýmir. I haven't."

"They'll be…startled. But it's time they knew the full truth."

"And we wouldn't want them to worry that you're also married to a famous actress," McKenna said cheerily. "I do still want to act, you know."

"And I'll enjoy watching you perform," Rob said.

"I found Mr. Froman's copy of the play," she said. "I've thought about changing it, especially the ending. She could learn that her mortal lover didn't betray her and she chooses him instead. And her father comes to accept her choice and blesses their union."

"It is fictional, after all," Rob said wryly.

She butted her shoulder against his. "I think someday, another century from now, when the horror of war is over and people have forgotten the damage the Aesir did, we can change the enmity people feel toward the Aesir. They may even start to romanticize the race."

"There is much to admire about your people," Rob said. "And in a hundred years, the Invisible College will be respected again. Magic will be useful. Where will we be in a hundred years, Miss McKenna?"

"That's the best part of all," she said, beaming at him. "Wherever it is, it will be lovely as long as we're together. We'll be able to watch it all happen. To nudge things along now and then. And we'll watch for the unwearying ones my father warned you about."

"That means no Skrýmir, then," Rob said.

She nodded in agreement. "Not until we know things are truly safe. You never know. The *strannik* might come back."

"If he does, we'll be watching for him," Rob said with a wary smile.

"I think I'm ready now," McKenna said, mustering her courage. She leaned up and kissed his cheek. "Thanks for letting me do this at my own pace."

"There's no need to rush. Should I warn them we're coming?"

"No," McKenna said. "Let's surprise them."

They began walking up Brake Street, and she enjoyed the sound of their shoes on the sidewalk. The trill of birds. She could have glamoured herself into being deaf again, but she wanted to hear their voices. Wanted to experience a conversation without looking from face to face and reading lips. Though she was grateful for all she'd learned and overcome.

When they reached the little gate, Rob bent to undo the latch and opened it. Hand in hand, they walked up to the front door and knocked, and her giddy excitement and nerves made her knees tremble. They looked just as Rob and McKenna had in that life, even down to the style of their clothes, which had definitely drawn some looks as they'd walked through the city.

McKenna made out the sound of light steps approaching. The door opened, and there stood her mother. She had a pleasant smile, full of wrinkles, and her hair was gray and neatly coiffed. Her smile faded into a look of astonishment and disbelief.

"I'm home," McKenna said, her voice thick. "It's me. I'm home."

Mrs. Foster looked to Rob, her eyes filling with tears, pleading for affirmation that this wasn't a trick.

At his nod, Mrs. Foster gasped and flew to her, pulling her into a fierce embrace. "McKenna!"

McKenna felt her own tears streaming down her cheeks as her mother hugged her, kissed her, clasped her face in her hands with a mixture of anguish and relief.

"I'm home, Mama," McKenna said. "It's me."

"How?" Mrs. Foster pleaded earnestly. "This is so hard to take, but I can't...I don't want to disbelieve this."

"We'll explain everything," Rob said. "Gather the rest of the family."

The welcome McKenna received tugged and yanked at her heart. Clara and Wickins arrived first. Clara looked so much like Mother the resemblance was almost frightening. Wickins was older and wiser looking, a professorial type in his tweed jacket. Trudie came bounding down the stairs after hearing all the commotion, and seeing the once little girl as a full-grown woman had McKenna in tears that dripped down her nose as she embraced her younger sister. Jack came down and shook Rob's hand, giving them both a smile.

"Where's Father?" McKenna asked chokingly.

And then he was there. She'd expected to find him in the parlor in his favorite chair—or one that at least resembled it—but he'd made it to the corridor before he'd stopped, transfixed, at the scene in the front hall. He squinted at her, mouth moving without words, and she ran to him and hugged him fiercely and kissed his cheek.

After the initial commotion was over, they gathered in the parlor. It was different from her memory, but it still had a Broadwood grand, and she wanted so badly to hear her mother play it. She and Rob sat squished together on one of the couches, grasping each other's hands as the emotions of the moment surged through her. The wallpaper was different. But it was close enough, and there, outside the open curtain, she saw a greenhouse very similar to the one that had been lost in the fire. So many memories of this life swirled within her.

"I don't think I can speak without sobbing," McKenna murmured to Rob. "Can you tell them?"

Eager eyes were fixed on them from every direction, as the family found seats around the room. It felt so wonderful to be there with them. She loved them and needed them still. Being cast off by her own father, who had never forgiven the mortals for the death of his wife, had robbed her of familial bonds. The Fosters were a refreshing reminder of the true meaning of family.

"It is so good to be here again," Rob said with tenderness. "To see you all. Let me explain all that I could not explain before. You know me as Robinson Dickemore Hawksley. But he is an invention. A glamour, if you will, that I chose before I came to Auvinen and met you all. My real name is Isaac Berrow. And this is Eiríka, the Erlking's daughter. But she is also McKenna, *your* McKenna. All her memories are intact. And so is her love."

"Do you mean she was never a Semblance?" Mr. Foster asked, his brow wrinkling.

"She was a Semblance for most of her life. Your daughter died during the fever as a child. That's when the Erlking put Eiríka's intelligence into McKenna's body. When she almost drowned in Siaconset, the magic began to unravel and she started to remember who she was. The magic failed in Nirshoye, and her intelligence was swept off again to join another life. Which it did in the form of Annalise Kauer when she was sixteen years old and her manager, Mr. Froman, killed her. But she is no longer a Semblance. All of her memories from all of her lives have been returned to her. The connection to her Aesir body is gone. And so are the Aesir. They have left this world forever."

McKenna could sense the various emotions the family was navigating. This was difficult information, but they all seemed to accept it.

"Are you saying, old chap," Wickins said, "that you are *the* Isaac Berrow? The founder of the Invisible College?"

"I am," Rob said with a humble nod. "Eiríka and I have been searching for each other for a thousand lifetimes. Remember the runes on my device? I came to learn of Eiríka when I was a student at the university. I was a Semblance myself and didn't know it. Eiríka came to me in another guise and taught me the truth about herself and the covenant we'd made with the Erlking. If we managed to find each other and marry each other one thousand times, the Erlking and the Aesir would forsake our world. That was the only way to end the war. McKenna and Robinson were number nine hundred and ninety-nine. Isaac and Annalise made it one thousand."

"That's why you were looking for a magistrate in Tanhauser," Mr. Foster said in amazement. "We'd heard reports the city was in ruins."

"We were there during the destruction," McKenna said,

finally able to find her voice. "Isaac tricked the Erlking into believing he was dead, so they left. Thanks to your help, Father, we found the captain of a ship who married us. That stopped the bombardment. We've been in the Lake Country celebrating. But how I longed to return and tell you the truth. A truth I didn't know as McKenna Foster until the very end."

Mrs. Foster put her hand on her nose, stifling a sob.

"I cannot thank you in words, but I will try," McKenna said, looking at each of them in turn. "I didn't know I was a Semblance until that accident in the sea. That's when I started to have memories of my past lives." She settled her gaze on her mother. "You were willing to protect me. Even if I was the enemy. You couldn't have known that I'd chosen to leave my father and my people because of my love for this man." She clenched Rob's hand. "I think the Erlking expected you to send me to an asylum for the deaf. Where I'd be lost and Rob couldn't find me. But instead, you treated me with love and compassion and gave me everything I needed to succeed in a world where Society condemned those who were different. There are no words that can express how I feel." She pressed her other hand against her bosom. "You were the best family, the best sisters, the best parents I could have had."

She noticed a little look of shame in Clara's eyes. Maybe she felt undeserving of the praise for how she'd sometimes treated McKenna because of her disadvantage.

"Clara," McKenna said. "None of us were perfect, me included. But I always knew you loved me. Trudie—you were so dear to me and I am so happy you've found love, even though your husband did try to stop our marriage," she said with a little laugh. "He will be the first one we will help separate from the Aesir soul locked inside of him. Wickins...you were amazing. Without your help, the inventions wouldn't have happened as quickly. And you saved many lives forewarning of the Aesir attack that day." She started to cry again and had to pause to compose herself. "Mother. You were my guardian. My defender. You gave up so much to be my mother. Papa...you are the father I finally learned to trust." She could barely get the words out.

She watched matching tears flowing down the cheeks of her family. Rob helped her stand when her parents did, and they embraced in the middle of the room. It was the homecoming she'd longed for. And one that was long overdue.

The sun was going down as McKenna and Rob stepped inside the greenhouse. The air was pleasantly warm. She was exhausted from the long, deep conversations they'd had in the family parlor. Music had been played, including a lovely violin piece by her husband, which she could finally hear and enjoy on the violin she'd purchased for him in that life. They'd talked about history, about inventions, and about Caddam House, which she wanted them all to visit.

"My head aches from all the crying," McKenna said with a little laugh as Rob shut the greenhouse door behind them.

The curtain to the parlor had been closed. Mother was overseeing the kitchen and had promised to have one of Rob's favorites, salmon chowder, available for dinner in an hour. They'd spend the night upstairs in McKenna's room. But she wanted an interlude with him in the place they had first kissed. Before either of them had remembered the truth of themselves.

"You must be exhausted," Rob said, wrapping her in his arms protectively.

"Not *too* exhausted, Husband," she said with a promising smile. "There are a lot of windows in Caddam House," she observed. "Now I know why I loved them so. It's nothing but a gigantic greenhouse."

He smiled at her and leaned down to touch foreheads with her. "I don't want to lose you again," he whispered huskily.

"Well, there are no more Semblances trying to hunt me. The *strannik* is stranded in another world. My people are gone and cannot come back. I think you can rest your anxiety for one evening, Mr. Berrow." She rubbed his back and then leaned her cheek against his chest.

"A thousand lives," he murmured. "I feel a little restless not having another goal. A purpose."

She pulled back and wrinkled her brow. "Husband. Let's focus on the moment, not the next thousand lives. And then the next. And then the next."

She leaned up toward him, and he bent down and pressed his warm lips against hers. Her fingers found his unruly hair as memories swam through her mind. So many lifetimes, so much heartache, so much love. In that moment, embracing him in the family greenhouse, she felt it had all been worthwhile.

She pulled away, saw the hunger in his eyes for more. She touched his mouth with her finger. "I haven't gotten tired of kissing you yet."

Let me not to the marriage of true minds
Admit impediments; love is not love
Which alters when it alteration finds,
Or bends with the remover to remove.
O no, it is an ever-fixèd mark
That looks on tempests and is never shaken;
It is the star to every wand'ring bark
Whose worth's unknown, although his height be
    taken.
Love's not time's fool, though rosy lips and cheeks
Within his bending sickle's compass come.
Love alters not with his brief hours and weeks,
But bears it out even to the edge of doom:
If this be error and upon me proved,
I never writ, nor no man ever loved.

— WILLIAM SHAKESPEARE

I think it was around 1981 that my parents traumatized me with the movie *Somewhere in Time* starring Christopher Reeve and Jane Seymour when it came out on HBO. It's the story of a writer who falls in love with an old photograph of an early American actress, which he finds in a hotel he's staying at. He falls in love with her and is determined to meet her, even though they are from different eras. The gorgeous scenes, the thrilling score by John Barry, and that impossible ending burned into my mind a love for that movie, and I've probably seen it twenty times. In July 2025, my wife and I were able to visit Mackinac Island in Michigan where it was filmed, a bucket list item finally achieved.

Many don't realize that the story of *Somewhere in Time* was inspired by author Richard Matheson falling in love with a portrait of Maude Adams, a famous early American actress. Maude Adams Kiskadden (yes...I borrowed her real last name for Kingfountain) was born in Utah in 1872 and became famous as a stage actress. One of her famous plays, *The Little Minister*, was used as inspiration for the play in this novel. The playwright, J.M. Barrie, was so impressed with her as an actress that he chose her to play the titular role of his most famous play, *Peter Pan.* Instead of modeling Annalise Kauer after Elise McKenna in *Somewhere in*

Time, I modeled her after Maude Adams and read several biographies about her, her estate Caddam House, and how singular and interesting a person she was in real life. I could have written an entire novel just about her backstory but decided you wouldn't want to deprive Isaac of finding his lost love any longer.

This series has been an emotional roller coaster to write as I'm sure it has been for you to read. But ever since being inspired by Alec and Mabel, Richard and Elise, I have wanted to create a story that spanned different generations and would connect, ultimately, with my other worlds.

You haven't seen the last of Rob and McKenna yet. I hope you will enjoy what I'm working on next, my continuation of the Harbinger series.

Because if you haven't figured the clues out yet, the Aesir are on their way to Kingfountain.

ACKNOWLEDGMENTS

I'm grateful for the longstanding partnership I've had with Amazon Publishing and their support for over a decade. They decided not to publish this book but allowed me to publish it with Oliver Heber Books. I'd like to thank Tanya Anne Crosby, the founder and publisher, for being enthusiastic about taking on this project and for the whirlwind effort required to write it, edit it, record it, and have it available to enjoy with the third book's release. I finished writing this book at the end of May 2025, and the fact that you are reading it now is nothing short of a miracle.

I've also partnered with Angela Polidoro for nearly as long as I've been a full-time author, and she has since become a bestselling author in her own right and informed me that she wouldn't be able to work with me in the future. Thankfully, she agreed to do one more dev edit for me so that she could conclude the Invisible College and help me deliver an ending that I hope you feel was worth it. I am so grateful for talented and skilled individuals like Angela who offer expert advice and creative support to authors to make our books even better. Thanks, Angela! I will miss the little emojis and comments you always include in the manuscripts you send back to me.

I'd also like to continue to recognize the input and collaboration of Wanda and Dan, my copyeditor and proofreader. It takes a village, as they say. I happen to have an amazing village. Thank you!

About the Author

Photo © 2025 Jeff Wheeler

Jeff Wheeler is the Wall Street Journal bestselling author of more than forty epic novels, including the Angel Sworn series, the Invisible College series, the Kingfountain series, and many more. Jeff lives in the Rocky Mountains and is a husband, father of five, and devout member of his church. Learn about Jeff's publishing journey in *Your First Million Words*, visit his many worlds at www.jeff-wheeler.com, or participate in one of his many online writing classes through Writer's Block (www.writersblock.biz).